Praise for *A World of*

'*A World of Other People* is a powerfully imagined, elegiac homage to love, heroism and poetry ... an intimate private drama, set against the immense and tragic backdrop of European civilization tearing itself apart'

Prime Minister's Literary Awards judges, 2014

'A fine, absorbing novel – darker than *The Lost Life* but equally eloquent and assured. Carroll's re-creation of a distant and now long-lost world is vivid and tactful'

Andrew Riemer, *The Sydney Morning Herald*

Praise for *The Time We Have Taken*

'Carroll's novel is a poised, philosophically profound exploration ... a stand-alone work that is moving and indelible in its evocation of the extraordinary in ordinary lives'

Miles Franklin Literary Award judges, 2008

'The result is a deeply satisfying encounter with the empty spaces that the suburb failed to fill both between people and inside them. Carroll takes time to tell an untidy story with a gentle sense of wonder. His prose whispers loud'

Michael McGirr, *The Age*

'It is the creation of a larger concept of suburban life in all its transcendent possibilities that makes this novel so special. Carroll's revelations of these beautiful insights into our utterly ordinary world make him a writer worth cherishing. His prose is unfailingly assured, lyrical, poised'

Debra Adelaide, *The Australian*

Praise for *The Gift of Speed*

'Carroll's gift for evocative storytelling ... had me captivated'
Australian Bookseller & Publisher

'A novel of tender and harrowing melancholy'
Le Nouvel Observateur

'Carroll's a rare beast in that he writes with great affection and understanding about life in the suburbs ... A lovely rites of passage novel that is oh so carefully crafted and captures the evanescence of time to perfection'
Jason Steger, *The Age*

'Carroll's writing is astonishingly assured'
James Bradley, *Australian Book Review*

Praise for *The Art of the Engine Driver*

'Subtle, true and profoundly touching'
Le Monde

'A veritable gem ... a beautiful discovery'
Elle France

'An exquisitely crafted journey of Australian suburban life ... fresh and irresistible'
Miles Franklin Literary Award judges, 2002

'A little masterpiece'
Hessische Allgemeine

Praise for *The Lost Life*

'Carroll's prose is limpid and assured ... [a] poised and beautifully burnished work. Carroll's control is masterly'
Andrew Riemer, *The Sydney Morning Herald*

'This is not so much a departure as an arrival ... Carroll's fiction is distinctive for the way his clean prose decelerates experience, puts aside the urgings of linear temporality, to reveal a richness that habitually evades us.'
Australian Literary Review

'Carroll's prose has a sublime rhythmic quality ... almost as if he has sung the words on the page'
Australian Book Review

Praise for *Forever Young*

'No Australian author has better evoked the sense of change, the ravages of time, the obligation to self as well as to others. *Forever Young* is on one level about nostalgia, without ever succumbing to it ... At every turn this exquisitely crafted novel can widen our notion of what it is to be human, then, now and, possibly, later'
The Sydney Morning Herald

'The title of this fine novel speaks ambivalently to a longing for lost youth, and to the desire to escape its sentimental claims'
Peter Pierce, *The Australian*

'Carroll ... transmutes the grey facts of daily life into light and luminous art'
Geordie Williamson, *The Australian*

Praise for *A New England Affair*

'This is a languid, angry, heart-rending novel, thoughtfully layered and passionately expressed'

The Australian

'Carroll has carved out a stark and simple portrait of yearning, stripping away any dizzy glamour of the role of an artist's muse to present a far sadder and more pragmatic study'

The Saturday Paper

'As always with Carroll, it is … the richness of ideas, the allusive, measured prose, the subtle cross references to other books and literary theories that captivate the reader'

The Adelaide Advertiser

'Carroll's quiet, measured style is imbued with breathtaking observations of seemingly small moments. His writing here invites contemplation and reflection on what we lose in life and what we have, who we think we are and who we aspire to be. This novel is so much more than the sum of its parts and it's impossible not to feel you have borne witness to something incredibly beautiful and true.'

Victorian Premier's Literary Award judges, 2018

'It is a deeply moving, intense and poignant novel of a love that never finds the right moment'

Mildura Midweek

Steven Carroll was born in Melbourne. His first novel, *Remember Me, Jimmy James*, was published in 1992. This was followed by *Momoko* (1994); *The Love Song of Lucy McBride* (1998); *The Art of the Engine Driver* (2001), which was shortlisted for both the Miles Franklin Award in 2002 and France's Prix Femina literary award for the Best Foreign Novel in 2005; *The Gift of Speed* (2004), which was shortlisted for the Miles Franklin Award in 2005; *The Time We Have Taken* (2007), which won both the 2008 Commonwealth Writers' Prize for the South-East Asia and South Pacific Region and the Miles Franklin Award 2008; *The Lost Life* (2009), which was shortlisted for both the 2010 Barbara Jefferis Award and the ALS Gold Medal 2010; *Spirit of Progress* (2011), which was longlisted for the 2012 Miles Franklin Award; and *A World of Other People* (2013), which was shortlisted for the South Australian Premier's Award 2014 and was co-winner of the Prime Minister's Literary Award 2014. He was a finalist for the Melbourne Prize for Literature 2015. *Forever Young* (2015) was shortlisted for the Victorian Premier's Literary Award 2016; and the Prime Minister's Literary Award 2016; and *A New England Affair* (2017) was shortlisted for the Victorian Premier's Literary Award 2018.

Steven Carroll lives in Melbourne with his partner and son.

Also by Steven Carroll

Remember Me, Jimmy James
Momoko
The Love Song of Lucy McBride
The Art of the Engine Driver
The Gift of Speed
The Time We Have Taken
The Lost Life
Spirit of Progress
A World of Other People
Forever Young
A New England Affair

STEVEN CARROLL

The year of the beast

FOURTH ESTATE

Fourth Estate
An imprint of HarperCollins*Publishers*

First published in Australia in 2019
by HarperCollins*Publishers* Australia Pty Limited
ABN 36 009 913 517
harpercollins.com.au

Copyright © Steven Carroll 2019

The right of Steven Carroll to be identified as the author of this work has been asserted by him in accordance with the *Copyright Amendment (Moral Rights) Act 2000*.

This work is copyright. Apart from any use as permitted under the *Copyright Act 1968*, no part may be reproduced, copied, scanned, stored in a retrieval system, recorded, or transmitted, in any form or by any means, without the prior written permission of the publisher.

HarperCollins*Publishers*
Level 13, 201 Elizabeth Street, Sydney NSW 2000, Australia
Unit D1, 63 Apollo Drive, Rosedale, Auckland 0632, New Zealand
A 53, Sector 57, Noida, UP, India
1 London Bridge Street, London, SE1 9GF, United Kingdom
Bay Adelaide Centre, East Tower, 22 Adelaide Street West, 41st floor, Toronto, Ontario M5H 4E3, Canada
195 Broadway, New York NY 10007, USA

A catalogue record for this book is available from the National Library of Australia

ISBN 978 1 4607 5769 7 (pbk)
ISBN 978 1 4607 1135 4 (ebook)

Cover design by Michelle Zaiter, HarperCollins Design Studio
Cover images: Woman © Malgorzata Maj/ Arcangel; Melbourne courtesy National Museum of Australia (1986.0117.2981); Crowd by Bettmann/ Getty Images; Lamp and textures by istockphoto.com
Typeset in Berthold Baskerville by Kirby Jones
Author photograph by Rebecca Rocks
Printed and bound in Australia by McPherson's Printing Group
The papers used by HarperCollins in the manufacture of this book are a natural, recyclable product made from wood grown in sustainable plantation forests. The fibre source and manufacturing processes meet recognised international environmental standards, and carry certification.

CONTENTS

PART ONE
Festival of the Id
Melbourne, October, 1917   1

PART TWO
The Milhaus Case
November, 1917   81

PART THREE
A Separate Peace
December 20th, 1917 – March, 1918   201

PART FOUR
The Beast Withdraws
Melbourne, November 12th, 1918   279

EPILOGUE
Paris, December, 1977   287

Part One

Festival of the Id

Melbourne, October, 1917

1.

Tall, that's how she looks. But she's not. It's the bearing. And the face: the broad forehead, strong jaw and dark eyes that miss nothing. Hers is not a face that the age calls beautiful. The favoured look is the English rose: clear skin, pink cheeks, cultivated and deferring. The best the garden has. But Maryanne is no English rose. Rather, her face is strong. Skin, swarthy. What another age might call striking – and in a way that suggests an intelligence that does not withdraw from male company or defer to it. But this is not another age. Nor is it *her* age: she is one of those who have arrived ahead of her times.

All the same, it is the age she *has* been thrown into. A particular place. A particular time. A nasty one. Ugly. Brutish. The very worst of humanity on display. And the prime minister, who looms up from a street poster she passes on her walk home, pointing his finger accusingly at her or anybody else in range, the very sight and symbol of the times: the prime minister, someone she can only think of, whenever she thinks of him at all, as a giant wart on thin legs. A thought that gives her passing amusement. One that Maryanne will repeat later to her sister, for she is known as a bit of a wag. Striking, yes.

Serious too. But with a comic eye for exaggeration. Always on the brink of an observation that tells people she's watching. And imagination: possibly too much of it.

It's not just her face and bearing that are striking, though. So is her belly. It is round and swollen, seven months pregnant, the baby only a couple of months from falling into the world. And what a world to be falling into. She has just stepped off her tram and is moving slowly, labouring towards the corner of Elizabeth and Bourke streets. The centre of the city on a grey spring day: late afternoon, slipping into twilight. Dust, whipped up by gusts of wind, stinging her eyes. Spring! Ratty spring. She pauses before the intersection. Her heart sinks. Normally thick with carriages, trams and the occasional motor car, it is now thick with people. Clouds in the sky swirl; on the ground the crowd sways. This way and that: a single organism, with thousands of arms, legs and eyes, emitting a continuous hum. A giant thing. A beast. All those faces, eyes, mouths, hats, ears, arms and legs surrendering themselves to this thing they have become. This mass. This agglomeration, now still, now swaying, and all the time emitting a continuous hum and occasionally erupting into a roar as if the beast were suddenly stirred for action. Or wounded. A groan that subsides into a hum, then erupts into a roar.

It is as if some fantastic metamorphosis is taking place in front of her. And a storybook beast is coming to life before her eyes. As if each of those faces has reached into the depths of its darkness and brought forth the beast that lurks there. Always lurks there, waiting patiently. Sometimes years, sometimes centuries. But always there. And now, its hour come, the beast roars, groans and writhes into life. The very worst of humanity has risen and become this collective thing to which each of those massed faces gives the gift of its darkness, so that the beast may slouch into life and the world hear its groans. For it has waited a long time, brooding in its cave, alone and forgotten, but always there. And now, its moment come, the world will pay.

Maryanne stands at the edge of the crowd, staring at the intersection. Is she the only one who can see it? She stands apart. Proud, removed. Seven months pregnant, as erect as anyone can be with a belly like that, pausing at the edge of the crowd, wondering how on earth she will make her way through it. Her home is on the other side. And so she *will* enter the crowd, pass through it without surrendering to it, if only to glimpse the beast from the centre of its black heart.

The Town Hall clock points towards six. Night will fall. She moves forward, entering the crowd. A large banner hangs from a building on the corner: a dark 'Yes' written across it stands out against a rising sun, while a wounded soldier on some foreign battlefield reaches out his hand for help. Brother … She doesn't read it the way she might a newspaper article or a book. She simply takes it in at a glance. Just another part of the swirling, swaying spectacle.

A soldier, an officer, is standing on the back of a truck draped in Union Jacks. The soldier's lips are moving. His mouth is opening and closing, but his words are lost in the continuous hum of the crowd. As she moves forward in laboured steps the crowd makes way. But they eye her suspiciously, as if knowing instinctively that she is not one of them and that she stands apart: moving through the crowd, but removed from it. Proud all right, just a bit too bloody proud. The beast, with its unerring nose for these things, has sniffed her out. But they part for her all the same. The beast has retained at least this much of its former life. And it is only as she nears the soldier who is addressing the crowd that she hears his words. They are yelled, blasted out into the crowd. Volley after volley. He could almost be speaking a foreign language. Or no language at all. Just a series of howls and grunts: each howl, each grunt, a variation on the previous one or a repetition of it, and all of them exploding into the crowd with an immediacy that makes ordinary words of reason seem weak. For this is a place without reason. And, every so often, the soldier raises his fist as the sounds he emits rise to a crescendo and the crowd erupts: the beast roars, groans, then settles back into a grumbling, continuous hum.

Just then the crowd surges towards the truck and she is carried with it. At its mercy. Her feet barely touching the ground. The officer continues, his utterances hurled into the crowd, but suddenly nobody is listening or even looking. And Maryanne is no sooner thrown to the front by the crowd than the crowd stops, and through a rare gap in the mass of bodies she sees two, maybe three, men rolling round on the bared street. A man's nose, like a burst drainpipe, spurts blood into the air. Police and soldiers appear as the crowd closes around the scene. She is stuck, can move neither forward nor back. And for the first time since entering the crowd she feels afraid because she has lost the power to choose where her feet can go. And pleas are useless for no one will hear or care. The mob has taken her feet and voice from her. And, at this moment, she is not standing apart from it. She is no longer removed from the beast, but just one more part of it: one more pair of arms and legs. But just as quickly as the crowd closed around the fight, it parts, and a man in overalls staggers past directly in front of her, what's left of his nose spilling blood. The crowd steps back, he makes his way towards the intersection and the Town Hall, and Maryanne, in his wake, follows.

The man disappears into the mob, half of which jeers and laughs at him, the other half taking him in. She is suddenly standing near the steps of the Post Office. And it is then, faintly at first, that she hears singing floating across the crowd towards her. Singing? It can't be. But it is. And as she approaches the steps she sees them, above the crowd on the highest steps of the Post Office, a heavenly choir. In full voice. But barely audible above the beast. And as she pushes and pleads her way towards them – old women, young women, all women, a women's church choir in full voice – she hears the hymn itself. The words float out across the crowd: 'Thou rushing wind,' they sing, 'that art so strong.' The crowd behind her erupts. The song is lost.

Reluctantly, men and women part for her and she is concentrated on leaving the crowd behind when she looks to the opposite corner and sees, standing on a makeshift platform, in top hat and black suit, the unmistakable figure of Archbishop Mannix himself. There is a gust of wind; he holds his hat. It is almost like watching a statue move. Mannix. And as much as she is drained by the effort of crossing through the crowd and as much as she wants only to leave it behind her, she is drawn to the tall, top-hatted man in a black suit who is about to address the beast assembled on the other side of the intersection: two assemblies, one beast. Behind Mannix another women's choir booms into full voice: 'In gladness let us sing ...' For a moment, the booming, unified voice of the choir conquers the noise of the crowd: 'Alleluia, Alleluia, Alleluia ...' But just as this choir begins, the other on the steps of the Post Office bursts into the sound or simply lifts its voice in response: 'Oh, thou rushing wind ...' And for the time it takes to complete the hymns, it seems to Maryanne, looking from one to the other, that these opposing choirs are doing battle. Hurling their holy choruses at each other, volley after volley.

In front of the Town Hall the soldier is still addressing the crowd from the back of the truck; booing, cheers and hooting mingle in the air. The beast roars and writhes. The choirs each rise to their crescendo, climax, then subside into silence. The air is strangely still. The spring wind stops and listens. Mannix begins.

The clear, crisp voice of Ireland carries across the gathered heads towards her. Unimpeded. As if the street were a church and they were all listening to Sunday's sermon. But they're not. And the lull is short lived. On the steps of the Town Hall behind her she hears voices calling out in the name of the dead. Vote 'Yes', the dead call. Vote 'Yes'. An egg is thrown. A stone. Another. A fight breaks out beside her and she flees, rushing forward away from it as the police part the scene, swinging truncheons. Mannix's words are lost for a moment. And because the crowd, like her, has rushed forward to avoid the fight, she has been swept closer to Mannix. His top hat sits firmly on his head. He barely moves. He is calm. The still point of the swirling crowd, which is soon subdued once again. The clear, crisp voice of Ireland is not raised, but she hears it well enough. A church voice; no, a cathedral voice. And she moves closer, drawn more by the voice than the words, in a kind of thrall. Then he does raise his voice and, suddenly, there is passion in it. He is talking of mothers and children, and death and war, and at one point he seems to be speaking to her alone. Their eyes, she is sure, lock. And for that moment she is not just some nameless part of the crowd, but once again stands apart from it, discernible from it, and the words that reach her of mothers and sons and death become personal: heard by the crowd, but addressed to her. Behind him, behind the choir now standing silently to attention, a giant banner bearing a giant red 'No' lifts in the breeze, dripping blood. But it is a blur, like the hum all around her. His eyes, she is sure, his eyes clear as his voice, remain fixed on her. She could swear she can see the whites of them and the black pupils. Intense. Fixed. And for a moment it is like staring into the eyes of God himself: all-seeing, all-knowing. The God from whom there are no secrets. The God to whom you can't lie. He knows! *Fallen woman!* She is exposed, bulging with her sin. Shame sweeps over her, and the sputtered cries of the day, hurled out into the crowd from one side to the other – duty, blood, death, Hun, mercy, war, loyalty, victory – all fade from hearing, and the sins of the world are suddenly concentrated in her. Wars don't matter, or ruined countries or bloodied fields. Only this matters. This shame that sweeps over her, telling her that the burden of sin is hers alone, and that she is bulging with all that is wrong in the world. And the whole bloody nightmare thousands of miles away is nothing to *this*.

She turns sharply from Mannix, from the judgement and the sentence in his eyes, and moves away from the crowd, which still writhes in all its black triumph. Men and women make way for her, but suspiciously and accusingly, as if they too know. As if everybody does.

She is once more standing apart. Looking back. On the edge of some awful force. And, for a moment, it is like watching history, possessed by the devil of the very worst in everyone, work itself out: the sum total of the crowd, the place and the hour – the beast they have all given birth to – slouching towards its moment.

* * *

Then she is free. She can breathe. The city has opened up. The streets are clear. The October evening is falling. Twilight is upon her. Shadows are forming. The day is cooling. Behind her, a window smashes. Yelling and curses follow. The pubs are closing and drunks are spilling onto the streets. Enemies will clash; friendships long and deep will be broken, never to be repaired, in these days of the beast. YES to conscription, and NO. NO and YES. Duty and death. Blood and sacrifice. In the distance the choirs start up again, faintly audible, hurling hymns at each other from opposite sides of the street: *In gladness let us sing ... Thou rushing wind ...*

She walks away from it all, a laboured walk up the hill to parliament. The air is purer and clearer and she breathes deeply, as if, in the midst of the beast, she had been suffocating and hadn't known it. The noise of the crowd behind her subsides, then slowly fades altogether. When she finally reaches the parliament she stops. The lights are on. Is the Wart inside? Possibly. The country's good is decided in there by the likes of the Wart. The building glows in the evening light like a touch of something out of ancient Greece or Rome. Impressive, yes – on the outside. She smiles to herself, leaves it at that and moves on. North, where the dome of the Exhibition Building is visible not too far away towards her suburb. The grey clouds have parted for the first time all day, and the setting sun, a giant egg-yolk, melts onto the rooftops and trees and over the dome itself. Somewhere, children are playing in the last of the light.

Children. Until a year ago she was a teacher at the Catholic school that she attended as a student: in the junior school, the lowest of all. Like her sister, Katherine, she'd finished school. Went as far as she could go. And not just finished school, but was very good at her work. Good enough to be offered the job of an assistant: cleaning blackboards, filling inkwells, standing on yard duty. All the things nobody else wanted to do. And she did this until she was old enough to take her own class. She wasn't qualified, and still isn't. But nobody cared. She certainly didn't. And she can still see herself when she first started. Impossibly young. Thrilled. Her own class. There were forty-seven of them. Either they mastered her, or she mastered them. So, every day, she beat them into submission, hating herself for it, for it was mutually degrading. But eventually she won. They were hers, she had them. Beaten brats every one. And every class after that bent to her will. But the effort was so great she could no longer feel or muster the thrill of first stepping into the class. She had beaten them into submission and they feared her. That was the price of respect.

But Maryanne no longer teaches, and she doesn't miss it. She stops on the edge of a park next to parliament and pauses: the scene is soothing, silent, apart from the tinkle of children. Then the clear, crisp voice of Ireland comes back to her. And the eyes. All-knowing. The God from whom there are no secrets ... Odd. She's been leaving her religion for years. Strange how these things creep up on you, catch you, and before you know it you're the all-believing girl you once were, trembling under the all-seeing eyes of a God you don't believe in any more. Shadows gather. The last of the day's light retreats. A couple, passing beneath a street lamp, nods. Here, at least, all is still and calm. A world at peace. Almost happy.

She moves on to a tree-lined street. Over her shoulder and out of sight, in a distant part of the sky, a silver jet glides through the air, shining in the last of the light. It slows, seems to hover, then prepares to touch down in another age. Another country: where night is becoming morning, autumn turning into winter. The son of the child she carries sits in that silver capsule as it prepares to land, staring out the window with pen and notepad on his lap, gazing back upon the scene: a woman, swollen belly, makes her way along a tree-lined street in the last of a spring day. She looks tall, but she's not. It's her bearing. A woman, swollen belly, makes her way along a tree-lined street in the October twilight; a story begins ...

She enters a small street that leads into the cluttered suburb she calls home and has called home all her life. The streets are closed in, the air dusk-thick. The grimy neighbourhood she calls home is deserted. Except for two boys who rush through a crossing in front of her. Then rush back. Their arms, which are wings, are outstretched. They are aeroplanes. They weave, they roll, they swoop. Rat-a-tat-tat sounds shatter the quiet stillness of the evening. She pauses, staring at them. This playing at war. So old. Ancient. This urge to kill and die. They play at war, and then they grow up and stride off to war as if they are still playing.

In the half-light they circle each other, dodging this way and that down the street. Wild boys. The father gone to a never-ending war, the wife left holding a baby girl who is only just walking. They are in front of her one minute, and flown into the night the next.

The house in which she grew up, and in which her parents died, one after the other, is not far now. Home. A refuge of sorts. Her life has been lived in this rectangle of land that calls itself a suburb. It is both home and alien, her neighbourhood: row upon row of workers' cottages, small and dark.

She stares at them, those cottage eyes, both welcoming and suspicious, as if saying: we take you in because we have to, you are ours; but also eyeing her suspiciously, pronouncing her proud – just a bit too proud. Cottage eyes, terrace after uniform terrace, staring back at her all along the street. She lifts her head, the orange sunset has gone, the yolk on the dome of the Exhibition Building has melted into the darkness. And somewhere out there in the night the beast will be lying down, resting, eyes eternally half-opened, or maybe it will be slouching and swaying home through streets like these, singing some football song or other, scales shining in the moonlight, before rising up again in the morning, and all the mornings and days after, until it gets what it craves and what it will not be denied: something … something *final*.

2.

The local priest, Father Geoghan, is sitting in the front room of the cottage when she enters. It is the best room in the house. The one set aside for important visitors. And a priest is an important visitor. Maryanne sits next to Katherine, who has come to stay with her for these last couple of months before the child is born. Katherine, who looked after her when their parents died: big sister and mother all in one.

Maryanne wrote to her, care of a post and telegraph office in some little bush town. To let her sister know. She was pregnant. Long story. But it was all right. She could do this on her own. And the next thing, Katherine walked through the door and dropped her baggage in the hallway. Oh no, she said, you can't do this alone. She moved into a small room beside the kitchen, big enough for a single bed and her things: a tent, a swag and a rifle. An Enfield. Army issue. Maryanne knows little of guns, but she has learned about the marvels of the Enfield from Katherine. Katherine paid a lot for it, but it was worth every penny. And she likes to talk about it. It is her prize, her protection, her provider. And she's a better shot than most. She can pick rabbits off from a good distance. And the odd snake. And if any tramp gets too near she's happy to demonstrate the marvels of the rifle. But they don't, because one look and they know she can use it. And so big sister, who has tramped most of the country over the years, doing whatever job came up, pretending to be a man if she had to – and nobody questioned her, not with a rifle like that over her shoulder – has come to stay.

Maryanne smiles, glancing now at her sister. We're not the ordinary run, you and I. Never have been. The room is dim, cool, with the slightly musty scent of rooms that are not used often. The priest turns from Katherine to Maryanne. Father Geoghan, her sister tells her, has come to see you. Katherine says this, at least it seems to Maryanne, almost with a bowed head. It's something she'll never understand about Katherine: she's battled droughts and floods and tramps, and heaven knows what else out there on lonely bush stations and farms, but she's still afraid of a priest. And the crucifix she's had since she was a girl, that has always hung over her in huts or in her tent wherever she's pitched it, and to which she prays every night before sleep, is as prized a possession as her Enfield. And so when she tells Maryanne that Father Geoghan has come, it is in the manner of one of the faithful, an unremarkable middle-aged woman who gives little or no hint of this other Katherine at all.

The priest wishes Maryanne good evening as though welcoming her into his house. Maryanne nods. He leans back in his chair and talks of the crowds, of the hour of decision that has come to them, and of the stirring words of the archbishop.

And they all agree they are lucky having the archbishop to champion their cause: a great man, a great cause. They reflect on this for a moment, and then Father Geoghan begins speaking to Maryanne in a quiet, measured voice.

He speaks, she watches. He is, she has felt from the first time she saw him years before, an old-young man: balding even then, drawn cheeks, inquisitor's eyes and prickly brows, and a voice that was always ten years older than he was, and still is, with a way of speaking that could almost have come out of last century's novels. An old-young man, a look that his simple, round spectacles add to. One of those who have never been young, who never seem to age because they can't, and one of those who have never known a moment of doubt. Fatal purity. Where did she read that phrase? She's forgotten. But he's got it, Father Geoghan, the disease of fatal purity. But as much as there is judgement in those eyes as he addresses her, there is also concern. He leans forward and rests his hand lightly and reassuringly on her knee as he speaks.

She looks down at his hand and he withdraws it. He has, he implies as he continues speaking, her interests at heart. He loves her as he does all his children. She could almost laugh. Thirty-nine years of age and she is still a child in his eyes. One of his children. A child! Of course. This is why he is here. Now she understands. His concern is not for her at all, but for the unborn child. And she now stares down at her swollen belly through the eyes of Father Geoghan: as if, already, the child is not hers but *theirs*.

He casually observes, drops it into the conversation, that he hasn't seen Maryanne at church for some time. Letting the observation sink in with a pause, he then addresses more directly the matter that has brought him here. He speaks in a voice that presents itself as reason: his Sunday voice. The Sunday voice she's heard before, listened to for years, but doesn't listen to any more. Measured and quiet. Quiet because it is also the voice of authority. And authority never raises its voice. Or it shouldn't. For, once it does, it is no longer the voice of authority.

Sin, the priest is saying with well-practised lines, is like a stain. You must imagine a clean white sheet of blotting paper. The sheet of blotting paper, white and unblemished, is innocence. When a single drop of ink falls on the paper it is no longer unblemished. No longer innocent. It has sinned. This, the priest says, is original sin. And he says this in a way that suggests that although he is perfectly aware that Maryanne knows this, she also needs reminding of it. We can't help that, he goes on. Not the original sin. We are all born with the blot of ink upon us. We don't choose it. He pauses again; Katherine nods. Maryanne says nothing. Betrays no reaction. She's heard this sermon before, the priest's lines so well practised now, she imagines, that he doesn't really need to think about what he's saying. The blot of ink falls on the paper, he continues. But it doesn't stop there. It spreads, as blots will. We don't choose that first drop, we are born with it, but every fresh drop we add thereafter is our choice. And with every fresh drop the stain spreads, wider and wider. Like a disease. A plague. We must stop the spreading stain. Or all will be stained black. He pauses, eyes peering deep into hers in a manner that suggests yes, we've all heard this before, I know, but we might do well to hear it again. And dwell upon it. The stain spreads; blackness will cover all, if we choose to let it. And you, Maryanne, who will do well to hear this sermon again, remember it and never forget it, must ask yourself who bears that stain?

The mood in the room changes. Becomes tense. Katherine is motionless, eyes fixed on the priest. Maryanne is torn between outrage and fascination. But remains calm. Father Geoghan continues, a voice soft as an executioner's. It will spread, as sure as God created time and made day and night, it will spread to others unless we act. Unless we take action now, before it is too late. For the good of others. We must act, do difficult things, so that stain cannot touch them and its blackness be not upon them.

Here he sits back and nods, his bespectacled eyes on hers, then straying to her belly, swollen with the fruit of fornication, and she knows exactly what he is saying. He is one of those born for inquisitions and revolutions. And he would take her child from her the moment he could: for the good of the child, for the mother, for everybody. He would take her child from her without conscience because his conscience would be clear. She has become her own stain. And the stain of shame will spread to the child, unless the child is placed out of her reach, and knows not its shame. Oh yes, this is exactly what he means, even if he doesn't say it – and all implied with the quiet, measured voice of concerned authority. A voice that brings with it centuries of battling sin. A voice that brings with it cathedrals of wisdom, chapels of humility. A voice that implies: we know all about these things. Trust us. Leave these things to those who know. Maryanne is both listening and biding her time, glancing at the clock.

Then she's not listening at all. Her eyes stray to the morning newspaper on a side table. The words 'Empire', 'Duty' and 'Yes' are written large across the open page. As is the name 'Milhaus': the curious case of Jack Milhaus, an ex-footballer accused of spying. A German. A high-flying angel one day, fallen the next. A case, an affair even, that rouses her curiosity more than it should, for she has no interest in sport or football or football's heroes. But the swiftness of his fall from grace *does* interest her. And while she's contemplating this, Father Geoghan's mouth opens and shuts like a fish in a tank. He is speaking and she is – to all appearances – listening. But she has ceased to hear him. And for the time it takes him to finish, she feels like a scientist coldly observing a specimen and finding it intriguing. So, this is it. This is the face of the religion she not so much lost as left: walked away from. This is it. A bland, pure face. Bland and merciless. Preaching a sermon she has heard before, and for which she has long since ceased to feel anything. A trick she has seen too often to believe in any more: an illusion with a long history, and no future. And it is this distinct sense of being on the outside looking in that allows her to feel like a scientist looking on while the priest's mouth silently opens and closes.

Then she *is* hearing him again because he has noticed her looking at the clock. The whore! The fornicating whore! She dares brazenly to look at the clock. And suddenly the quiet, measured voice of authority is no longer quiet but raised, and the cathedrals of wisdom, the chapels of humility, are ranting. And what she imagined he was saying, what he was implying, has become actual speech. The priest roaring at her like a three-headed dog, telling her that the child must be saved. Can be saved. And that he knows what must be done. The face, bland a moment ago, is now flushed, red, about to burst, transformed with passion and outrage. Spitting words. How dare she look at the clock when he is speaking. Whore! Fornicating whore! Is she listening? Really listening? Father Geoghan is stirred to outrage. God is stirred to outrage, and his bespectacled eyes are suddenly burning into her, and she's not sure if these questions are being spoken in fact or imagined. And, for a moment, she is rocked by this eruption, and the trembling fear of the believing child she once was suddenly rises up in her, and the all-knowing, all-seeing, bespectacled eyes of God are staring mercilessly into her. *Do* you understand, child? And, for a moment, she *is* a child again. Helpless and cowering. Oh, these people. These people … they never let go. She feels his power. She is a child. Silent and stunned. Yes, yes, Father, her silence would seem to be saying. Yes, she understands. She is a fornicating whore. She has become her own stain. The child must be saved. Yes, yes, Father. You are right, Father. You are always right. You bring cathedrals of wisdom with you. Yes, Father. Yes. Take the child. She is unworthy. Take it. She understands.

'All for the best,' the priest continues, rising from his chair, voice rasping, but shaky, almost on the verge of breaking. 'Believe me, I *know*!'

And it is then that he stops, eyes wide, looking from Maryanne to Katherine, and back again. The eyes of a man who suddenly realises he has gone too far. Said too much. Done the unforgivable, and lost control.

He settles back into his chair, staring at a country scene on the wall, his last words still humming in the quiet of the room.

Something, Maryanne tells herself, something has been said. But what? Something significant enough to bring Father Geoghan to a sudden stop. The mystery at the heart of Father Geoghan has been momentarily laid bare. But what is it? And, for a moment, all that priestly certainty, the cathedral wisdom, the fatal purity, dissolves as he sits there in front of them with a vague, lost look in his eyes. And the only certainty is that something happened, but what?

The eruption subsides as quickly as it started. A practised trick, a stunt she knows only too well, but which somehow got out of hand. Ran away from him. But one to which, all the same, Maryanne succumbed. A trick that still works. The inquisitor's look goes from his eyes and Father Geoghan recovers his composure, leans back in his chair, flicks an imaginary speck of dust from his trousers, his voice now soft and controlled.

'You want what's best, Maryanne. Your sister does,' he says, turning to Katherine, who, it seems to Maryanne, is now eyeing the priest in the way she might well look upon an actor who has fluffed his lines, asking herself if she can still believe the performance once the mask has fallen away. 'Everybody does. You understand,' the priest continues.

His composure is back as if nothing has happened, and there is a hint of a smile on his lips. Yes, you understand, the smile says. Of course you do. Once our child, always our child. His smile spreads: the performance resumes, the role and the man united once more. Welcome back to the fold. Once ours, always ours. You understand, my child. And you know what must be done.

All the talk of stains and shame returns to her. But if she feels any shame at the moment, it is the shame of her silence. For having failed her child. For having been weak when she should have been strong. When she should have stood tall, she shrank and became a child again. And shame turns to anger, and she'd suddenly love to wipe the satisfied smile off the priest's face. Or go and get Katherine's rifle. Just one shot over his head.

As if the matter were decided, he begins to talk – casually, calmly, the voice of authority once more, as if this is some small matter that can easily be remedied – about a foundling home he knows of. Not far. Just to the north of the city. It is run by the Sisters of St Joseph. Has been for years, he nods. Trust us, we know about these things. We know our trade, the trade of human souls. We've been doing this for centuries. There's no soul lost that can't be saved. No stain that can't be stopped. The child will be placed out of reach where it will not know its shame. Trust us. He leans back in his chair, a biscuit in hand. A contented smile lighting his eyes, a smile that says: I have this day saved a soul.

And now that Maryanne has had time enough to calm herself, and step back, her anger recedes. He talks again to Katherine of the coming vote, of the inspiring words of Mannix, and Maryanne is free to study him again, as a scientist might an insect.

Father Geoghan. Surely he must have been a child once.

And it is only then that it occurs to her that he must have a Christian name. A priest has always been simply a priest. Hardly human. Which, she only now acknowledges, is why the occasional waft of his tobacco or the scent of his hair tonic has always come as a bit of a shock. Father Geoghan, a man? But the shock always faded as did such questions. And so, for as long as she can remember, she never considered the possibility that he might have a Christian name – or have once been a child. Of course, he does – and was. All the same, it's quite a jolt to be thinking this, even for Maryanne. But the more she contemplates it, the more intrigued she becomes with just what his name might be. The name that his mother used to call him in from the street, the name that his father spoke, that his brothers and sisters (if he had any) teased him with. She dwells on this while he chats with Katherine.

She doesn't know his Christian name and never will. So, she decides, she'll have to give him one. *Who* is he? Father Geoghan, Father Geoghan, Father ... Yes, of course. Kevin. And this causes her to smile briefly, for it is a little like deciding that God himself must have a Christian name, and calling God Kevin. The name sticks. And, suddenly, she's staring at the freshly christened Father Kevin Geoghan – and imagining him as a child.

Little Kevin. Kev. Playing games, toy soldiers. Babbling all sorts of babble to himself, in a world of his own, a child ... but no, she can't see it. Always an old-young man. She squints at him, a slight shake of the head. Kevin. A bland name, like his face. Never, she tells herself, trust the bland. Never trust the banal. For underneath the quiet voice that moves easily from the topic of the vote to talk of this foundling home, where the Sisters of St Joseph will take matters in hand, is a man of extremes. Of fire and ice. And violence. Like that sudden eruption a few minutes before. A trick, yes. But real enough. And violent enough to get out of control, to let things run away from him. Like a quietly spoken revolutionary who'd think nothing of lining you up against a wall. And she thinks of this because revolution is in the newspapers, a world away in the cities of Russia.

This Father Geoghan is one of them. In another life the custodian of revolutionary change and the iron laws of history.

In this one, the custodian of human souls and God's will. It is all the same. Maryanne's eyes stray from the priest to the bookshelves that line the walls of the room. Books that belong to both her and Katherine, for they are both readers. Were brought up to be readers in a reading family, and one of the many lessons found in those books, for Maryanne (especially at this moment), is that the same types recur all through history, through revolutions and inquisitions, wearing different uniforms and robes and under different banners. But always the same types: and, among them, the Father Geoghans of this world, past worlds and worlds to come. They will always be there. And there is, with these thoughts, something suddenly unnerving about the presence of the bland-faced Father Geoghan in the room, a man who enters other people's houses as if they were his own, who speaks of stains and souls with practised ease, and who accepts the gift of tea, which he sips with thin lips, and biscuits, which he nibbles.

What *has* made the likes of you, Father Geoghan, Maryanne asks herself as she gazes at the insect priest. What unfamiliar parts of my world do you come from? She shifts her eyes to Katherine, now nodding warily at the priest, but nodding all the same. As girls, as young women, Maryanne and Katherine believed it all: God, heaven and sin. Now only Katherine does, but her faith is fervent enough for two: her crucifix, like her rifle, her constant companion. Maryanne's faith left her gradually. Day after day, she lost the will to sustain it. The strength to believe it all. A magic show she saw once too often. The mirrors, the tricks, the sleight of hand, the musty, rich scents of the church – all no longer a mystery. And there was sadness in the way she left it, like leaving her childhood behind. At first she missed the occasional Sunday mass, then at some point she stopped going altogether: ceased to kneel down before a God she no longer believed in. There's just us, she thought one day, looking around at streets and houses and people, just us. And it was frightening and exciting at the same time: being both free and alone. A new feeling, one that she kept to herself. A change that left her looking at the world the way someone might from a distant age that sees things differently.

Katherine is still listening to the priest, but saying little. She's reserved, even, as if to say my faith is strong, as it always has been, but you, Father Geoghan, you are another matter again. People err, she might be thinking, but faith is always faith – in spite of its guardians. And that, dear sister, Maryanne tells herself, is the difference between us. For let me tell you, when they come for you, when they come for your belly, when they walk in off the street and into your best room like a king strolling into some corner of his kingdom, telling you that what you thought was yours is actually theirs, the look of faith leaves your face. That's what tells us that the magic show – the magician's robes, the mirrors of stained glass, the smoke of incense, the holy choirs – has lost its magic. The mask is ripped away and the holy book becomes just another storybook.

More and more she has this odd, sometimes disquieting feeling of being one of those who are thrown into life in advance of her times. One of those whose world is still out there somewhere, still forming. Swirling around in distant dust and skies, a remote corner of the universe. She is travelling towards it but will never inhabit it, her true world. Maryanne looks at Father Geoghan, not so much listening as observing him, even a little sadly now, like bumping into an old teacher who once filled her with fear.

And as the priest rises, he looks at her again, looks right into her eyes, seeking assurance that his words have been understood and his counsel taken. But although Maryanne's manners, the look on her face, are cordial enough, the way she would be for any guest, he finds no such assurance. There is no hint of a bow, no deferring. She simply stares at him. We are equals, you and I, Father Geoghan, the look says, so shall we drop the play-acting? The look is noted.

'I sincerely hope we understand each other, because if we don't – and I'm sure we do, but if not – you may find it difficult to step inside our schools again. We must be so careful, you understand. The young are so impressionable. And we can't be giving them the wrong impression.'

It is his last piece of advice. And it is delivered in a tone that says: believe me, we mean exactly what we say. We trained you, we gave you the shelter of work and we will take it from you as easily as we gave it to you. It is advice that Maryanne takes in silence.

Father Geoghan turns to Katherine, who, eyes narrowed, scrutinises him while taking in the meaning of his parting words. He nods farewell and is reassured by her returned nod, though he does not notice Katherine's reserve, her sudden formality. He turns back to Maryanne, eyes cold and steely, as if to say, you have much to learn from your sister. Maryanne shows him the door that opens onto the street, now dark, but with spring still in the air. And without further speech, abruptly even, he is walking away, bespectacled eyes looking down at his feet, footsteps audible at first, then fading: a dark figure dissolving into the inky night.

3.

Maryanne lingers in the doorway, staring into the inky night, watching the retreating figure of Father Geoghan. Her belly larger and heavier with every week. Lately, the more she looks at her belly the more the feeling comes over her that what is in there, the life inside her, can't possibly come out, that its emergence is an extraordinary mystery that will only be solved when the moment comes.

On the other hand, what happened to bring about Maryanne's belly was common, some might even say grubby – and like nothing else that had ever happened to her before. Or will again. Two people, by a mixture of accident and design, stepped outside the rules. If she had been a society lady, he a gentleman, it might be called a scandal or an affair: Madame X and her lover. But the reality is, in the world that Maryanne moves in, it is more than likely not called anything, because nobody talks about these things. Perhaps a knowing nod or a sigh. Or a reference to 'that business'. But most of the time, these things are simply not brought up. Certainly nothing as grand as an affair or a scandal.

She had come to a country town to teach. The town's teacher had enlisted, and her school sent her to the town, famous for its mineral water. She was the logical choice. Experienced, single. And low on the list of senior teachers. Besides, nobody else wanted to go. So she did. And straightaway she liked it. It was a pretty town. A little Switzerland in the Victorian countryside. At least, that was how it looked when she stepped off the train. You could have adventures in a place like this, she imagined, as she made her way up the main street to the school.

He was a shopkeeper. Viktor, spelled the German way, from a long line of German shopkeepers. Drapers and haberdashers. In her first couple of weeks she passed the shop often enough, for it was near the school. And the shop stood out because its displays were eye-catching. One day, a roll of material in the window caught her attention, and she bought it from him for a dress. That was the start.

And she'd like to think it was his charm (for he was charming) or a certain tenderness in his voice (he was nothing to look at) that stirred her. A tenderness that told her that she interested him. A look on his face that suggested we don't get your type around here often. City types. Smart eyes. Something new. Is that what he saw? He smoothed the cloth with his soft, draper's hands and spoke of the material like a tailor with a client – at one point draping it over her shoulder, letting it fall and nodding with approval: a gesture that, professional as it was, had planted within it the seed, the hint, of a liberty. And which she didn't mind him taking. The effect was immediate.

Awoke her to a sense of possibility. It was, in fact, flattering. Not something that Maryanne – striking, not beautiful; not what the age calls beautiful – was used to.

But as much as she might point to all this and say that's what happened, there was something else beside the charm and the flattering attention. He was a shopkeeper, after all. It was his job to be charming. No, even if she didn't admit it to herself at the time, she was stirred by something else: the indefinable but unmistakable feeling that this man represented what she could only call a last chance.

She leans in her doorway, staring out into the balmy night, the priest long gone. A last chance for what? She was thirty-nine; if life hadn't already slipped by it soon would. Worse still, it was slipping by predictably. An ordinary, dull life stared her in the face. When all the time she knew that she, like her sister, was not the ordinary run. Never had been. She'd always felt different. Destined for something other than what she was getting. Always felt that life ought to hold in store for her something else. Something more. But life was miserly. Life wasn't giving away anything.

After she settled in, that sense of adventure soon faded. The pattern of her life quickly reassembled itself. She was alone, and would stay alone. This would be her life. A spinster. A school teacher. A bush school. Taking junior students. The headmistress taking the other class, the older ones. Nothing changed. Only the view from the window. This was it, her life. She would teach in town and country, beating her students into submission if need be, until she lost her strength or her will to dominate them and fell by the way. Just another leaf off just another tree. Passing away quietly, soundlessly, for all the world as though she'd never existed. One of those who come and go leaving no record, apart from the bare facts of their birth and death certificates. No story. Just two dates. And she had come to accept this.

Until the town's draper stepped out from behind his counter, suggesting to her the indefinable but unmistakable hint of an opportunity, and the conclusion that if life, miserly life, wasn't going to give her that something more, then she would have to take it. Perhaps someone really could have adventures in a place like this.

Perhaps her life didn't have to amount to just two dates on a certificate or a gravestone. There could be a story in between. A happy one. A sad one. Or even an ordinary one, for suddenly the ordinary run, the prospect of an ordinary life, filled her with something that at first she couldn't name, until she realised it was hope: husband, children, house. A chance to live just like everybody else. And, at the same time, she asked herself if this business of telling herself that she was *not* the ordinary run was a sort of compensation. That, deep in her, all she wanted was the ordinary life.

She went back to the shop after that first purchase, always mindful of the window displays. Viktor was proud of them, asking her whenever she came to the shop what she thought, the way a painter might ask about a painting, and it occurred to her after a while that his windows were artistic. Stood out from everything else in the town. One Saturday morning, in particular, she passed the shop and her attention was immediately caught by rolls of cloth: blue, grey, green, flowing down the window like rivers to where men's shirts and jumpers lay artfully arranged. Oh, yes, he was good at it. She could see that. But it wasn't the displays or the trifles, the buttons, needles and thread, that she returned for over the weeks that followed.

She looks around the dark city street: the wind has dropped, the night is quiet and calm, good for thinking. No, it wasn't the trifles. He knew it, she knew it. At some point, be it an exchange of glances, a compliment or a smile of greeting, they came to an understanding that something was happening beyond the purchase and sale of cloth and thread. And even when she discovered he was engaged to be married (a long engagement that the town had puzzled over, but was losing interest in), she kept returning. For the news of a long, drawn-out engagement was an opportunity. Carried a hint of indecision.

So she returned and returned, until one day he closed the shop for an hour after school and they walked up the hill to the botanical gardens that overlooked the town. Here, with no one about, they were free, for the town rarely bothered with its gardens. This chance, this opportunity to change her life so that it would never be the same again, she told herself, would never come again. This was one of those moments. One of those tremendous moments that change things forever, and from which most people run. And as much as Maryanne may have felt the impulse to turn and run, she wanted this thing more, whatever it came to. And so, amid birdsong and exotic trees, in the dark privacy of a corner of the gardens, she closed her eyes and let it happen.

* * *

Where was the child conceived? It's something she's thought about frequently over the last five or six months. For, somehow, it has become important. As though the environment in which a child is conceived determines the nature of the child. Was it in those gardens, amid birdsong and exotic trees, on a secluded bench, or was it in that drab back room at the school that was her accommodation? Her head tells her the latter, for that is where most of their meetings took place. But her heart tells her the gardens: a child conceived in birdsong and nature. In the end, the child will tell her, from the moment it appears and opens its eyes. For the eyes will tell her all she needs to know of the child's nature: the bright eyes of birdsong and bush, or the sombre, brooding eyes of a drab back room in a country school.

But as much as it may have been a dingy, dark room, painted in regulation brown and cream, there was an hour in the late afternoon when the sunlight flooded in. A mellow sun. And it was during one of those hours, while Viktor was pulling his trousers up as she sat fully clothed on the narrow bed (they never saw each other naked), her hair down, her head leaning back against the window, the sun behind her, that he stopped slipping his braces over his shoulders and stared at her. She didn't notice at first, but he kept staring. A long, puzzled stare.

'What are you looking at?'

The question was a mixture of curiosity and concern. Even alarm. Was something wrong? Still he looked at her, almost in a trance, without answering.

'Viktor,' and there was distinct concern in her voice this time, '*what* are you staring at?'

'You.'

She looked back at him with a frown. 'Me?'

'Yes.'

'Why?'

He spoke like someone trying to explain something that had only just occurred to him and which he didn't really understand himself. Some mystery that he hadn't yet found words for.

'You look different. Sitting there,' he said slowly, pointing at her, then letting his hand fall to his side. His face still puzzled.

'How?'

He said nothing, seeking the answer in her face.

'How? How do I look different?'

'*Schöne*,' he said, almost in a dream. '*Schöne Frau.*'

Such strange-sounding words. The language of the enemy. But wonderful. Like something out of a fairytale. And Viktor changed, it seemed to her, by the words he spoke. Not the Viktor he was a moment before.

'*Schöne* ...' he repeated, almost whispered, slowly and thoughtfully, as if it were the only word that said what he wanted to say.

'Which is?'

'Beautiful. You look beautiful,' he said, still in a daze.

She sat in silence, lingering on the words and what they meant, the wonderfully strange sound of them hanging in the air.

Hers, she knows, is not a face that the age calls beautiful. Striking is the best she gets, and not often. But when he spoke to her that afternoon, in their hour of sunlight, in a voice that was both deeply puzzled and trance-like, what the age called beauty or what any age calls beauty ceased to matter. Her skin prickled, her eyes widened, her body shivered as it would before some wondrously momentous event, and she *felt* beautiful. Never mind what the age thinks, never mind all those English roses. He believed it, and she felt it.

The local children call out in the night. A baby cries somewhere in the next street. *Schöne, schöne Frau* ... She whispers the words to herself, lingering on them once more as she did that day. It was the only time in her life anybody called her beautiful. And she firmly believes it *will* be the only time. The beautiful, she imagines, nodding in the dark street, hear it all the time until they cease to hear it. But hearing it once, when she never thought she'd hear it at all, was like one of those special moments in church when church mattered, when a rousing hymn and a bright sun lighting the coloured windows could still move her. Only this was brighter and sweeter. Hear the word time after time, like the beautiful do, and you cease to hear it at all. Hear it once and you never forget it. He believed it, she *felt* it.

'*Do* I?' she finally asked, when she'd recovered sufficiently to reply at all.

He nodded, then, as if snapping out of a spell, and finished slipping the braces over his shoulders. He then sat in the only chair in the room and, holding her stare, nodded again.

For Viktor, she suspected even back then – drunk on unfamiliar feelings and unfamiliar sounds as she was, yet clear-headed for all that – it was a dangerous moment. For it is, she imagines, staring out over the street, in moments such as those that people fall in love. Or say they have. Or think they have. And she fancifully asks herself: did he, in that moment, fall in love with her in German? Did she? A forbidden language; a forbidden love?

For Viktor was engaged. And she only had to look at him to see the mind of Viktor, who believed what he said but, at the same time, could scarcely believe he'd said it, weighing up the moment. And, judging it dangerous, he laced his shoes and put his coat on without speaking further. Almost as though he didn't trust himself to speak further. He merely muttered something about the time and the shop, and she nodded. She understood.

And with this understanding hanging in the air, and with the room's allotted afternoon sun almost run out, he closed the door behind him and slipped out along the side of the school and over the small yard that led onto the main street. Unobserved. Or so he imagined. But Viktor's departure *was* observed, every furtive step of the way, from the senior classroom window where Mrs Collins, the headmistress (a woman six years older than Maryanne, whose husband was away at the war), noted Viktor's exit, and that he was possibly coming from the direction of the junior mistress's room, or possibly not. But, above all, she would have noted that the town's draper was departing like a thief from a crime scene, and it was this, more than anything, that would have raised her eyebrows and roused her curiosity.

Maryanne knows this because as soon as he closed the door on her she rose from her bed and followed him out into the laneway, unseen. She leaned against the school wall, watching him, on the point of calling him back. But she didn't. It was only when he was gone, as she slowly turned back to her room, that she saw the fleeting, but unmistakable, figure of Mrs Collins disappearing from her window. And in that moment, she drew the inevitable conclusion: Viktor had been observed. Mrs Collins knew.

Afterwards she sat on her bed looking about the room. A room now changed. Dingy, but with its moments of sunlit danger. And words – *schöne, schöne Frau* – the likes of which had never been spoken in the room before, still hanging in the air.

* * *

After the doctor told her (it was a school half-day and she'd gone to him because she had mysteriously lost her appetite, didn't *feel* like eating), she floated up the hill to the gardens in a dream. Not just in the sense that everything looked and felt like a dream: people in the town floating by, she herself unaware of her feet on the ground, trees a luminous green, roses a golden yellow. It was more than that. As she floated up the hill, she had the distinct feeling of looking at everything for the first time. Really looking at things, and feeling them: their movements, their vibrations. The sort of sensation that, one day, people in another age would call a 'trip'.

But it was not just the dreamy look of everything – familiar streets, trees and sky made new – but the sudden turn of events as well. She walked in a dream in which the strangest things were possible. She was pregnant. No matter that she was thirty-nine and beyond having babies – at least she'd thought she was, having entered that zone of irregular 'visitings': whether early or late in life she doesn't know, because she doesn't talk about such things. No one does. But none of that mattered now. Here she was: thirty-nine, pregnant and floating up the hill to meet the father who knew nothing of this, and whom she knew was the father because there wasn't anyone else. Never had been. And she knew it would stay that way: that there would only ever be one man in her life.

How could such a thing have happened? Of course, it *was* a dream. She wasn't just floating up the hill in a dream – she was dreaming. True, the doctor had told her she was pregnant, that she had probably conceived about seven or eight weeks before. But he was in the dream too, and the words he spoke to her were words spoken in a dream. None of it was true. Of course not. She would wake any minute. But she could feel her feet on the ground now, and she knew that she wasn't dreaming – even if everything was dream-like. The most unbelievable thing had happened. And, at some stage, she started to think of this sudden turn of events as a miracle. As much as she might have thought she was beyond babies, she was going to have one. A miracle. Not exactly an immaculate conception – she *was* rushing up the hill to meet the father – but a miracle all the same. Fate had singled her out.

And as she swept up the hill to meet Viktor, she was bringing news of her miracle with her. The most unbelievable, the most wonderful, of events. And she was as light as air as she reached the top – the gardens deserted as they always were – and saw him sitting on the bench where they always met, amid birdsong and foliage. He looked at her and waved, smiling. He had no idea. How could he? She had only just found out. And in that moment, having floated up the hill, she was suddenly both light as air and heavy with her news. How to begin?

He rose to greet her and told her he had closed the shop. They had an hour. She could have smiled. Since when did they ever need an hour? As he stood and spoke to her, he seemed to enter the dream. For he spoke to her slowly, with a soft, tender voice. More than charming, with a tenderness she felt sure she'd never heard before. And with a light in his eyes she'd never seen before. Beautiful. They were living the most beautiful dream, and as much as she wanted the dream to go on and on, she had news of a miracle to deliver. And all the time – seconds, minutes – in which he spoke of the shop and the hour they had, she was bursting with this news until she could hold it in no longer.

'I'm pregnant,' she blurted.

And in that moment, the dream dissolved. His face went blank. She was no longer floating. Her feet were heavy on the ground. A flock of birds screeched into the air; the harsh everyday world, a world without beauty, colour or living dreams, the world she'd known and lived in all her life, reasserted itself and the dream collapsed. She was the forbidden love he spoke to in German. A fairytale. That was where they existed. That was the part she played in his life. She was a fairytale character in a fairytale far removed from the everyday world. But she had just stepped out of her part and into another for which he had no use: for nobody gets pregnant in fairytales. And from the moment she stepped outside that fairytale world and that fairytale life, everything came crashing down around her.

There was no uncertain pause on her part, wondering how this news might be received, for she saw all of this straightaway.

'*Pregnant?*' he eventually stammered. The soft voice was gone. The light in his eyes was now a glare. He turned from her and looked around the gardens, taking in the distant departing screech of the birds.

'You're sure? How do you know? Who have you spoken to?'

The questions were shot over his shoulder with a backward glance.

She explained. The doctor. The verdict. Baby conceived about seven or eight weeks before. Yes, the doctor was sure. Staked his reputation on it.

He eyed her, up and down, as if she were lying. Worse, as if she'd planned this weeks before and he'd walked right into a trap. Crafty bitch ... It was all there in his eyes. Eyes that not so long ago had seen the beauty in her that no one else had ever seen now saw only a crafty bitch. And the same Viktor who was too afraid to speak, afraid of the danger of those moments when people say things they *think* they mean and in which they fall in love, or think they do, now shot questions at her over his shoulder without care or concern. And at some point she realised she was crying. Crying, for heaven's sake. When was the last time she'd cried? Years ago. She hadn't allowed herself the luxury of tears since she was a child. But there she was, at the top of the hill, thirty-nine, pregnant and crying. Never so achingly alone.

He kicked the dirt and looked around the gardens again. Rigid, apart from a deep intake of breath and a sigh that was instantly comprehendible: What a mess!

'You'll have to go away.' He spoke without even looking at her. 'You can't stay. The whole town will soon know. The town will talk. You can't stay.'

That was when he turned to her. Whether he could see her tears, she couldn't tell. He didn't speak of tears. He didn't come near her. He didn't touch her. He could barely look at her. Suddenly, he was an engaged man. Had responsibilities. Commitments. Duties. Promises to keep. Honour to consider. He threw these things at her as if speaking to a child. Couldn't she see that? No, he seemed to conclude, she couldn't. Or wouldn't. Crafty bitch ... He sighed again. What a mess!

She had brought news of a miracle, while between sighs he talked of his responsibilities. What on earth did she expect of him? And with that question and in that moment, she drew breath. What did she expect? She barely knew. For a moment there, while she floated up the hill, she may have expected ... something. Improbable happiness, some sort of wonderful ordinariness. How could she explain? She barely knew herself. He stood shooting questions at her without care. She stopped crying. And she knew, right then, that she should have expected nothing. She'd been a fool.

It was, she knew instinctively, one of those moments we never really recover from. She will be seventy and the memory of what has just happened will always be recalled with pained surprise. Her eyes might have been wet from fresh tears, but iron entered her, body and soul. And she knew, with absolute clarity, that she would never forgive him.

She wanted nothing of him now. He was unworthy of the miracle. She saw this in an instant. And for a moment it felt to her as though her conception *were* immaculate. That he had nothing to do with it. Could not possibly have had anything to do with it, such was his unworthiness. He'd been revealed for what he was and had always been – a small-town draper. Talking of his responsibilities and his honour, of the family business, when she brought miracles. Something tremendous.

But most people run from the tremendous, and Viktor was just most people, after all. He was running. Even as he spoke, he ran. And honour? She had to laugh at that, for the town's gossip had informed her weeks ago that the town saw no honour in him. He had already received white feathers in the mail or delivered under the shop door. Viktor, spelled the German way. Viktor Muller. Why hadn't he changed any of that? Why wasn't he in uniform? He was not a young man, but men older than him, like Mrs Collins's husband, were in uniform. He was either a coward or a spy. Someone ought to report him. Have him locked up. No, the town saw no honour in Viktor Muller. Nor did Maryanne. No, this child was not born to be fathered by a small-town draper, or to be taught the trade of the draper and haberdasher: words she now mentally spits into the inner-city suburban night air. The child, she knew from the first, was going to be larger than that, and from the moment of its conception had outgrown the father.

He said something about meeting the next day, and she guessed why: money, an address to write to when the time came.

'We should walk back separately,' he added.

'But nobody ever comes here, Viktor. Isn't that why we do?'

And it was then, as if on cue, that a third figure entered the gardens. And not just any figure. Mrs Collins, who never seemed to leave the school, stood on the edge of the lawns, her progress halted by what she saw. She stared at Viktor and Maryanne without greeting them, not even a nod, drawing her conclusions, then straightening herself and finding her privacy in another part of the gardens.

'Damn.' Viktor looked down at the sandy pathway. 'That's all I need! I'll go first.'

And with that he wheeled around and strode away, Mrs Collins nowhere in sight. His path curved, dipped, and he was gone. Maryanne was left standing by the bench, palms on her stomach. She had floated up the hill in a dream, bearing news of a miracle. The dream had dissolved the moment she told him, but the miracle was still there beneath her palms. Fate had singled her out. For *this*. A fate unlike any she'd contemplated before coming to the town. And as she set off back down the hill, alone, never so achingly alone, it was also with an odd sense of resolve. Alone, but singled out. Different. The bearer of a miracle. And her life, until now devoted simply to getting through from one day to another, would be devoted to this.

* * *

She returned to her room after school to find a note slipped under her door. Mrs Collins was waiting to see her in her office. Such a serious, high-minded woman. One of those upon whom the worries of the world seemed to sit; one of those who looked at you in a manner that says: Don't you understand?

I am Atlas; I bear the weight of the world. Its injustice and wrongs. Somebody has to. For the world is all wrong. And I must set it right. I am chosen. And yet, all the time through the first interview when Maryanne had arrived at the school, she'd had to suppress a smile. In case the smile became a giggle. And that would never have done. And all because of an old childhood rhyme she'd forgotten about until the name Mrs Collins brought it back.

Mrs Collins lost her drawers;
Won't you please lend her yours?

But Maryanne wasn't smiling that afternoon. The note was a summons. And she knew why. Maryanne dropped her classroom things on her small desk and walked back into the school, up the silent and deserted hallway to the office.

Without speaking, Mrs Collins pointed to a chair on the other side of an imposing desk. She signed a piece of paper then looked up at Maryanne as if, it seemed to Maryanne, she were studying some nasty mark on the carpet.

'A certain gentleman,' Mrs Collins began, going straight to the matter, 'a certain gentleman from the town, a gentleman engaged to be married, I might add, has been seen leaving your room.'

Her voice was controlled, but only just. She glared at Maryanne across the desk.

'By whom, Mrs Collins?'

'Do you deny it?'

'Deny what?'

Mrs Collins straightened herself, her voice rising in response to the sheer cheek of the question. 'That this gentleman was seen leaving your room …'

'I can't be responsible for what people see or think they see, Mrs Collins.'

'The same gentleman,' Mrs Collins added, as if Maryanne had never spoken, 'the same gentleman you were seen with this morning in the gardens. Do you deny that?'

Maryanne was weary. Her day had already been long. Her life would never be the same again. And although she had floated up the hill in a weightless dream, she was now beginning to feel the weight of the change. She was heavy with it, and the questions added to her weariness. But among it all there was this miracle that had happened. A child. She could scarcely believe it. And as much as Mrs Collins sought to impose her disapproval and displeasure upon her, Maryanne kept returning to the prospect of a child. *Hers*. The world is big, she was thinking; a baby small. The baby will look to her for *everything*. And she will give it that everything, while, small at first, it grows into the world. A mother. She will be a mother. She was only beginning to comprehend it, in all its wonder and terror.

She was contemplating all of this, in a world of her own, when she became aware of Mrs Collins's eyes staring at her. No, glaring, demanding an answer.

'We met and spoke in the gardens. That is true. People meet and speak there all the time.' She paused, adding, 'Does it matter?'

'Matter!' Mrs Collins almost jumped from her chair. 'Do you deny he was ever in your room?'

More questions. And she knew this was a difficult question. If she said yes, she'd be lying. And Maryanne doesn't lie. If she said no, she'd be bowing to her inquisitor and confirming the gossipy suspicion of the small-town spy in Mrs Collins. There was a third alternative. She could simply place herself above such questions. For something mighty had happened. Something that swept her up and soared above all this. What *of* talking in the gardens with a certain gentleman? What *of* her room, and who visited? 'Beautiful, *schöne, schöne Frau* ...' he'd said. And it suddenly occurred to Maryanne that *that* was the moment: that was the day the baby was conceived and that was why she was suddenly beautiful. There was a reason for Viktor's sudden observation, one that neither of them understood at the time. But which she now did.

'It's seems,' she said, choosing the third alternative, 'that you've already made up your mind.'

'So, it's true?'

'Did I say that?'

'Answer me.'

She was doomed anyway, with mightier things on her mind, and was strangely calm, as though two people she knew were talking and she was merely watching. 'Is this any of your concern? *Why* do you ask, Mrs Collins?'

Looking back, it was as though Mrs Collins was a bomb set to go off, and Maryanne's casual reply the detonator. And there was a part of Maryanne that was intrigued, almost amused, by the spectacle. She was clearly going to be sacked, so what *was* the point of all this?

'*Why?* This is my school. *Mine.* Do you have no shame?'

The exploding Mrs Collins delivered the question with a roar, the noise lingering, then tapering into silence. All that was lacking, it seemed to Maryanne, was the dust and smoke.

Mrs Collins lost her drawers …

Make the powerful comical and they are no longer powerful. How, Mrs Collins, did you lose your drawers? It wasn't something Maryanne had ever contemplated before, and for the first time it occurred to her that it was not such an innocent little rhyme after all. How indeed?

Mrs Collins rose from her chair, turned round and, with her back to Maryanne, contemplated the main street beyond the window, a view that Maryanne, from her chair, vaguely took in too. A large banner with a giant 'Yes' was stretched across the Masonic Lodge opposite. A dog yelped at anything that passed. A truck drew up, a soldier got out. A crowd began to gather. When Mrs Collins turned back to her she was composed: one of those who could switch their moods on and off in a moment. Perhaps it came with the weight of great responsibility.

'You will leave this school at the end of the week,' she said, adding that it was just as well the holidays started the following week.

Yes, Maryanne thinks, standing in her inner-city doorway, looking onto the street: there was no scandal, nothing so grand as an 'affair', just an unfortunate business that did not need to be spoken of again.

Mrs Collins resumed her seat and opened a drawer, pulled out an envelope and passed it across the desk to Maryanne.

'There's a week's wages. And two weeks for the holidays. Be thankful you've got that.'

There was a touch of pity in her voice, or perhaps it was just despair, that said: Aren't you too old for all this, you silly woman? She turned back to the view from her window: the crowd gathering on the dusty street, the dog kicked into a whimper by the soldier. 'What a world,' she said, shaking her head, as if to add: They sack silly young maids for this, not women of our age.

She wrote a name and address on a sheet of paper and handed it to Maryanne. 'There, that's the headmaster of a school near your home whom you can contact. I'll write to him.' She handed Maryanne the sheet of paper and nodded towards the door, as much as to say, our business is done. You are now off my hands. And Maryanne took the sheet of paper with a vague thank you. A vagueness that Mrs Collins took to be casual, if not insolent. She stared at Maryanne with a look that this time pronounced her trouble: trouble that she was glad to be rid of.

Maryanne was tired as she closed the office door behind her. She returned to her room, lay down and drifted into a deep afternoon sleep. But before she drifted off she heard the echo of a softly spoken 'beautiful', and closed her eyes, convinced that that was it, that was when the baby was conceived and that was why Viktor suddenly saw beauty in her when no one before had. *Schöne, schöne Frau* ... There was a reason ...

* * *

Her meeting with Viktor the next morning before work was a quick exchange, almost between strangers: he constantly looking about in case they were seen, while he gave her a roll of notes and an envelope containing an address she could write to when the time came, or if she had to. She told him she'd been sacked, and he rolled his eyes: one person knowing about them, in a small town, was one person too many. What a mess! But he shot her a glance that also said, it's all for the best. Then, still anxiously looking about, he took a step back and offered her the slightest of bows, as if they'd been dancing, the dance had got out of control, and now the dance was over. He turned and was gone. A different Viktor. A changed man. Or, perhaps, the Viktor he always was. And, she knew, a Viktor she would never forgive. For Maryanne is one of those you only cross once. Once trust – like faith – is broken, it stays broken.

She looked down at the roll of money in her hand, wishing she could have flung it back in his face as he had flung back the gift of her miracle. With no wedding ring on her finger, she knew then there'd be no end of the Mrs Collinses of this world ready to pronounce her a whore, and with the roll of notes in her hand, part of her felt like one. But the fact, the pathetic fact, was that she needed that money. That money would help sustain her. Sustain *them.* And she could tell, just by the weight of the roll, that there was a lot of it. And the security it gave her outweighed the indignity of receiving it. He had wheeled off, without looking back. And she was alone in the gardens. She could have wept all over again. Eve, after Adam stormed out on her. But Eve wasn't alone, was she? She had this gift. Eve was no longer one, but two. She drew comfort from the thought, and stroked her belly in silent communion. And felt an odd sense of strength, that she had been singled out and she could do this. She *was* different. Different from what she had been and would have been had she never come to this place. She might have been alone in her garden, watching the rapidly diminishing figure of Adam storming off, but she had never felt so alive. Never so filled with purpose.

By late Saturday morning she was standing on the station platform. The view of the town hadn't changed. It was still pretty. A little Switzerland in the Victorian countryside. And, above it all, the gardens and the many wandering paths it contained and which she could easily picture. No, the town hadn't changed. Or the view. But the viewer had. She'd arrived in summer, now autumn had fallen. A short time. But enough to make her life different in such a way that it would never be the same again. And between the inevitability of two dates, there was now a story, the indignity and the security of a roll of notes in her handbag, and a swelling in her belly that would soon begin to show. The egg from which a story would be hatched.

* * *

That was how it happened: common, grubby even, a gloomy back room painted in regulation brown and cream, hurried meetings and brief farewells before sneaking off. And yet like nothing else she had ever known before or would again. All changed.

Maryanne stares out into the night. That touch of spring is leaving the air. The street is empty and still. She feels a sudden shiver. The yellow light disappears from the doorway as she closes the door and steps back inside, leaving the inky darkness to spread over the streets, cottages and rooftops of the suburb.

Inside, Katherine is reading the paper, but looks up when Maryanne enters the room.

'Gone?'

Maryanne, still dwelling in that strange, fairytale world she entered and lived in for a short while, looks at her, puzzled. *'Gone?'*

'Father Geoghan,' Katherine replies, as if to say, who else?

Maryanne nods as she sits. 'Yes, gone for now.' She pauses, her mind returning to the priest's visit. 'He means to wear me down.'

Katherine says nothing, scrutinising her sister as she ponders the comment, both concerned but also alive to her sister's flaws. Don't think I don't care, Maryanne, the look seems to be saying, but don't think I don't know you. You imagine something, and just because you imagine it, you think you can make it real. As if the world will bend to your will because you imagine it so, but are you taking on more than you know? Look at you, you're exhausted already.

Maryanne sighs, glancing at her sister. Yes. That's it. That's what she's thinking. Little sister, too much imagination for your own good. Living some dream that is bound to collide with life and shatter because the world doesn't work like that. Taking on something that is bigger than she understands. A permanent little girl with great expectations and grand dreams deciding things inside the grown-up Maryanne. Yes, that's how Katherine sees her sister. Not quite grown up. And she may well be right.

Maryanne studies her. They barely look like sisters. That they don't think alike doesn't surprise her. There is a seven-year difference between them, and since the death of their mother giving birth to their younger brother (neither mother nor child survived), Katherine has been both a mother and older sister. Their father, a police constable, continued to bring money in until he dropped dead one day on the street. But it was Katherine who ran the house. It was only when Maryanne was grown and working at the school that Katherine announced one day that she was off. Off? Off where? To see the country, said Katherine. She'd always wanted to see the country. All of it. She would travel it, she would find work, whatever came up. She would send money, to help keep the house. And so she did. She returned every year with tales of her travels, and then was off again. That was twenty years ago, and she is still travelling the country, for the country, she tells Maryanne, is large; she only has one life and fears she will never see it all.

And as much as Maryanne enjoys her tales, she's always shaken her head at the many requests she's had from Katherine for them both to explore the country together. It's a wide, wide world out there, Katherine would tell her. Come with me. But Maryanne likes cities and towns. They're different. But what Maryanne will never understand is how she can walk the breadth of the country and not be cowed, yet defer to the likes of Father Geoghan in a way Maryanne has long ceased to do. So it's with a puzzled look on her face that Maryanne addresses Katherine.

'How *can* you still believe it all?'

Katherine is a bit put out, for the tone of Maryanne's question bears little of the respect for an older sister that it should. 'Believe what?'

'God, heaven, hell,' Maryanne answers. 'We're not children any more. How can you believe any of it?'

'How can you *not*?'

Katherine's response – impatient, like a parent talking to a clever child, one that may well be just a bit too clever for her own good – is said in a way that assumes this is all beyond question.

Of course, Maryanne muses, contemplating her sister's way of looking at the world: take away God, heaven and hell, and nothing makes sense, does it? And we can't live in a world like that. It's *got* to make sense. But that's just it, it doesn't. At least, not the way they tell you, dear sister. Certainly not the way the Father Geoghans of this world tell you. But perhaps, for Katherine, it's a way of not being alone out there in the bush. And she's never thought of it like that before: God as a sort of companion, someone to talk to. Like a mate. Perhaps, in the end, they found different Gods. Katherine's is company, a friendly ear at the end of the day around the fire. *I have warmed both hands*, Maryanne suddenly finds herself thinking: an old poem, but whose? *I have warmed both hands before the fire of life, it sinks ... something, something ...* Is that the way Katherine sees it? Is that the God she found, and sticks to like a friend? Someone who's *there*. Beside her, while she warms her hands by the fire. Whereas for Maryanne, there was only ever the God of Fear.

'Oh,' Maryanne eventually replies, almost lightly, picking up the conversation, 'I might still believe in hell.'

'Is that a joke?' Katherine says, her frown suggesting that if it is, it's not funny. 'You've picked up some clever ideas since you stopped going to church, haven't you?'

'Oh, it's no joke. I saw it today. Hell, I mean.' Maryanne turns the tea-pot round in her palms, nodding at the newspaper:

'Duty', 'Hun' and 'Yes' written large on the open page. 'And it was frightening, but … fascinating.'

'That wasn't hell, that was your imagination.' And Maryanne notes again that Katherine uses the word 'imagination' in a way that suggests there's something unhealthy about having it when you're grown: something that will eventually get you into trouble.

Maryanne ignores her and continues as if her sister hasn't spoken.

'There were two choirs on opposite sides of the street. One on the steps of the Post Office, the other lined up behind Mannix.'

Katherine nods slowly at the mention of Mannix. A great man, the nod says: a great man we are lucky to have fighting our battles; come at just the right time, as the great do.

'It was like watching opposing armies. All praying to *their* God before battle.' Maryanne pauses a moment. 'Rocks, eggs, drunks, choirs, fights, blood and this … this madness. As though everybody, every single last one of them, had given up their minds.' She turns to Katherine, suddenly intense, almost, it seems to her sister, frightening. '*That's* what I call hell. And it wasn't my imagination. I *saw* it.' An odd smile lights her face. 'And it was fascinating. Horrible, but fascinating.' She pauses again, caught by a thought. 'And Father Geoghan …'

'What of him?'

'Do you really think he believes in God?'

'What sort of question is that?'

'I think,' Maryanne says slowly, 'I think he believes in hell. I think he believes in hell more than anything else. That he'd be lost without it.'

'And what,' Katherine asks briskly, changing the almost sacrilegious subject, 'were you doing walking round the city?' She doesn't add with a belly like that, but she doesn't have to; the look says it all.

Maryanne answers her calmly, knowing how preposterous her words will sound. 'I get restless. Confined. I have to get up and go out or I feel like I'll go mad. I have to go ... somewhere. And today I went to a suffragette meeting. Oh, they don't go around calling themselves that. What *do* they call themselves? Women's Peace Army? I think that's it ...'

Katherine stares at her, concerned. '*What?*'

'I've never been to one before.'

'You've been with those types?'

'What types?' Maryanne asks with what she knows is a maddening incomprehension.

'You know what types. Everybody knows. Those women who stir things up.'

'I just wanted to see for myself. And they're no different from you or me.'

'Not like *me*, they're not!'

'That's just it: you're just their type, don't you know?' Maryanne smiles at her sister, remembering the meeting. 'I felt ... at home. For the first time in a long time. Nobody staring at me: no wedding ring, swollen belly. If it wasn't quite home, at least I felt welcome. They gave me tea afterwards, and a card, and invited me to visit their offices whenever I wanted. Then I left and walked headlong into the mob.' Here, she stares long and hard at her sister. 'And, believe me, the difference was night and day. Things making sense, and then no sense at all. A place of reason, and a place of no reason whatsoever. *That's* hell.'

Katherine stares back at her sister with a mixture of admiration and reproof and shakes her head. The sympathetic reproof of an older sister who is sure *she,* not Maryanne, knows how the real world works. But she's wary too, for there's an intensity in her little sister, a sort of waywardness that was always there: laughing in church, giving the boys the eye, or giving them more of her eyes than was good for her. A kind of recklessness, a hunger for something more than life was giving her. And now this ... consorting with these women. Bad as Bolsheviks. And the look on Katherine's face also asks: Maryanne, aren't you a little old for all this?

A silence hangs between them briefly, a stand-off, before Katherine speaks, changing the topic once more. Changing her tone. Now it's personal. Two sisters talking of something that matters: something that *really* matters.

'Will you go to the home? See it?'

Maryanne strokes her belly, scarcely believing what her sister has said. There is accusation in her reply. 'Do *you* think it's theirs?'

'Perhaps we should see it.'

'*Do* you?'

'No! But let's see the place. And not because Father Geoghan says. Just to find out. No harm.'

'You don't think I can do this, do you?'

'I didn't say that. But don't you think we ought to see it? So we know, if we ever need to?'

Maryanne leans back in her chair, staring at the best ceiling of the best room in the house, her earlier suspicions now confirmed, eyes and head suddenly aching with tiredness. She doesn't think I can do it. They all want me to farm the child out. Give it up. The priest thinks it's theirs. Mannix thinks it is. God thinks it is, and God wants what's God's. Men and women in the street she's known all her life look at her with either pity or contempt. And Eve, fallen woman, expelled from her garden by Mrs Collins, who lost her drawers, suddenly feels the loneliness of her expulsion, while stroking her belly. Now, it seems to her, huge: like the job in front of her.

The world will call the child a bastard. A bastard child. She's never spoken the word. At least, has no memory of ever using it. And why should she have? Or thought about it, until the child. But out there the world will call the child a bastard: a cruel word. One of those words that wound. And as she dwells on it she is suddenly *in* some cruel, distant playground. She *is* her child and the child's pain is hers, as the blow of the word comes down upon it. And she knows she can bear her own pain, but not this, not the pain of her child. And, not for the first time, she's asking herself: what if they're right, after all? Father Geoghan and all the Father Geoghans? Will not the child be best removed from the stain of its conception, so that it knows not its shame? And then, and only then, the words 'bastard' and 'illegitimate' will *not* rain down on it and mark the child for life. So that it will not one day look about in that distant playground and see that everybody has gone, because no one will play with the bastard child.

And what if they're right, after all? For a moment, she almost agrees. Feels the weariness of a long day and a long evening taking effect. Weighing her down. Feels the resolve and the strength of the day going out of her. They wear you down, these people. They come back for you again and again. For that won't be the last of Father Geoghan.

Her eyes droop. She's tired. No, exhausted. It's true, she can't do this. She barely has the strength to look after herself. They're right. They're all right. They were all along. The enormity of it all is suddenly apparent. It had been there all the time, only she never saw it. Or never wanted to see it. A child! Not just for an hour or two, babysitting for a friend on Sundays, but forever. At her age. And lately, she's been feeling her age. For she has just progressed from thirty-nine to forty. And there is something in the change of numbers that makes her feel too old for all this. How will she work when the money finally runs out? If Father Geoghan is right, the school won't take her back. How will she find the hours in the days and nights – and where on earth will she find the money for all the things she can think of and all the things she can't think of yet because she doesn't know what she's in for? Hasn't the faintest idea. And the enormity of it all, like some laughing Jack springing from a box, is suddenly obvious. Staring her in the face. She can bear the looks she gets in the street, in shops and on trams. Knowing looks. Day in, day out. She can bear that. She's grown. But can she bear passing that weight on to her child? Have them all staring at the child the way they stare at her?

Yes, she can bear her own pain – but her child's? And even if she could, should she put the child through it? Is it fair? Wouldn't it be better all round to give the child a clean break? A chance in life, a better chance than she can give it. And the strength seeping from her, she closes her eyes in surrender.

'Yes, I'll go to the home. I'll see it.'

'We both will,' Katherine says, eyeing the weary frame of her sister. 'Just so we know. No harm.'

'No.'

Maryanne has almost succumbed to sleep when she hears Katherine clearing the table and snaps her eyes open.

'Let me help.'

'No.'

'But …'

Katherine shakes her head. 'There's no need. Rest.'

Unresisting, Maryanne sinks back into her chair, and immediately dozes off, vaguely aware of the sound of cups, the pot, the plates, being taken to the kitchen at the back of the house. When she opens her eyes again the room will be cleared, everything will be gone. Simple. And in that moment, eyes closed while the room is being cleared, she can see how much easier and simpler for everyone it would be. Just close your eyes and let somebody else clear things up. Take matters off your hands. So that when you open your eyes, as she does now, there's no sign that anything – cups, plates, pot – was ever there.

4.

Row after row of cots. All in neatly arranged aisles. Stretching out across a vast hall. It could almost be a factory. But the babies are not made here, they're brought here. Every now and then a tiny hand reaches up into the air: a tentacle testing space to see if anyone is out there. And finding nothing, returns to the security of the cot. So many, and all so quiet. What do they do to make them so quiet?

Maryanne is walking slowly along one of the aisles, Katherine behind her, and a nun, elderly and calm (as though she's been doing this all her life and seen it all, which she possibly has), beside her. She talks like a kindly factory owner giving Maryanne and Katherine an inspection of her plant. She points to this child and that: mostly the babies of young girls, too young to look after themselves, let alone a baby. Young girls running wild, their fathers gone to war or gone to drink. And their mothers, worn out by a lifetime of having one baby after another, too tired to look after their own – let alone the children of their children. And so here they are. God's children now.

And then, the nun goes on, there are the mothers who just can't cope any more, the mothers who finished up with one baby too many and went a little mad for a while. And the husband-less mothers and the wife-less fathers with babies they can't keep, as much as they might want to. Which brings her to the babies that nobody wants. Never intended for the world, never wanted. Little white elephants. She smiles at one cot after another, reeling off their names. If they're lucky they'll be adopted out to good religious homes. Or go to their special callings. If not, there is the orphanage. But all God's children now, the little foundlings.

Foundlings. The word is all wrong, Maryanne can't help but think. Because they're not found. They're given away. Abandoned, even. And suddenly she's picturing a world of abandoned things: children, toys, homes. All the things that nobody cares about or wants any more. Cast-offs at white-elephant fetes. Like these babies. No matter what becomes of them, they will always have an abandoned look: an emptiness in them that a mother or father might have filled. Thrown into the world, casting around, picking themselves up and going through life with that lost look forever in their eyes. And so many. But you can't call it the thrown children's home, or the lost children's home, can you? So it's the foundling home, and she guesses there's a bit of hope in the choice of words. But only a bit. For the very word, foundling, will always remind her of abandoned animals.

At some point Maryanne decides she's seen enough. She tells Katherine, and her sister, gazing thoughtfully on the rows of cots, nods in silent agreement and they turn around,

Sister Bernadette (for that, they have discovered, is her name) leading the way. There are occasional cries from a cot here and there, but the place is eerily quiet. And every now and then a little hand reaches up into the air, testing, once again, to see if anybody is out there. And finding nothing, falls back again to the security of the cot. And so it will be, Maryanne imagines, throughout the morning and the afternoon and the evening: all the mornings, afternoons and evenings. A hand will rise into the air, and retreat. Rise and retreat. Until, one morning or afternoon, someone comes along and takes that hand in theirs. Or does not come along, and the little hand tires of testing the air and eventually gives up.

That baby, that one or that one, Maryanne tells herself as they leave the hall, could be my child. Testing the air, and finding nothing there, until it gives up. But she knows before she even leaves the place that the hand of her child will never become one of these tentative feelers, because she will never give the child up. And, for this, it has been worth the visit. Well, Katherine, we've seen the place; now we know.

Suddenly, she can't wait to get out. There are hurried goodbyes and thank-yous at the front door, Sister Bernadette watching them leave with the kindly eyes that have seen it all and know full well that this one has got away from them. For as enormous as the task of bringing up the child by herself may seem to Maryanne, the task *will* be her life's work. Her life *will* be different from anything she ever imagined. And when her child's hand reaches into the air – morning, afternoon or evening – it will discover that there is someone out there, someone who loves it. Not God's child, but *hers*.

As they are walking up the path to the front gate of the home, Maryanne comes to a sudden stop. For there, not far from the path (and they weren't there when Maryanne and Katherine arrived), in a leafy part of the grounds is a small group of pregnant girls. One of them, Maryanne guesses, is no more than thirteen or fourteen. Katherine stops too, at first puzzled, until she follows Maryanne's gaze.

The girls – and Maryanne, at what seems the terribly advanced age of forty, can only think of them as girls – are sitting on benches in the shade. All dressed in simple smocks, pregnant girls. Possibly on a break from their duties at the home. There are roses and geraniums in bloom. Without the need of being told, she is certain that none of these girls will leave the home with their babies. There they are in varying stages of pregnancy, chatting or silently sitting with their thoughts.

Suddenly, two of them jump up and begin chasing each other around the group. Girls, she tells herself again, still with the child's impulse to spontaneously play, throw caution to the wind, and be children again. The group looks up at the two girls; laughter chimes in the morning air. The game finishes; the chaser and the chased sink onto their chairs, faces flushed and grinning. A stolen moment.

Maryanne looks back at Katherine, slowly shaking her head. They move on, leaving the scene behind, having been unobserved the whole time. But the memory of hands like feelers reaching into the air and that garden of pregnant girls stays with her long after: throughout the afternoon, and the days and months that follow.

* * *

Steam from the engine trails past the carriage window as they leave. She watches the station recede. Broadmeadows. It is a name that suggests pleasant English fields of grain or grass, swaying in a gentle summer breeze. But these paddocks of Scotch thistle and scrub are hardly what she calls meadows. The foundling home is only nine or ten miles from the city, but it may as well be in the country. White smoke – which, years from now, she will learn is the sign of a good fireman – obscures the view like sudden cloud, then parts just as quickly to reveal open paddocks, occasional houses and the odd shop of a small farming community. And, in the distance, Maryanne can see what appears to be a mansion.

The train slows for the next station, for the small farming community has a station, as well as a flour mill and tall silos that rise before her like a medieval castle. A landmark, she guesses, visible for miles around. And as the train slows she is drawn into the view, as if being drawn into a painting. One that moves. Is alive. And it is strangely entrancing, as if the place itself has cast a spell on her. Or perhaps she is just tired, the way travelling makes you tired. The way Katherine is tired, close to nodding off in front of her. She turns back to the view, drawn into it again. She's never laid eyes on this place before, and yet she knows it. Feels an odd connection. Strange, she muses, how some places speak to the very heart of us. They *think* us, and we cannot resist.

The train huffs to a stop just before the station platform begins, almost as though it just felt like it. And Maryanne finds herself looking down a dirt road. A picket fence here, a street lamp a little way ahead. Two people are walking down the road: a soldier and a woman. She may be his wife, or a friend or sister, but the way the soldier is walking – his stiff upright carriage, the tilt of the head when he turns to her, that touch of formality – suggests she is the rather formal mother of a rather formal family. At least, it does to Maryanne. Besides, mothers are much on her mind. The soldier – an officer, for he wears an officer's hat – is carrying not a rifle, but a tennis racquet.

The train moves on then stops in the station. A horse and jinker, the driver holding the reins, wait on a sandy pathway that runs alongside the platform. The train moves on again, a cloud of steam obscures the view and when it parts the view is gone. Changed. She is no longer drawn into it. The spell is broken. But she can't help wondering about the two people, and the odd image of a soldier striding off down that dirt road and into battle, carrying not a rifle but a tennis racquet, comes to her. Then she pictures a battalion of soldiers, an army of them, striding into battle, not with rifles but tennis racquets.

Volley upon volley of white tennis balls flying forward and back and forward again over the net of the front line: white tennis balls, flying and bouncing from one side to the other, occasionally dropping into no-man's land, where, no doubt, they would be collected at the close of the day's play.

It's a fanciful thought that amuses her for a minute or two. But it's just that. Fanciful. For the world has given birth to a beast. It is the Age of the Beast. Everywhere, in everything. And the armies of the beast are not clutching tennis racquets but rifles: firing off not white, fluffy tennis balls, but shells and bombs. Huge weapons to squash tiny tin soldiers. It is everywhere, this mood: a mass surrender to the beast in all of us. In shop windows, draped across public buildings, in every eye on every street, in the newspapers and magazines everybody devours on trams and in stations, howling with death and darkness and accusation, as if written by the three-headed dog of hell itself. An awful time to be born into.

And the Milhaus case, one of those scandals that consumes a city from time to time, in the newspapers day after day after day: a story to set the beast's nostrils twitching with the smell of blood. And, for a moment, Maryanne can imagine what it is to live through the worst of a revolution, like the one sweeping over Russia right now and over the pages of the newspapers; can imagine what it's like to be there when history shrugs, and the Father Geoghans of this world have their hour of mastery over human souls. But it's the here and now she can't escape. Ugly days. Days of a dark sun, even in glaring spring.

Maryanne draws herself up in the carriage seat, rubs her belly, and looks out to this world she barely recognises any more as hers, as if about to do battle with the beast herself.

Neither Maryanne nor Katherine has spoken since they boarded the train. Now Katherine, speaking slowly, drowsily, with a puzzled and thoughtful frown as she gazes out the window, asks, 'Just what do they give them to make them so quiet?'

Maryanne nods. 'I was thinking that too.'

'Babies aren't quiet,' Katherine adds, with the authority of someone who's delivered a few in her time on remote bush stations, miles from doctors. 'Not *that* quiet.'

They fall into thoughtful silence, staring out the window. Neither of them has said as much, but it is understood, silently agreed upon, that they have seen the home. And will not be seeing it again.

Gradually, Katherine's eyes close and she nods off to the rhythmic clicking of the rails. Maryanne sits, haunted by the memory of tiny feelers testing the air, unable to sleep. But she is also comforted, has drawn strength from the visit, because her sister now thinks she *can* do it. Or, at least, thinks she *must* do it. And although Katherine has been beside her these last weeks, looking after her, doing what she's always done, she's now *with* her. In spirit, and Katherine's, Maryanne notes, smiling at her sleeping sister, is a big spirit. And when she gives, she gives everything. And Maryanne sits, as if warming her hands by the glow of that spirit.

One stop comes, then another. And another: Essendon. It's a wonder, she muses, looking out the window, that they haven't got around to changing that name. But they haven't, and here this place is, complete with a station: a little Germany on the fringes of the city. She amuses herself with alternative names for a moment or two while passengers get off and on, but can come up with nothing satisfactory, and perhaps that's what happened. Nobody else could either. And so here it sits, this little Germany: a foreign land now receding as it slips from view. Then it is gone.

There is a novel on her lap. Hardy. *Tess of the d'Urbervilles.* She finished the book on the way to the foundling home and both likes and doesn't like it, just as she both likes and doesn't like Tess. A sad but annoying girl. And that's all she'd be if it weren't for the old family name, the local squire and the squire's mansion and land. Money and a grand old name – that changes everything. An irritating girl becomes a heroine, and her story becomes tragic. A pure woman no more. If it weren't for the squire and the horse, wouldn't it be just plain pathetic? What if Tess were just an annoying girl with a vivid imagination who fell on her back in an open field with a farmhand and wound up with a swollen belly? Or in a city laneway with a factory hand? Or in the back room of a school house with a small-town shopkeeper? Not the same story. No woman fallen from purity there.

But Maryanne can't picture Tess riding into the forest on anything but a squire's horse, her arms around the squire's waist; the horse, rehearsed in its role, slowing to a trot in the moonlight; and Tess minutes from being a fallen woman. We might all be fallen, she faintly smiles, thinking of Father Geoghan on his Sunday pulpit, only some are more tragically fallen than others. Almost makes the fall worthwhile.

Maryanne's story, the thing that fills out the years between two dates, has no squire, only a shopkeeper. A draper and haberdasher, from a family of shopkeepers. No grand family name, no title, no family estate to come begging to, no wild ride into the forest on a black steed, no moonlight fall. And as much as she might like to imagine the child being conceived in the gardens amid birdsong and trees, it was more than likely in the dingy room at the back of the school: a dingy room with its allotted hour of afternoon sun and talk of beauty, but cramped and dingy all the same. Is that a story worthy of a miracle? To be jilted by a lord, deprived of the family fortune and cast out into a cold world that doesn't care – that is one thing. But to be jilted by a small-town draper – that is another.

And so, with the book on her lap and staring out the carriage window, her thoughts turn to the story life has given her, and the one that life didn't, but *could* have.

Yes, to be jilted by a small-town shopkeeper is unfortunate, at best. But to have the giant door of the family mansion slammed in your face, that is another thing altogether. Tragic. Noble. Worthy of a miracle. A story to stir more than just a shrug. Or a shake of the head before getting on with things. To have a titled door slammed in your face – *that* invites sympathy, compassion, sorrow. And anger, for there is injustice in slamming the giant family door in the face of a pure woman: it casts her into a contest she can never win. Maryanne nods slowly, looking out the window. *That's* a story, like doing battle with some ancient god after it's taken your virtue and cast you aside: pounced on your innocence, then, well satisfied with its sport, gone off laughing. And you, left huddled on some windswept, lonely road, the seed and fruit of the god's sport in your belly. Yes, that's a story.

But she's in a country without lords or squires or an aristocracy. And all those ancient gods have long since left the scene. But there are lords of sorts, and mansions of sorts: landowners with acres and acres of countryside, fathers and sons who'd think nothing of casually pouncing on a woman's innocence, then casting her aside and slamming the family door in her face. Not quite gods and not quite lords, but godlike and lordly enough to make it a struggle that is nobly lost before it's begun. Uneven. Unjust. Almost tragic.

She opens the book at the last page. The black flag of Tess's death is raised. Two observers of the sombre spectacle kneel in prayer, then rise. Homage is done. A tragic tale has been told.

There is much to be learned from literature, and Maryanne is learning. The story must be large, a noble yet futile struggle against the gods of the day. And so Viktor, draper and haberdasher, is transformed, somewhere between the stops of Kensington and Spencer Street stations. No longer a shopkeeper from a line of shopkeepers that goes right back to some muddy little German town by a muddy little river, but a wealthy landowner. A married one. With a respected place in the community's life. Marked out for politics. A future prime minister, even. She tilts her head from one side to the other, weighing it up. Possibly. Someone she might read about in the newspapers one day and say to herself, I knew you when …

So Viktor – wealthy, married, respected – packs her onto a cart (she has worked as a maid in the family mansion that overlooks a vineyard) and dispatches her to the nearest town and then to the city. Never to return. Just after he's given her a heavy bundle of notes. An indignity, but one she must endure: a pure woman, fallen from purity, watching herself being paid off like a whore. And so, with the fruit of having fornicated with the gods of the day swelling her belly, she catches a lonely train to the city, where slowly, bit by bit, those with whom she comes in contact learn her story. A story worthy of the child. Worthy of the mother. Worthy of them all. A tragic tale of tragic origins that the child will come to learn, pass on, never question and never forget.

And who will there be to say it didn't happen? She looks out the window, surprised by the inner city. There is much to be learned from literature. Life, Maryanne muses, watching the drab, soot-covered railway yards come into view, gives us little enough. And so, when we can, we have every right to give our lives a little something that life hasn't. Who's to know?

The train pulls into Spencer Street station. Katherine wakes. On the platform, Maryanne waits for her sister while she gathers an umbrella and the magazines she never read. Beside Maryanne, the engine hisses and blows steam into the air. Like an animal in winter, sighing. And she is drawn to the engine as if it were alive, sighing steam and stamping its feet like a tired cab horse, speaking to her the way animals speak. Tired and in need of food and rest and a pat. It lives and speaks, this engine. And she is drawn to its tired sighs. And while she is staring at the engine, the driver, his goggles on his forehead, cloth cap pulled back and shirt and tie under his overalls, pops his head out the cabin window. He nods at her, a smile across his grimy face, and she nods back. And in that moment she envies him, for it is a face and a smile that want for nothing. This man, she is convinced, has the happy, contented eyes of someone who is doing what he was born to do. How wonderful. How splendid. He waves and disappears into the cabin, and she is left gazing at the engine, which is hissing, exhaling long, tired but contented sighs of white steam. Alive.

Katherine emerges, waving the umbrella. Steam floats in clouds along the platform, following them as they make their way out to the street and into a hot burst of spring sunlight that seems to dissolve the sisters on contact. The smell of steam and soot evaporates. The spell with it. Everything is suddenly pale and washed out by the late spring sun.

The first thing they see when they step from the station is a great banner stretched across a building on the corner: 'ENLIST, THE EMPIRE CALLS'. 'VOTE "YES"' another banner screams in bold letters, while a poster beside it shows a laughing Kaiser and grinning Huns. There is a crowd on the street. The beast has reassembled itself, swaying this way and that, as the beast does. A speaker shouts, the beast roars. And at some point Maryanne could swear that the beast turns its vacant eyes to her, collective in its scrutiny, and lets out a slow, menacing snarl – recognising, with a deep, unerring instinct, one of those who stand apart.

She stops, and Katherine glances at her, a question in her eyes. But she knows why her sister has suddenly stopped. She is afraid. Katherine looks at the crowd and sees a crowd. Maryanne, she knows, looks at the crowd and sees something else. Something that scares her.

'Do we have to go this way?' Maryanne almost pleads. 'Must we go through it?'

'It's just a gathering of people,' Katherine says quietly, trying to calm her.

Maryanne shakes her head. 'It's not, you know. It's not.'

'Trust me,' her sister says. 'Hold my hand.' Katherine extends her hand with a look that says: take it, trust your big sister. She'll guide you through.

And so with Katherine leading the way, parting the crowd with an umbrella that she gives every impression of knowing how to use as a weapon should the need arise, as if, indeed, wielding her rifle instead of an umbrella, they make their way through the swaying mob, surrounded by it, but removed from it. A seething mass, swaying this way and that, erupting into roars and hisses, craving something … something *final*.

Together they reach that part of the street where the crowd thins and eventually peters out and where the trams are still running. On the tram the passengers part, a seat appears. Maryanne sits. Or rather, *they* sit: mother and child. A portrait of a story: a story that she will not only tell the child but which will pass down through the generations of the family unquestioned, a story that, one day, when her memories and what happened and what *might* have happened have mingled with the years, she – the story-teller – will eventually come to believe herself.

Part Two

The Milhaus Case

November, 1917

5.

The Milhaus case has captivated the city. No, possessed it, like a dream that stays on into the day, and on into the next and the next. Maryanne follows it in the newspapers, for the newspapers are possessed by it too. They feed the crowd and the crowd feeds the papers. And every day brings a new detail. It is an inexhaustible, bottomless well. Every day the city comes to the well of endless loathing, and draws up its bucket of sustaining bile. The beast smells blood. And the head of Milhaus is the sacrifice the beast howls for; the very image, the symptom of sick times.

Maryanne sits at the kitchen table. She lifts her eyes from the paper. The baby is moving, revolving inside the universe of her belly. She waits till it settles, then returns to the paper. Milhaus: the angel who fell. Milhaus, who tumbled from the heaven he'd occupied for years and seemed destined to occupy forever. Adored by the city before the beast was born, and who seemed to be one of those that the years and misfortune could never touch. Then the beast was born, and wide, adoring eyes turned to slits of scrutiny. *Who is Milhaus?*

She looks at the photograph in the paper. Handsome, she concedes. One who moves in a different world from her. The type that would have no end of society women making eyes at him. Like actors do. But Jack Milhaus isn't an actor; he was a footballer in a city that worships the game it invented and all those who play it. Especially the best. And Jack Milhaus was the best. Untouchable in life, untouchable on the field. Blessed. Then he fell, a fall as swift as Lucifer's. And the city felt betrayed: Milhaus, the angel, was revealed in his true image, and had been a devil all along. The beast rose up, and every day the newspapers fed it.

To Maryanne, who is finishing breakfast, the newspapers are as fascinating as the beast itself: they are dictated by the beast, its urges come to life and given words. And she reads them in the same way that she reads a horror story. Except horror stories aren't really that scary – the beast is.

From the start, when war was first declared, the city's eyes turned to Milhaus and there were murmurings about him. Why hadn't he enlisted? His team mates had enlisted, why not him? Was he better than the team? They could be dispatched, but not him? Did he really believe he was above everything? And everyone?

She watched her city change. At first, when far-off war was declared, there were joyous crowds waving flags and singing songs of king and empire, linking arms, hanging from office windows, gathering in city squares and streets, smiling in the winter sun. Swaying together as one. A city, a whole country, no longer at the edge of history but on the brink of leaping headlong into it, so that nothing would ever be the same again. Everybody laughing in delirious delight just to be alive at this glorious moment: savouring at last, after years of waiting and craving, the blessed release of war. Of glorious death. *God be thanked Who has matched us with His hour.*

Where are the poets of glorious death now? Even when the smiles faltered, even when the innocence was wiped from everyone's faces, as it was always going to be, the tears that were shed were for glorious death. Blessed war with the gift of death. Everywhere – on the streets, in trams and shops and tea-houses – Maryanne heard the inescapable talk of war and felt the hunger for annihilation.

And then one day a million pairs of eyes looked up from a million newspapers filled with the names of the dead, as if to say: We never really thought *this* would happen. That it would come to *this*. But it had, and everything really had changed and nothing would ever be the same again and there was no going back. The smiles turned to blank faces of disbelief, which soon turned to anger, to sneers. And the laughter to howls of sorrow and rage. All of which had to go somewhere. Somebody was to blame. And so the beast that was always lurking in the laughing crowd, craving something – something *final* – began to reveal itself, becoming clearer with every day, until the transition was complete and it roared into life.

Maryanne watched, horrified and fascinated, as the beast rose up in city squares, on corners and back streets, scales shining in the sun, glinting in the moonlight, howling for death and vengeance. The beast was them and they were the beast, and had been all along, just waiting to be conjured up to feed upon the sickness of the times. And every day, everybody went to the well of loathing and drew up the very dregs of the worst of themselves, the sustaining slops that the beast craved and which kept it alive.

Women she knew were handing out feathers in the streets to men not in uniform. Older men and women, fathers and mothers, whose children had gone to war, were suddenly shaking their fists and spitting upon young men on trams, in theatres, on street corners. While in the evenings, barmen hosed out onto the streets the blood and vomit of public bars where brawls had broken out all across the city. And under cover of night, neighbours went to war with each other, throwing rocks through the windows of Hun businesses where they'd shopped all their lives. Children, she observed on schoolyard duty, suddenly weren't playing with their old friends any more, barely understanding. She watched families split, friendships torn apart and never put back together. Gradually, the sun turned black. Blue skies filled with swirling grey clouds. Everything changed: familiar people, a familiar city, *her* city, became alien and strange – and the beast, like some fairytale monster come to life, was born.

And Milhaus was the very thing it was looking for. Somebody was to blame; somebody would pay. Maryanne has no interest in football, or any sport at all. And she doesn't understand why anybody does. But she has followed the Milhaus business, before it became a 'case', from the beginning. And it wasn't the arguments this way or that that captivated her, but the hatred and the vitriol it unleashed, as every day the city pressed to the news-stands.

And she wonders now, staring at the newspaper picture, whether the beast would have bothered if Milhaus hadn't been so gifted. Isn't this the way, she ponders, that these angels, these half-gods, we create – a link between us and the gods – can only remain hovering up there in the heavens for so long before we drag them down?

In time, the newspapers were not just asking why Milhaus hadn't enlisted but why he hadn't changed his name. Everybody else had: Mullers became Millers (though not Viktor), Weiss became White. Not difficult, they said. He loses a few letters from a common alphabet, and gains a few others. Milhaus to Millhouse. No great matter. Others, he was reminded, were losing arms and legs. So what was wrong with Milhaus? It was a small gesture to make, but a patriotic one. Did he not love his country, a country that had taken him in from far away, given him a home and given him the game of football? Did his loyalty lie somewhere else? Was the country he loved far away? And after being asked again and again by the newspapers why he hadn't changed it, Milhaus finally snapped back: Because it's my *name*!

And Maryanne admired that in Milhaus. He didn't bend to the crowd. Like her, he was not one of the crowd. Not one of them. And it was at this point that she started to feel an odd connection, an affinity with him, as if whatever happened to the one somehow happened to the other. Entwined fates. Kindred spirits. If Milhaus comes through, so will she and so will the child. It's silly, she knows. Just superstition. Like crossing the paths of black cats or walking under ladders. But once these things take hold they're hard to shake.

Then everything took a dramatic turn. Milhaus was arrested. Not because he wouldn't change his name. That was forgotten for the time being. Suddenly, there were more important matters. For Milhaus had a job. It seemed fantastic that a god of sorts should work, but this god was a public servant, with, it seemed, access to information crucial to the country's defences. The very country that he refused to change his name for. The very country that he had proven *not* to love. The very country that had given him the game of football and turned him into a god. But then he was arrested for treason, and Milhaus fell from heaven into the lap of the waiting beast. The city felt betrayed. He had presented himself as a glittering angel, even a god, and was now revealed for what he always was.

Maryanne puts the paper on the kitchen table. Katherine is out working, as she is every now and then, washing and cleaning the large houses of those who can pay for her services. Maryanne has the house to herself, which she likes. Inside the paper there is a diagram of a rubbish bin, and beside it an impression of a screwed-up, handwritten note, which has been flattened out to be read. The diagrams and others like it, surrounded by advertisements for boot polish and furniture, fill much of the paper, because this is the evidence against Milhaus. For sometime after the war started, the government put a spy inside the Swiss consulate: a cleaner. Information was passing through the consulate and going to the enemy. Or might be. Such was the advice received by the government. The cleaner was the government's eyes on the inside. And she eventually came up with the letter that is now as famous across the city as Milhaus himself. The writer of the letter was ready to sell secrets. The consular official who received the letter screwed it up with a laugh, so he said, and threw it into the bin. The writer of the letter, it seemed (and it is a long, detailed article she is reading over a second cup of tea, for she has long been eating for two), had assumed that this Swiss consular official would be happy to pass information on to the Germans. But he had assumed badly. Hence the laugh, and the automatic response of screwing the letter up and tossing the paper ball into the bin, where it lay all day until the cleaner came that evening, gathered the paper from the bin and passed it on to her boss. Maryanne shakes her head slowly; no wonder he laughed. It's all so far-fetched. A few years ago, everybody would have laughed. Not now. Now, nothing is far-fetched any more. Everybody is ready to believe anything.

A few days later, Milhaus was arrested. Experts studied the writing in the letter, compared it to that of a number of public servants inside Defence, and Milhaus was plucked out. The writing was his. Confirmed. The experts couldn't be wrong. Even though Milhaus claimed he was not even in the city the day the note was supposedly passed on. He was in the countryside, he said, went to a nearby town on a day's break. By himself. No witnesses. And no witnesses came forward. All Milhaus had to offer was his word. And that wasn't worth much. Milhaus, the god who had played everybody for a fool, who refused to change his name, who placed his personal feelings above the interests of his country and who proved himself *not* to love the country that gave him the gift of football, was a spy. No matter what he said. The blond-haired god who soared across Saturday-afternoon skies, drawing gasps of wonder from packed playing grounds, had fallen to earth with a thud. The devil had been unmasked. Maryanne finishes her tea and puts the cup back on the table.

The beast was roused, put its twitching nose to the air, and smelled the nectar of warm blood. Cries of innocence – from Milhaus, his lawyer – were drowned out by the roars of the beast. The smell of warm blood was in the air. And now that the trial has begun, the newspapers contain diagrams of the rubbish bin every day, as well as the screwed-up letter and a drawing of a machine gun, the details of which he is said to have been ready to pass on (and which looks like something out of last century's wars, but nobody cares). And it doesn't matter what Milhaus says. Innocent? He *would* say that. He has played them all for fools. He has no wife, no children. Has never settled, never really put down roots in the country that has given him so much, and to which, in return, he would not even give the gift of a name that would show them that *this* was his country and these were his people. No, he has played them all for fools. For behind that smiling face, all along, was the snigger of the laughing Hun.

But the Hun isn't laughing now, is he? Whenever he is taken through the streets from the police wagon to the court, crowds gather, jeer and shake fists, while the newspapers watch; the crowds feed the papers, the papers the crowd – there seems to be no end to it. It is *there* every day. A new detail. The Milhaus case captivates the city.

6.

It is late in the morning when she steps out onto the street. The streets are empty, the children are at school: restless and wriggling, no doubt, ears tuned to the sound of the lunch-time bell, when they can burst free of their cages. The memory of spring mornings like this, watching all that caged-up energy yearning for release, is almost pleasant. It is warm and sunny. A day to make you forget all those things you don't want to know. Just up in front of her on the narrow footpath, a mother and two children – too small for school – are walking towards her. Maryanne pays them little attention; her eyes are on the blue sky and the late spring sun shining bright over the rows and rows of dark cottages. Huts from the Dark Ages.

She is thinking of different things: dark huts, the mineral-water town, the gardens that overlook it, Viktor and whatever he might be doing at this moment, Milhaus, Katherine and the baby – always the baby, moving this way and that, revolving inside the universe of her belly. And she is so preoccupied with the sky, the sun and her jumble of thoughts that she pays little attention at first to the sight of the mother taking both children by the hands, and dragging them to the other side of the street. Even when she notices that they have stopped, she imagines they have paused to say hello, chat even. It is that kind of morning: one for bright, spring greetings. The beast has taken a holiday: she smiles across at them, about to speak. It is only when she sees the glare in the mother's eyes and fear in the children's that she understands.

The mother, who has a husband at the front and five brats to look after, whom Maryanne has known for much of her life and who lives a few streets away, takes a bunch of feathers from a bag and flings them into the air, as if tossing a hand grenade or poisonous powder at Maryanne. The four of them, on opposite sides of the street, watch the feathers float and flutter to earth, the mother suddenly yelling at Maryanne.

'Give *that* to your fancy man!'

The smile falls from Maryanne's face. Whatever spring greetings she was about to offer are forgotten. Her shoulders sag, the sparkle gone from her. A moment ago she'd been happier than she'd been for so long. Life was good. People were good. The beast had taken a holiday. Now, this. The children are holding tightly to their mother. She is their rock. They are safe where they are. But on the other side of this small inner-city suburban street is danger, like a stray dog gone wrong, carrying a disease. Maryanne is that danger, and she sees alarm in the children's eyes, while the last of the feathers settle and the mother's words ring out as they fall.

'The Hun's whore! Go back to your fancy man! Whore …'

With that, the mother strides off, dragging her children behind her.

Maryanne is shivering and shaken. Fragile, like that burst of happiness she felt. All changed. No, the beast doesn't take holidays. The sun is obliterated, the warmth blown from the air; the street like streets from bad dreams where shadows lurk. Unreal and all too real. Are we all damned? She looks about her, as if having been thrown from the skies and only just landed this minute. Row after row of dark huts sit in moody, sullen silence. Dark, like a village scene from the Middle Ages. Or further, much further back. It is as though everybody has burrowed up from underground, from the very centre of the earth, and brought up hell with them. From the centre of the earth and from the centre of ourselves. She has known this woman for years, and yet never known her. But amid the suddenness of the incident (a suddenness that leaves her asking if it really did happen), she is also asking: how could she know?

And as she goes over everything, she comes to the conclusion that there is only one answer: Mrs Collins. Mrs Collins had a friend, headmaster at a nearby Catholic school, who might do the right thing by Maryanne, and she, Mrs Collins, undertook to contact her friend. Maryanne was told which school, but she hadn't contacted the headmaster. Clearly Mrs Collins had, and this friend, upon receiving Mrs Collins's report, presumably saw no need for privacy. To keep it to himself. Indeed, may well have felt a public duty to let people know that there was a Hun lover among them. A Hun's whore. How else could it have come about? It is the only conclusion that makes sense, if there's sense to be found in anything.

She watches the feathers being blown along the road. It's not so much the glare in the mother's eyes as the children's fear that stays with her as she slowly leaves the street and makes her way down towards the gardens, leaving the gloomy medieval huts behind her, to board a tram at a stop near the parliament where the Wart sits: one of those dark magicians who conjure up the hell in everyone.

He has recently made a public pronouncement about Milhaus. Of course, he would. He called out to a crowd gathered along the banks of the river, asking them if we really wanted those kinds of people in the country. And the beast bellowed back: not just one thunderous, explosive NO, but a succession of them. On and on it went, followed by cries for the blood of Milhaus, until the beast, exhausted for the moment, fell silent. The newspapers reported the meeting in all its detail, dwelled on the words uttered by the prime minister – 'honour' and 'blood' and 'death' and 'sacrifice' – and how he held them all in his sway.

The tram travels along a city street, lined on either side with bright goldrush buildings that inexplicably lift Maryanne's spirits. The goldrush that changed the city overnight is not so far removed in time from where she sits: not fresh, but not *quite* history. Not so distant that she can't imagine swaggering miners, pockets bulging, standing on the footpaths and marvelling at the city that gold built – that *they* built. *In gladness let us sing* ... The buildings, decorated with gargoyles, ancient flowers and old European gods, line the street with quiet satisfaction. They sparkle and she feels a sudden rush of ownership. *We* did that once. The loud, crass, swaggering best in ourselves somehow made beautiful things. The bombs of this never-ending war are too far away to bother these ornate and intricate facades. The war will come and the war will go, and when it's gone these buildings, these monuments to a not-so-distant time, will still be lining the street, the quiet satisfaction that beams from them in the midday sun unruffled.

As Maryanne descends from the tram, she hears a howl and a cry coming from the front of the Town Hall. And she looks round to see a group of women sharing a newspaper. It is spread open and flattened against a wall, the women at the edges of the group pinning it there. Somebody is sobbing. A further howl rises from the group and people passing stare without stopping; a man, stepping up from an underground toilet and onto the footpath, pauses for a moment and moves on. How did this happen? A few years earlier, anybody – everybody – would have stopped. Now, nobody does. And it's not that they don't care. It's just that there's only so much care to go around.

Maryanne nears the group of women. She can now see in the newspaper what she knows to be column after column of names. Death fills the pages. A woman, fashionably dressed, possibly on her way to some fashionable club for lunch, collapses onto the footpath, howling one moment, sobbing the next. And all over the city, women like her – and fathers and mothers, and sisters, brothers, cousins, lovers and friends – are opening newspapers or staring at noticeboards on town halls and post-office walls in silent, breathless dread. Maryanne can almost hear the wings of dark Death beating in the air, then tapering into the sky, and knows they will descend again with the next day's newspapers bringing the next day's roll call of mortality.

She's seen it all again and again. Everybody has. Every day a new howl joins the old howls on the great march to death. The fashionably dressed woman suddenly leaps to her feet, tears streaming down her face, and screams at a young man walking past, following him down towards the station, crying and screaming until she is dragged back by her friends. Just a group of women: going to lunch one minute, dressed for a day out, and all changed the next.

Maryanne can't help wondering whether there is also some part of them, neither spoken of nor acknowledged, that longed for an end to all the waiting as much as they dreaded it. Longed for something ... *final*. Like hearing the screeching brakes of a runaway tram and both dreading and longing for the crunch of a collision all in the one moment of horrible anticipation.

Surely some deep longing for it all has been conjured up by the magicians of darkness. Why else would a whole civilisation rush to the killing place? And so when the Wart speaks of death and blood and honour and sacrifice, are the hoarse cries that follow only cries of anguish, or are they also of some deep, unspeakable longing? Unspeakable pleasure. Everyone ecstatically mad. Is this not when the beast rears its head, roused by the magic words of 'blood', 'death', 'duty' and 'sacrifice'? And so when the beast howls it *sounds* like a howl of pain, but is it not also the howl of some deep craving, some deep pleasure that cannot be expressed any other way? Maryanne asks herself this, wondering if she too has not gone mad even to be asking it. *God be thanked Who has matched us with His hour.* Death, oh glorious ... if this is what it takes so that we shall *never* be the same again, then let death rain down.

Maryanne turns from the group of women. Are we all damned? And mad? For as deep as that woman's sorrow is, the worship of death that put everyone on the great march to war is everywhere too. The dark conjurers who summon up the hell in all of us – the beast in all of us – have held sway. The beast demands death. The beast craves it. Not just pain, but the deep pleasure of unutterable sorrow, the rapture of unspeakable loss, of oblivion. And it will not be satisfied until the last drop of blood has drained into the mud of ancient battlefields and swamps and there is nothing left.

Maryanne's legs feel as though they are about to give way and fold beneath her. What a time, what a time to be bringing life into the world when all it craves is death. A spring breeze blows the dropped newspaper gently along the footpath and up the street. Maryanne wavers on the spot before boarding her connecting tram. I can't do this ... I can't ... I ...

She gets out at the library and spends the next hour sitting in the blissful sanctuary of the domed reading room to which she comes most days, driven, often as not, by sheer restlessness, this need to be *out*, to walk through these days, through this valley of death that she can't tear her eyes away from. She sits for an hour: the huge domed reading room her cathedral, and the wisdom this cathedral contains her scriptures. After her hour, and it has not escaped her notice that the hour she regularly spends in the reading room is equivalent to the hour she would once have spent at mass, she places her books on a trolley, a trolley that, in time, some quietly stooped custodian of the library will push from one letter of the alphabet to another, shelving the books, all in their place, as if the library in all its alphabetically arranged order were a model of how the world ought to be. Or could be. Was once, and will be again.

From the library she takes a short walk away from the city and pauses at a narrow sandstone facade, complete with gargoyles, glinting golden in the sun, and once again, uplifted, she feels that odd sense of possession. *We* did this once, in all our crass, swaggering finery. And she thinks 'we' because at that moment she possesses her city; it is hers as much as she is its – the best of it. And we will come through, she murmurs, staring down at her belly, we will come through somehow.

* * *

What Katherine might think, Maryanne can only imagine, for Maryanne is about to take the lift up to the offices of the city's suffragettes. Although, they don't go around calling themselves that. Not to her. Officially, they are the Women's Political Association and Women's Peace Army, which, when Maryanne first read about them, sounded very earnest and daunting. Not her sort of thing at all. But the more she heard about them, the more she wanted to know. She's never been one to troop off in a gang, and she's never belonged to any party or joined any movement, but she was curious. And curiosity won out. So she's been here before, she knows the way up the five flights that lead to the offices, and the women who frequent them know her. This is also one of the few places in the city, along with the library's reading room, where she feels at home – though it is perhaps not so much a cathedral as a wayside chapel for Maryanne and a soup kitchen, for they fed people here during the big strike. It is a place that is many things.

'Back again,' a young woman says, then disappears into a discussion. It's always the same. Busy. Lots of talk. Somebody always running round with a sheet of paper in hand or carrying a stack of pamphlets. Maryanne rarely says much, and nobody minds: swollen belly, no wedding ring. Nobody cares.

'Here, what do you think?'

The same young woman thrusts one of the pamphlets under Maryanne's nose. The gesture is not only eager, but is posed, Maryanne suspects; something in the manner of saying:

well, let's see what the people think. Maryanne smiles, she is evidently one of the people. Or so the young woman imagines. One look at her and Maryanne knows she is from what the northern half of the city calls the 'other side of the river'. Posh. Private school. Privileged. And there is presumption in the way she thrusts the pamphlet into Maryanne's hands that annoys her. But, at the same time, this young woman is keen to know what she thinks, and Maryanne can't help but be flattered. And also anxious. She's never been asked to give her opinion before. The question is also posed in the manner of a welcome: a way of saying that Maryanne, one of the people, is also one of them. And there is something reassuring in being welcomed into their company. Something that makes her feel less alone.

She gazes at the pamphlet, which announces a meeting to be held the next month. An important meeting. A meeting the times call out for. The words 'peace', 'sisterhood' and 'new world' rise to meet her in large letters, but she barely takes in the rest before the young woman speaks again.

'Well?'

The young woman smiles, radiating, Maryanne can't help but think, a fantastic innocence. It is evidently her work and she wants to know what Maryanne thinks. And straightaway Maryanne knows that it is the last thing she will tell her. Her impulse is to say that the world doesn't want peace, only death – don't you see it? It's everywhere. Sweet glorious death and exquisite tears. That's all the world wants. It wants to gorge on tragedy so that nothing will ever be the same again, then collapse into deep, pleasurable sleep. And let them, let them have it. I'm tired of them all. Let them have the death they crave, until the last of the craving is wrung out of them and they are exhausted by it and finally look forward to just living and we can start all over again with what's left. Then, perhaps then, they will listen to your words. But not now. Throw your pamphlets to the wind and see where they land. She wants to say this and all the things that are bottled up in her, which have been brewing inside her all through the year, and which she's never told anyone. All the strange visions that come to her, too strange to tell, constantly, haunting her: visions of hell and beasts and death. She'd like to say all of this, but this young woman radiates such fantastic innocence that she can't. And so she finds herself looking up and saying, 'They're wonderful words. Really wonderful.'

And they are. She believes they are. Just too wonderful for the times. The young woman, no fool, eyes her suspiciously.

'We'll know just how wonderful if people come.'

'I hope they do. I really hope so.'

It is just as the conversation seems finished and the young woman is turning away that Maryanne sees a small pile of leaflets demanding 'Justice for Milhaus'. She picks one up and reads it, and the young woman turns back towards her.

'You know the case?'

Maryanne speaks without looking up. 'How could I not?'

'And what do you know?'

'Only what I read in the papers.'

Here the young woman raises her eyebrows and rolls her eyes. She and Maryanne nod in silent agreement, as if to say, ah, the papers!

'I can't read them any more,' the young woman says.

'I find I can't *but* read them. It's like lifting a rock and seeing what's under it. You can't take your eyes off them. At least, I can't. They show us who we are now. What we are. As though we looked deep inside ourselves, and *this* is what we found. People are …' Maryanne shakes her head.

She doesn't say that she's developed this odd connection with Milhaus, the feeling that they are both on the outside looking in on a city gone mad; the feeling that whatever happens to him happens to her. The way we sometimes make these connections: if the sick dog lives, so will I; if Milhaus comes through these times, so will I.

'… people are being led,' the young woman says, finishing Maryanne's sentence for her.

Maryanne's eyes are alight. 'You think so? You really think so?'

'Yes–'

Maryanne is becoming bolder with every moment and doesn't let the young woman finish. But it's not rude, and the young woman doesn't take it that way. Maryanne's finally got a chance to say what she thinks, and she's going to say it. And the young woman, far from put out, is looking at her with a touch of admiration, perhaps amused admiration, as though just discovering that this middle-aged woman, swollen belly, but ordinary-looking really, albeit with striking eyes that are now lit up, is a bit of a surprise package. And Maryanne is looking back, gauging the amused respect in the young woman's look, while also gauging that, smart as she is – and oh, she's sharp all right – she needs a little lesson in life as well. From one of the people.

'They didn't *need* to be led. Don't you see? They were just waiting for it. Ready.' She closes her eyes, the memory of the mother and her children just a few hours earlier suddenly vivid again. *Give that to your fancy man … Hun's whore …*

'Perhaps. All the same, people need someone to blame. To hate.' The young woman pauses. 'And Milhaus was born to fall and be hated. The perfect scapegoat. This whole scandal was concocted to make you vote yes. Not *you*,' she adds, pointing at Maryanne, 'but people. Enough people voting yes will give the prime minister what he wants. A spy, one of our own, among us only helps. Make people scared enough and they'll do whatever you want. The papers, the prime minister–'

'The Wart.'

'The what?'

'I call him the Wart. Can't you see it? I can. This large wart on thin, spindly legs.'

The young woman looks at Maryanne with questioning eyes, then laughs. Soon they are both laughing and the women behind them, deeply engaged in discussion, turn round, a puzzled look in their eyes, as if to say, what *is* that sound?

The young woman is laughing because she *can* see it. Of course, a wart. Like those cartoons of politicians and kings: bullfrogs in suits, walruses wearing spectacles – a wart on legs. She nods at Maryanne, a nod that says: yes, I can see it. A wart. And he will always be a wart now. Their laughter subsides. The young woman turns serious again.

'Imagine how alone he feels.'

'Milhaus?'

'Yes. Hero one minute, villain the next. The enemy. A Hun.' She pauses, lifting one of the leaflets. 'The world loves you one day and turns on you the next. How alone. How strange.'

'Indeed.'

'He has no family. No wife, no children. No mother, it seems. At least, no one's ever seen her. No father. No brothers or sisters. No one. Nobody visits. Or wants to.'

'*Nobody?*'

The young woman looks at her quizzically. Surprised. 'You didn't know?'

'I didn't.' Maryanne turns worried eyes to her. 'Nobody visits at all?'

'No.'

'How awful.'

'If only someone would. Just so he knows, he's not alone.' It's offered as a sort of wish, but to whom or what, the young woman doesn't seem to know. Her voice is vague, as if she's thinking aloud. Maryanne nods slowly. The young woman continues. 'The Germans have a word for people like him.

Wunderkind. Wonder child.' She laughs. 'The Germans always have a word. What a language!' And here she looks directly at Maryanne as she speaks. '*Das Leben gehört den Lebenden an, und wer lebt, muss auf Wechsel gefasst sein …*'

The effect is immediate. She is, at once, back in that drab little back room listening to Viktor speak, transported by the sound of the words and the sound of this young woman's voice. And it is like hearing an old fairytale, or the words of some ancient magic spell, a spell that Maryanne instantly falls under. And it is not just Maryanne, for this young woman is transformed by the words she speaks, possessed by them, almost speaking from another time. It is thrilling, and it's not just the sound of the words themselves: it is hearing the language of the enemy again, such a beautiful language and such beautiful sounds, spoken aloud in a public place. And it is not just Maryanne who is enthralled, for the women behind them have stopped talking and are listening in wonder at the sheer strangeness, the foreignness, of these sounds.

There is a long silence, the young woman seemingly oblivious of the effect she has had on them. And, as if having fallen under her own spell, she seems to be slowly returning to the here and now, a sleepwalker waking and becoming aware of everyone around her again. And, smiling at Maryanne, she slowly repeats herself, '*Das Leben gehört den Lebenden an …*' then trails off into dreamy silence.

And without thinking it or willing it, immersed in that same dreamy silence, Maryanne murmurs, '*Schöne.*'

The young woman looks at Maryanne anew. 'You speak German?'

'No,' says Maryanne.

The young woman's look is an inquiring one that seems to say, that may be the case, but you know at least this much. And how did you come by such knowledge? And it is then that she shifts her gaze from Maryanne's eyes to her belly and, with a faint raising of her brows, answers her own question. And it is then that she repeats the word the Germans have for those like Milhaus: slowly, lingering on all three syllables. '*Wun-der-kind.*'

Maryanne, unable to speak for a moment, asks herself if she's read the comment correctly, then gathers herself. 'And the wonder child had to fall?'

The young woman, snapping out of her dreamy state, back to whatever it was they were talking of – Milhaus, of course; yes, Milhaus – nods before answering. 'Perhaps.'

Maryanne nods back, convinced that some odd sort of bond now exists between them. At least, more than it did before. Enough to prompt her to ask, 'What is your name?'

'I'm Vera,' the young woman replies. 'And you?'

'Maryanne.'

They smile, reach out their hands, and shake.

'Cheerio, Maryanne,' Vera says. 'Must go.'

And with that, Vera finally turns back to the group of women behind them, who are once again deep in discussion about the planned meeting. 'Peace', 'sisterhood', a 'new world'. Fine words, Maryanne notes. Even wonderful. But she's still dwelling on the effect of hearing the wondrously strange language of the enemy spoken in a public place and can't concentrate on the women's conversation.

She glances down distractedly at the leaflet on the table in front of her: 'Justice for Milhaus'. *Nobody.* No mother, no father. Why didn't she know? She didn't know, she concludes, because the newspapers didn't tell her or anybody else, in case Milhaus became human and people started to feel sympathy for him. For that would never do. She picks up the leaflet and puts it in her bag.

She leaves the offices unobserved and slips out onto the street. Instantly, she feels as if she is wandering through some strange land again, full of strange people who ought to be familiar as *her* people, but aren't. Ugly eyes, warped faces. Warped by the times. And she can't help but hate everybody she passes. Hate them with a passion that she knows has to be stopped, stopped now, or she'll turn *into* them. Were they led, or were they always just waiting there? *Give that to your fancy man ...* Feathers fly into the air. The mother she's known most of her life disappears from the street, her children trailing, fear in their eyes, dragged from the danger of the Hun's whore. The feathers settle. A gust of wind blows them away, and her thoughts turn back to Milhaus. *If only someone would.* Vera's wish and those wonderful, foreign sounds that poured from her haunt Maryanne. *If only someone ...* How lonely, indeed. No mother, no father. Nobody. How lonely must he be?

With strained steps she approaches her tram and sits heavily, her bag on her lap, Vera's wish weighing upon her. *If only someone would.* Someone who could say, I *know* what this is like. I know what it's like to feel that, in a world gone mad, you're one of those who haven't: who can see what's happening. You live it. I live it. Every day. And as the tram rolls and lurches down the slope towards her stop at the Town Hall, an idea is forming. How lonely, indeed. The child moves inside her, then settles. Not long now, not long. She rubs her belly. And suddenly Milhaus is not a … What was the word? *Wunderkind.* But a lonely child. Like the one she carries. Just a boy. Alone in some vast playground, wondering where everybody went.

She steps off at the Town Hall for her connecting tram. The women, dressed for lunch, have gone. So too the sound of wailing. And the newspaper, long since borne gently on a considerate spring breeze to its final resting place. Fresh casualty lists await fresh wails of sorrow and rapture, rapture and sorrow. And the great march to death goes on. Feet tramping down to the station, eyes fixed on the footpath. Nobody looking up. Everybody marching.

7.

A stately black car is parked by the steps of the parliament, shining the way only black can. When Maryanne steps off the tram it is not Parliament House that catches her attention, as it usually does, but the car, the chauffeur casually smoking nearby, chatting to a policeman. He presumes the right to park there and the policeman guarding the car vindicates his presumption. They surely reserve privilege such as this for royalty and prime ministers.

She nears the car, for her path from the tram stop to the footpath leading into the park takes her past it. But she is anxious, for this car in all its black majesty says do not approach. And as she nears, the policeman stops chatting to the driver and eyes her suspiciously, for anybody approaching this car, commandingly perched by the parliament steps in the late afternoon as if to catch the last of the sun, is to be considered suspicious. He stares at her intently: full belly or not, she may be trouble. One of those troublesome women with troublesome ideas who seem to be everywhere now.

The car is no more than ten feet away. Behind Maryanne, another tram arrives, people step off and the policeman's attention swings to the small group of workers crossing the street for home at the close of day. She peers, eyes straining, at the back window of the car. Then stops, suddenly frozen. For there, staring back at her, is the face of Mannix himself. His eyes, clear and unclouded by doubt, fixing on her. Taking in her face, her swollen belly. And once again, it is as though the all-seeing eyes of Mannix know everything. And she is not staring at the face of the archbishop but the face of God himself. And God knows, knows everything. *Fallen* woman, don't think I don't know. Nothing escapes me. Escapes us. We bring cathedrals of wisdom to your small life. And all must kneel down before us.

And just as she is about to avert her eyes, for his gaze, casual in its omniscience, is too much, she sees the profile of a second figure in the car. And straightaway she recognises it: the bald dome, the nose like a growth on the dome, the spectacles perched on the nose. The Wart. Both of them, sworn enemies and on either side of the great Yes and No of the day, sitting in this stately black motor car by the steps of parliament. *Chatting.* Can it be? Mannix's eyes shift from Maryanne back to the Wart, and she leaves the car behind as she steps into the park for the walk home. How long they chat for, what they talk about, she can only guess. Not that she dwells too long on it. For it is the eyes of Mannix that stay with her as she makes her way home.

And when she enters the house, when she steps into the kitchen, where Katherine has prepared their dinner, her impulse is to turn the photograph of Mannix on the mantelpiece around so that it stares at the wall, not at her. She reaches out, then withdraws her hand. No, she decides, she will leave him there with his all-seeing eyes and his cathedrals of wisdom, and she will stare him down as she would stare down all the others. I don't believe … I don't … I don't believe in you and your magic show any more … You can't touch me, you can't touch … you can't … she chants, silently addressing the framed portrait. I am beyond you now. And I will *not* kneel.

When Katherine turns to her with a simple potted pie steaming in its dish, she smiles and sits. Katherine joins her at the table, folds her hands and closes her eyes as she whispers grace. Maryanne looks on silently, then turns to the photograph of Mannix and meets those all-seeing eyes.

Katherine finishes and they begin the meal in silence. Then Maryanne announces: 'I saw him today.'

Katherine looks up, puzzled. And annoyed. It is one of Maryanne's annoying little habits – assuming you know what she's thinking. Maryanne had, in fact, nodded in the direction of the portrait on the mantelpiece as she spoke, but Katherine hadn't noticed. 'Saw whom?'

'Mannix,' she says, as if it were obvious. 'And not just the archbishop. The prime minister as well.'

'Together?'

Maryanne nods.

Katherine puts down her knife and fork. 'Impossible.'

'In the back of a motor car by the steps of parliament.'

'No, I can't believe it.'

'Chatting away like old friends.'

Katherine stares intently at her sister. 'You're telling me God sits down with the devil?'

Maryanne nods. 'They live in different worlds, these people.'

'They stand for different things.'

The portrait on the mantelpiece is Katherine's. Along with portraits of their mother and father. Mannix, to Katherine, is almost part of the family: archbishop, of course; a touch of God on earth; and a sort of distant relation. And so when anything is said about him she takes it personally, as if he were in the room. Which, more or less, he is.

'Perhaps,' says Maryanne. 'But you have to wonder if they're really so different from each other, after all.'

'Not different?' Katherine speaks, astonishment in her voice, not so much in her role as big sister, but more like a mother pointing out a fact of life her child seems not to have noticed. 'Not different? They're as different as day and night!'

'I don't mean what they think and say. Or even in their hearts; what they believe. I mean … if you have power, isn't it just possible that the only other people who understand what it's like are those who also have it? Does it get lonely, and do they seek each other out?'

'Who put this nonsense into your head? Those women?'

'Nobody did. Isn't it just possible? And every now and then does the prime minister seek out the archbishop, and does the archbishop seek out the prime minister? Does the "Yes" need to speak to the "No", and the "No" the "Yes"?'

Katherine looks at her sister, concern in her eyes. 'Are you well?'

'Perfectly.' Maryanne pauses.

Katherine understands, and she doesn't. She is as smart as anyone, as well read. But she's lived for years in a world of quick decisions: of the right thing to do and the wrong, the smart thing to do and the silly. And the judgement in her eyes is clear: don't get too smart for your own good. Or too fancy.

Maryanne looks down at her plate. 'I saw it, clear as day. The "Yes" and the "No", sitting in the back of a motor car, chatting away like old friends.'

Katherine corrects her. 'You saw them together, talking. But whether they were chatting, or even chatting like old friends, is something else.'

'I saw what I saw.'

'But *what* did you see?'

They finish their meal and sip tea, saying nothing. Maryanne, swirling the tea leaves and watching them settle, puts her cup down. 'I've decided to visit Milhaus. Or try.'

Katherine shakes her head. 'Are you mad? You shouldn't be doing any such thing.'

'It will distract me.' Maryanne almost shivers with a sudden wave of energy she doesn't know what to do with. 'I just get *so* restless. I have to *do* things. Just so I know this is still my life. Not everybody else's.' She looks up at Katherine, a look that says: you must understand this. 'I will *not* be confined. Oh God,' she says, wringing her hands, 'confinement. The very word gives me the shivers. Like being put in jail. Oh, a very nice jail. But jail, all the same. No. I must do things. And I *will* visit Milhaus, if I can. Believe me, it will distract me. And not just from this,' she says, looking down at her belly as if the wise, understanding eyes of the child itself were staring back. 'But from everything. Everything out there, the whole mad city … it's enough to make you mad yourself if you let it.' She lets out a deep sigh. 'Besides, nobody visits him. He has no wife, no children. No friends. Everyone's given up on him.'

'How do you know?'

'I just do.'

Katherine stares at her with dawning comprehension. I knew it: you've been with those women again, those meddling women. Haven't you? I don't like them. She doesn't say it. She doesn't need to.

Maryanne smiles. 'I know what you think. It's those interfering women. But it's not, it's me.' She pauses. 'And you think I'm in no state to be deciding all this.' She laughs, a thoughtful one. 'Go on, say it.'

Katherine smiles back, a slight, slow shake of the head. 'Would you listen?'

Maryanne raises her eyebrows, asking herself the same question: would she indeed? 'Besides,' she adds, 'we've got a lot in common. A woman in the street called me the Hun's whore today.'

Katherine puts her fist on the table. 'Which one?'

'Never mind,' Maryanne says, eyes blank, the whole nasty business coming back at her in a sudden rush. 'She had her two children with her and crossed the street when she saw me. Then she threw feathers into the air and called me the Hun's whore.' Maryanne shakes her head slowly, looking down at the floor. 'I suppose it was the worst thing she could find to say.'

'And what did you say?'

Maryanne smiles. 'I told her I was going to tell my big sister.'

Katherine sighs, rises from her chair and places her arms around Maryanne. 'She'd better not open her mouth if I'm there.'

'The thing is, I didn't say anything.' Maryanne closes her eyes and lets out a childish whimper. 'I tried to, but nothing came out.' She looks up at Katherine. 'I tried, I really did.' She quietly shakes her head from side to side again. 'I can't do this ... I really can't ...' She rests her head on Katherine's breast: Katherine, big sister and mother, mother and sister. 'I can't ...' Maryanne leaves her head there until the whimpers run out, then lifts her chin. 'I just want to tell him he's not alone. And that I know what it's like.'

Her head falls back on Katherine's breast, Katherine stroking her hair and whispering words of comfort. 'I'm here, I'm here ...'

She looks up again at Katherine, who seems suddenly older, careworn, then at the table and the dishes. 'Let me help with the dishes.'

'No, you need to rest.'

Maryanne rises and places her hand on Katherine's. 'Please, it will distract me.'

With this they laugh shakily and begin gathering the plates and knives and cups, and before they know it, Katherine is saying she'll wash and Maryanne will dry. And Maryanne is saying she will wash and Katherine will dry. Their voices are suddenly young and each knows they are re-enacting some childhood scene: the squabble over who washes and who dries. And soon Maryanne is standing at the sink, washing the plates, and passing them to Katherine, noting how calming, and strangely satisfying it is.

Her mind wanders back to the events of the day – Milhaus, the feathers – and then she's not thinking anything. She's reached that point of blissful forgetfulness, of just mechanically doing something. The day, the city, the feathers – all dissolving like the grease from the plates. All gone. She finds herself smiling broadly at Katherine, and sees Katherine smiling back. And later that night, lying in bed, she will remember this as she drifts off, and realise they were happy and were having fun.

8.

Maryanne has been standing in the hallway, staring at the front door, for too long. The walk from the kitchen to the door takes a few seconds only. But not this morning. This morning she reached the halfway mark and stopped. Froze. Her legs won't move. She tells them to, but they are stubborn. And she's really not sure how long she's been standing there. But she knows it's far too long. And she's starting to feel ridiculous. The more she tells her legs to move, go on, step forward, the less they listen. And just stand there. Stuck to the spot. Her exasperation mounts as she tells herself to stop this. Just stop. But she can't. There's a voice inside her saying: Don't go. Don't go out there. There are monsters out there with scaly skin and claws, and feathers of hate to fling in your face while they call you the Hun's whore. Don't go.

Her stomach heaves and tightens. A sick weight sits there. And it is so tempting to stay inside all day, not go out again and confine herself to the house. For suddenly confinement feels good. The world frightens her, and she doesn't want to go out into it. Not this morning, not today, not … And so she stays, glued to the spot, midway between the kitchen and the front door. And as much as she tells herself not to give in to this voice, this voice which is her and not her, familiar and strange, kind and sniggering, as much as she tells herself not to listen, she does. And the voice holds sway. And time mounts, and if she does not snap out of this she will stand in the hallway, glued to the spot, all morning. All afternoon. For Katherine is out. It is Sunday. Katherine is visiting an old friend, the house is empty and there is no one to snap her out of this madness. And she knows it is madness, but she is powerless to laugh it off. And the more she stands there the more ridiculous she feels, and the more her anger rises: with herself, her legs, her useless legs, and the door – the damned door.

It almost sniggers at her. Come on, open me. I'm just a door, open me and let the world in. What are you afraid of? You've been opening and closing doors all your life, and I'm just another door. Or am I? And as she stares at it she's aware of the distance between herself and the door, and covering that distance, let alone opening the door, seems beyond her. Somehow, overnight, she's lost … the what? The thoughtlessness, if that is what it is. Lost the ability to open a door without thinking about it.

And the thought of turning round and going back to the kitchen or her room is so tempting. All she wants to do is sit down in the kitchen and not go out again. Never go out again. And her legs *would* turn, and would take her back; she knows they would. And the sick weight in her stomach would leave her. This voice, familiar and strange, is telling her to turn back. There are monsters out there, who will fling feathers of hate into your face and call you the Hun's whore. All the way down the street, and the next, and the next. All the way. This day and the following, on and on. Don't go out there. And all the while the door is staring at her, saying: Go on, open me. I'm just a door. Or am I?

And just as she's about to scream, she feels the child inside her kick. And she stares down at her belly and could swear the child is staring back: puzzled and concerned and fearful, all at once. And straightaway she knows she must overcome her own fear, so that she may ease the fear of the child. The child must not feel her fear. She must hide it. She must *never* let this child down. It kicks again, this time impatiently, almost saying: Come on, what are you waiting for? Just get on with it. And she swears she can actually hear the child's voice: a wise child, a wise voice, a grown-up voice coming from the curled-up baby. Saying, just get on with it.

She looks longingly back down the hall to the kitchen. A good room. Safe. But a room, all the same. A square. And you can't live in a square, can you? A child can't live in a square. Unless you're a square peg.

And *that* is when her legs move, and the voice inside her is silenced, and she covers the short distance to the door, by now just a door, and, hands trembling, opens it onto the world. Daylight spears into the hallway, blinding her, and she stands there for a moment, waiting for her eyes to adjust, then looks about. And there it is: the street. The street she's known all her life, there all the time while she stood in the hall. Just a street. And closing the door behind her, she steps out onto the footpath, nobody about, into a bright spring morning. All monsters banished for the moment, the feathers of hate blown away by yesterday's breeze. And as she makes her way to her regular tram stop, she is telling herself she must never let that happen again, telling herself that the voice she heard, familiar and strange, her and not her, was the voice of madness. The very voice, that if you listened to it too often, would delight in making you mad.

She turns towards the park and the parliament, smoothing her belly, easing the child's fear, telling the child it has done well. That it was just the kick she needed. That, already, they have gone through much together. And will do this, together.

The parks, the streets, have that deserted Sunday look. She waits for her tram in the sun, a pleasant spring sun, for far longer than she would during the week. But she doesn't mind; it allows her to look back calmly on the morning and the Maryanne who stood so long in the hallway, afraid to leave the house, as if she were someone else. And she was, for that Maryanne was not her. And she resolves there and then that *that* Maryanne will not come back again, and she will not be cowed by the beast ever again.

She looks up as her tram arrives, almost sauntering towards her at a slow, weekend pace, the tram that will now take her to Milhaus. For it is Sunday, visiting day. And Mr Milhaus will have a visitor.

* * *

If the beast is a glimpse of hell on earth, then these are hell's dungeons. Day and night, it's all one in here. When the guard shuts the door behind them, he shuts out the day. And everything is not only dark, but Maryanne has the immediate feeling of being hundreds of feet underground. There is no day, no sun, just this hopeless feeling of being underground, while the world up above goes on.

'Don't get many visitors,' the guard says, as though visits and intrusions are all the same and her presence is an annoying fact of life, like not finding a seat on the train or dealing with a salesman at the door.

He leads her over a stone walkway between rows of cells. Each cell has a small square opening on the door for the guards to peer through when they choose. The rest of the time they're shut, as they are now. Lamps, as in a laneway at night, light the way. She is suddenly afraid. Not that there is any threat. She is safe. It is simply *being* here that is frightening: the lamps and the cold stones and the shadows. It's an alien world, like being in the black heart of the beast, or its belly, and already she wishes she hadn't come and can't wait to get out. The place is stifling and she's been inside less than a minute. What must it be like to be stuck here in this never-ending night? And because she feels as if she's disappearing into the very shadows and darkness of the place, she speaks up, tense and on edge, if only to hear her own voice.

'Do the cells have a window? Does any light get in?'

'More than they deserve.'

Maryanne turns to the guard, frowning, but he doesn't notice.

'These people are the scum of the earth,' he goes on. 'All of them. Scum.'

He looks at her, shaking his head, disgusted. Some scum's whore, he's no doubt thinking, with more scum in her belly that'll wind up in here like they all do. Scum are born that way and stay that way and all finish up here. She doesn't like the guard. He doesn't like her. They don't say another word as on they go, lower and lower, it seems, the dingy lamps lighting the way. A voice here and there from behind the iron doors. A groan. A shout. And everything cold. Spring outside; dark and cold as winter inside.

At the end of the long walkway they turn to their right and the place opens out. Maryanne looks up for the first time and sees the stairs leading to two more levels of cells above her. She turns around and looks all the way back to the distant door she came through, level upon level upon level of tiny cells between it and her. Dungeons from a storybook world of monsters and half-humans and three-headed dogs. A place of cold flames, muck and swamps straining upwards to an underground sky that's never seen the sun.

It is when she turns back to follow the guard that she catches sight of something from the corner of her eye. Dangling. Hanging there. And even before she swings round to face it fully, she knows what it is: the rope, the beam, the lever. Just *there*. And so simple. So matter-of-fact. Like a bucket and a mop. And so close. Everybody, prisoners and guards, must surely look up whenever they pass, and must surely hear death's drop, the clank of the trapdoor or the thud of someone at the end of the rope. Surely, they must hear. And she can't help asking herself if, one day, Milhaus will dangle from that rope.

'He's this way.' The guard points to another wide walkway, cells either side. Though she now sees that some of what she took to be cells are bath-houses. Two prisoners mop the stone floor while their guards look on, the slap, slap of the mops the only sound.

She's on the point of shaking her head and saying no, this is all a big mistake. She can't do this. She can't stay in this place a moment longer. She looks back to the door through which she came, and through which she can leave any time she chooses. Don't get many visitors. But she *has* chosen to come and she can't go. Not now. She's here. One of these cells is Milhaus's. But which one? The whole prison smells of danger. And it's as though the place can smell her fear. She must get out and never come back. Still, she walks on beside the guard.

'Here.' The guard points to a half-open door. A small cell. She can see a table. A pair of folded hands resting on the table. And it's only then that she realises this is not Milhaus's cell; it's what the guard says is the visitors room. But it's a cell, all the same.

'You've got ten minutes,' the guard tells her, then stands by the open door.

When she asked at the jail entrance to visit Milhaus, the policeman on duty asked her why. Absurdly, she hadn't thought of this. What should she say? To let him know he's not alone? And someone cares? That the entire world hasn't turned on him? To let him know that there is more to the world than the beast? That the beast doesn't roar for everybody? After a long silence, noting that the policeman was becoming suspicious, she said that she had taught Milhaus. When he was a little boy, a little boy with a gift for drawing. Way beyond his years. A little boy who could have grown up to be an artist, and who, in his own way, did. Only his studio was the football field. A little boy in the classroom with a gift for drawing, and in the playground a gift for the game. And when she said it the policeman nodded, though with a look in his eyes that suggested he'd never heard such nonsense. Then he nodded again, as if to say, nonsense or not, he thought it was a good story or maybe even believed her. Which didn't surprise Maryanne because she almost believed it herself. Where did it come from? She doesn't know. But she knows what Katherine would say: too much imagination. Does it matter? It was the right story at the right time.

And what did Milhaus make of it when they told him he was to receive a visitor? A teacher from long ago whom he couldn't remember. But perhaps he imagined that he did remember. Remembered the name, but not the face. Perhaps, in his memory, she's already become someone else, acquired the face of some long-ago teacher, whom he may have liked and has vaguely pleasant memories of. After you've been locked up in this place for any time, she imagines, any pleasant memory, however vague or invented, would be welcome. Perhaps Milhaus is simply curious. Or needs a break from the boredom and the horror.

Whatever the case, she is about to find out. And Milhaus – the name, the story, the case that has absorbed the city and left it returning to the slops bucket of its loathing and hatred every day, wanting more every day, but never sated; Milhaus, the god who fell, whose fate feels entwined with hers – is about to become fact.

Milhaus is smaller than she imagined. Perhaps it's because he is shackled, for as soon as she sits opposite him she notices his handcuffs. But there is power in his presence too. What is it? The intense stare? The composure? The strange calmness that surrounds him? She's not sure, but it's there. This power. Almost as though he could break his handcuffs at will, whenever he chose. The power of someone who has that something extra; his whole body, tight and coiled, ready to spring into spectacular flight at any moment. But at the same time there is something lost in his look. His foot taps continually as he stares at her. Cool blue eyes search for something familiar in Maryanne's face one second, turn vague the next.

While she in turn is telling herself that there, just a few feet from her, on the other side of the table, is *Milhaus*: a name that is its own story. His foot stops tapping.

'Who *are* you?'

His voice is smooth and cool, like an actor's. Once more she feels like leaving. It's all too much. It's madness even being here. But here she is. Who does she think she is, indeed.

'You don't know me,' she half whispers, half stammers, leaning forward. 'I never taught you.'

He eyes the face and the swollen belly of this woman he has never met before, then he too falls into a whisper. 'No. I knew that.'

'You did?'

He nods slowly. 'Why are you here?'

She looks away, composing herself, then turns back. 'Because …' and she breaks off, silently rehearsing her reason in all its preposterousness, but deciding that, preposterous or not, it is true. She continues. 'Because I wanted you to know that you are not alone.'

He leans back in his chair. Puzzled and suspicious. Wary. She can see that. And why wouldn't he be? She could be anyone, here for any number of reasons. Possibly even sent to spy upon the spy.

'You came here to tell me *that*?'

'It seems so. If you like, I'll go. I should never have come. This is madness,' she says, rising from her chair.

'No.' He waves his cuffed hands. 'Stay.'

They are silent. The tapping of his foot starts up again. His eyes don't leave her and she can barely stay still. It's crazy enough to be true. She's crazy enough to believe, he seems to be thinking. Even to trust. Maybe. And Maryanne decides that the vague, faraway look in his eyes is also a sad one. As if he's sleepwalking through a sad, dark dream he woke to one morning and can't escape from.

'The crowds, the newspapers. They don't speak for everybody. There is a group. A women's group, not far from here. They campaign for your release. Have you heard?'

'No.'

It is a long, drawn-out no. His face still puzzled. His look suspicious. 'No, I haven't,' he adds, as if it were a matter of no importance.

And he also states this in the manner of saying: I don't know you. I've never met you before. Why should I believe you?

'They are making up a petition. It will be published in the papers. Mannix himself has signed it.'

He shows no reaction to the mention of Mannix. No reverence, no loathing. Just indifference.

'A petition? Why?'

'*Why?* Because you are innocent.'

His foot stops tapping. He laughs. A short, hollow laugh.

'Innocent?' He shakes his head slowly, as if to say, what does that mean?, the slap, slap of the mops on the floor beating time outside. Or measuring it. Milhaus pauses. 'The crowds don't bother me; I've put up with crowds all my life.' He breaks into a short, couldn't-care-less laugh. 'What the hell does it matter anyway? We're all guilty of something.'

'What does it *matter*? How can you say that?'

There is a beyond-it-all look about him, a dangerously casual air. 'Well, does it? Everybody's made their minds up. It's all decided.'

'You mustn't say that.'

'It's true. Why bother?'

'No, no. You mustn't give in to them. You're young. You've got your whole life in front of you.' Here she pauses, staring directly at him to emphasise the point, stressing the enormity of it. 'Your *life*!' She pauses again, gathering herself. 'We are only given one. Think of all the things that are out there waiting to be done. All those years waiting to be lived. Your *life*!'

He falls silent for a long time, staring down at his cuffed hands as if asking himself what sort of life he has, manacled like this. And although the silence is uncomfortable, he seems to be working through some line of thought, which he may or may not share with her, so she lets it be. He sighs, taps his fingers on the table. Perhaps she has struck a chord, for he seems to be dwelling on what she's said, circling some enormous question. Time passes. A minute, perhaps two. Then he looks up.

'Do you have someone you can trust?'

'Yes,' she says, puzzled. An odd question.

'Who?'

'My sister.'

'Ah,' he nods. 'A sister. You're lucky.'

He looks back at his hands, speaking to them, not Maryanne. 'How do we know who to trust?'

She pauses before answering, dwelling on what it must be like to be Milhaus. Your whole world upturned overnight. Somebody, somewhere, turning it upside down. But who? Someone you knew, or thought you knew. Even trusted. Suddenly pointing the finger at you for whatever reason so that, overnight, everything is utterly changed. And will surely never be the same again. But who? Well might he ask that. Who wouldn't? It is then that she realises he is staring at her, waiting for an answer.

'You just know.'

He is silent, looking about the small room, possibly saying to himself: Is that it? Is that all you can say? And she wouldn't blame him, for it doesn't feel like much of an answer.

His focus returns to her. 'What if you don't?'

'There must be someone.'

He laughs, then shrugs. 'What if there isn't?' He pauses, weighing things up, the way someone does when they're about to say something they might regret. 'I'm not even sure I trust my lawyer.'

Milhaus falls silent again. She ponders him, frowning. She knows nothing of football, but, she is thinking, perhaps he is one of those who play in a team but are never *of* the team. Is that possible? One of those who only ever rely on their own genius, and never trust the team. And so has gone through life never having to trust anyone. Until now. His hands are folded, his eyes closed. He could almost be praying.

At this point the guard steps into the cell. 'Time.'

She looks round, surprised; it has been a short ten minutes. And, in another way, an eternal ten minutes. She stands as the guard leads Milhaus from the room. He glances back at her, still wary. Unsure. A look that asks, almost pleads: Can I trust *you*? You come with a story crazy enough to be true ... but can I? And again he has the look of a man who has never known *who* to trust because, protected by his genius, he has never had to. And now desperately needs to know.

Then he is gone and she is led along the same dark corridor that she entered by and is soon standing in the full glare of the street, looking back at the grey face of the jail. People pass. Horse-drawn carriages clop by, a motor car rumbles along. The sun is high in the sky. Milhaus will be back in his cell, somewhere back there in hell's dungeons. Milhaus, the person who is no longer simply the case, the name that is a story unto itself, the god who fell, the traitor who betrayed them all. Back there in his cell, foot tapping on the stone floor, a shaft of light through the bars of the window. The image of a woman he's never met before, telling him he is not alone, clear in his mind. But wondering who she is. He didn't even ask her name. She never gave it.

Maryanne is drained. Exhausted. Palms sweating. There are no tea-houses or cafes in this part of town. She's hungry and thirsty. She passes the courts and makes her way down the street, past the library, to a familiar building where she knows she will be welcome. The women always make her welcome. There she can sit and rest. Revive herself for the trip home.

And there she can tell them where she has been. And what she has seen. If she can find the words. Then she remembers. It is Sunday. They won't be there. And so she makes for home. She can wait, they can wait, until tomorrow.

9.

'You spoke to him?'

It is not the usual crowded scene in the office, and Vera's question turns heads. Vera: this young woman with skin like fresh cream from the posh side of the river; this young woman whose voice and bearing talks of money and an expensive education; who speaks the most wondrously strange language, the language of the enemy. But with whom Maryanne feels such an odd affinity.

'Yes.'

Vera smiles at her, eyes alight with admiration and a touch of awe. 'Good heavens!' She pauses, then adds, 'And?'

'What do I think?' Maryanne raises her eyebrows, not sure what to say. 'I don't know. He's alone, yes. Suspicious, yes. Of everyone and everything. Who wouldn't be? But ...' She tries to gather together impressions that she hasn't yet had time to think about properly. 'It's hard to say, but I couldn't help but think he was holding something back.'

'You don't doubt he's innocent?'

Maryanne calculates her answer. 'He laughed when I said he was innocent. That we all think he is.'

'Laughed?'

'An odd laugh. Said we're all guilty of something.' She pauses, slowly returning to Vera's question. 'What do I think? I don't know. His eyes don't miss anything. But there's something lost in them too. Almost as if he's not in the room. In a dream. Sleepwalking.'

'Lost?'

'As if he's woken up in a strange land.'

Vera glances down at the sheet of paper in her hands, and when she speaks it's as if her mind is on two things. 'Imagine it. You've got everything one minute, and nothing the next. The crowd cheering for you one day, and baying for your blood the next.' She looks up from the paper. 'Who wouldn't be lost?'

And as she speaks, Maryanne's picture of Milhaus, the lost boy in the playground wondering where everybody has gone, comes back to her. Along with the nagging feeling that he was holding something back. Or that there was a story somewhere inside the story. 'Yes,' she says. 'Who wouldn't be?'

Maryanne sips her tea and munches absentmindedly on a biscuit. The two women are silent. She forgets Milhaus for the moment. Once again she contemplates this young woman with whom she has nothing in common but with whom she feels this affinity; this young woman who gives every impression that her life is blessed, full of possibilities in a way that Maryanne's is not.

'What are you going to do?' The question pops out of Maryanne.

'Do?' Vera asks, looking up from writing on her sheet of paper.

It amuses Maryanne; the women here are always writing something down, always rushing around with sheets of paper in their hands.

'With your life,' Maryanne adds, a touch of envy in her voice.

'My life?'

'Yes.' Maryanne nods as she says this, a thoughtful nod that suggests her life and Vera's will be as different as today and tomorrow. 'When this is all over. I mean the vote, the war. It will exhaust itself. It *will* end. What then?'

'Good heavens!' Vera smiles, as if counting her options. At least that's the way it appears to Maryanne, who is calculating the years of difference between them. Twenty years, or near enough, she concludes. A generation. And as she contemplates this, she's also dwelling on that curious feeling that these are not her times. That she's been dropped into these awful years by mistake. That her times are out there, travelling towards her: a silver jet about to land in another age. And perhaps that's it, the source of this affinity, that in this young woman with whom she has nothing in common she catches glimpses of the life she might have lived. Or the lives. But which she won't. For as much as she may feel that her times are out there, travelling towards her, she will never step into them. Never calculate her options. Not the way Vera will. But when she's with this young woman she catches hints of what it must feel like. To be able to take such things for granted.

'I want to change things.' And as much as Vera says this with what seems to Maryanne to be an impossible innocence, the morning still on her cheeks, there is also something quite steely in her resolve that she hasn't noticed before. Even hard. As well as something else Maryanne can't place: a sort of thoughtful distance in the eyes, which, in anybody else, she would call sadness. 'I want to leave the world a different place. Better.'

Maryanne, distracted by these hints of another Vera behind the privilege and clear skin, nods, conceding that she just might.

Vera puts down her pen. 'Will you see him again?'

Maryanne smiles: this is the other thing about Vera – talking about one thing one minute, another the next. Mind like a butterfly. But a dazzling one, flown in from other times.

'No.'

'Oh?'

'It's exhausting. I can't do it again. I couldn't bear to be in that place again. It's like nothing on earth.' She slowly shakes her head. 'Besides, he knows now. He knows he's not alone. And I'm not so sure he really wants company. Or has ever been happy in it. Or perhaps *I'm* not the company he wants.' She puts her cup down, her mind back on the mystery of Milhaus, gathers her coat and hat, and slowly stands.

Vera notes the effort that goes into it. 'When is the baby due?'

'Not soon enough.'

Vera stands with her, concerned, suddenly looking older.

'And what of the father?'

'There *is* no father.' She says this more sharply than she intended, then corrects herself with a small laugh. 'I don't mean it was an immaculate conception. Of course, there is a father. There just may as well not be.'

Vera looks at her in silence, as though not having thought of this and not knowing where to go from here. Not knowing whether to inquire is to intrude, or to not inquire is to be cold and uncaring. It's all there in her face, even as she speaks. 'I can't imagine having children.'

'Nobody can.'

'And not in these times. Not here, not now. And not by myself.' She pauses, calculating just what she can say.

'I've got my sister.'

'Good,' Vera says, seizing on it. 'A big sister?'

'Yes.'

'I wish I had a big sister. You're lucky.'

And there is something oddly disconcerting in being told by Vera, of all people, that she is lucky. 'Yes. I am. You're quite right.' She pauses. 'No big sister?'

'No.'

'Big brother, then?'

'No,' Vera says slowly. And, once again, with a kind of distance in her eyes that, in anybody else, Maryanne would call sadness. Then Vera's face brightens. 'I always think of having children as something other people do.'

'Until it's *you*.'

'Sometimes I try to imagine it.' Vera shakes her head, as if trying: a husband, a house, a child or two; the husband leaving for work every morning – a kiss – and returning every evening – another kiss. No, that's the problem, her expression suggests, I *can't* imagine it. Not for me. At least, that's how Maryanne reads things. And then, weighing her words, she asks: 'Is there someone? Is there a young man?'

Vera shakes her head. 'No. Well, there was.'

Now it's Maryanne who doesn't know what to say: whether to inquire further and risk intruding, or say nothing and risk seeming cold and uncaring. In the end, she leaves it at that, wondering just what that means. *Was*.

When she has her hat and coat on, Vera hands her a pamphlet for a meeting. An early-evening meeting in the gardens by the parliament. The day and the time on the pamphlet. 'If you can make it,' she says. 'And, oh!' she adds. 'We're going on a little march tomorrow. To hand out the pamphlets for the meeting. The more the merrier.'

Maryanne smiles and says she may come. Why not? They nod their farewells and Maryanne waves from the lift as she closes the door.

On the street, everybody looks down at their feet. Oh, *this*. She'd forgotten. And she braces herself before joining the flow. An army, marching from one day to the next. No one breaking ranks. Marching to the station; to the good fortune of a free seat on the train; marching to work and home again, to be greeted with an evening kiss as mechanical as a signature on a form. Maryanne feels a shiver run through her with the thought. Not for her. Not for Vera either. *We're not the ordinary run.* It's not, Maryanne imagines, what Vera would call living. And who can blame her? She wants to change things, and she just might.

Maryanne smiles. Make a difference, indeed. Wouldn't that be something? She boards her tram; it rattles down to the Town Hall. Indeed, wouldn't that be something? To imagine you *could*? You have to be young to think like that. To imagine things differently.

* * *

The next day, when she gets off her tram to join the little march of theirs, she is running late. She stops on the Town Hall steps, suddenly aware of a commotion ahead of her.

There, approaching the Town Hall, is a small group of well-dressed women of varying ages. They are in a line, spread across one half of the street, and the traffic behind them – buggies and a few motor cars – is blocked. The drivers, part of the commotion, are yelling at the women, telling them to get off the street. But these women are not budging. There is Vera, in the centre of the line. And beside her, all around her, faces Maryanne recognises from the women's offices. They have placards saying Vote NO and are chanting words of peace, calling for an end to war, handing out pamphlets to the small crowd watching them.

They are festive, smiling, urging people to join in and swell their numbers, and as much as they know they are holding up the traffic, they will not be moved. Protected by their innocence, or so it seems to Maryanne, they march towards her. And Maryanne is suddenly afraid for them, for their numbers are so few. They call again and again for people to step forward, but nobody from the gathering crowd on the footpath moves. And all the time the traffic behind them builds, the crowd gathers on either side of them, and they start to look tiny. Easy prey. But they seem not to notice the position they are in or the jeers and sneers of the crowd.

And it is then, seemingly from nowhere, as Maryanne is about to step onto the street and join them, that the police descend upon the march in numbers. Ten, a dozen, she's not sure. Two of them on horseback. And she looks around, wondering where on earth they came from as the large flanks of a horse, its legs as tall as she is, press close, and the rider, high above her, directs the horse towards the women, its hooves clattering on the street as the crowd suddenly retreats. And while the horses divide the crowd from the marching women, the police on foot reach Vera and her colleagues. And straightaway they grab them, wrenching them from the street, twisting their arms behind their backs and pushing their heads forward. In an instant, a festive, peaceful march has turned violent. And Maryanne watches, helpless, as Vera – Vera for heaven's sake, cheeks as fresh as the morning – is grabbed by one policeman while another locks her hands behind her and she is handcuffed. As they all are, their numbers are so few.

Once handcuffed, they are dragged from the street and marched like criminals caught in some lawless act towards a waiting van, which, like the police themselves, seems to have appeared from nowhere. And as they are marched away, Vera sees Maryanne, catches her eye and calls something out, but there is a man in a three-piece suit walking beside her, newspaper in hand, yelling at her, and in the din Maryanne can't hear what she is saying. Vera calls again, but it is at this point that somebody spits on her, and Vera, turning in horror, no free hand to wipe the spittle from her face, stumbles and falls to her knees, her hat tumbling to the ground, while all around her the women are being dragged to the waiting van. The policemen yank Vera to her feet, hauling her to the vehicle, her face terrified, her legs limp as she attempts one last time to call something out to Maryanne, who rushes forward to help her, only to be stopped inches away by a huge hand forcing her back. She sways on the spot, everything spinning around her, trying to steady herself, and when she looks for Vera she has disappeared into the van. They all have. All the women, suddenly vanished.

The police disappear as quickly as they arrived, and the man with the newspaper, who only a few minutes before was yelling at Vera, his face distorted with hatred, strides off along the footpath. The traffic, its way now clear, moves on. The crowd thins, and within minutes, it seems, everything is normal again. As though none of it ever happened. And it is only then that Maryanne sees Vera's hat on the street and rushes out to retrieve it, dusting it on her skirt as she walks back to the footpath.

What was she calling out? Maryanne, her body trembling, remembers that huge hand telling her to go back, and the frightened look on Vera's face. A look that said, or seemed to say, that she had heard and read of such things, but had never expected them to happen to her. And the frightened looks on all the women's faces might be read the same way. Both frightened and shocked that this had happened. At the same time, Maryanne asks herself if she could have done more, but she knows that, if anything, she'd been reckless enough.

And it is only then that she realises there are tears in her eyes. And not tears of sadness or self-pity. But tears of sheer helplessness and outrage. How dare they? Is there no end to this beast? This beast that dons suits, reads newspapers and yells, screams and spits before returning to the paper and home. And she realises also that it is the first time that the beast has reduced her to tears. Stinging tears. For as much as she's sought to stand back from it, today it scooped her up in its scaly claws and dragged her into its madness.

She sits on a bench near the corner and waits until she feels ready to rise. She holds Vera's hat in her hands, turning it round and round while people pass, eyes on the footpath as they tread home or to the station or tram stop, the street now just a street. The yelling, the clamour, the horses – all gone. No sign that anything happened, apart from a couple of placards lying on the footpath, people stepping on or over them, a few pausing to read them.

And for the first time Maryanne ponders the brutal efficiency of the police. For they looked well prepared for the action. Knew exactly what they were doing. Almost as though someone had told them that at such and such an hour, at such and such a place, a small group of troublesome women would be disrupting the city. And suddenly the words of Milhaus come back to her: who can you trust? Did someone from within the group betray them? For it was an ambush. And she shakes her head, asking herself if this is what her world has come to.

When she's ready, the trembling gone, she rises from the bench and walks back towards the tram stop from which she stepped no more than half an hour earlier, when the sound of a commotion caused her to pause and turn. Her tram comes and she hauls herself aboard, deciding what to say to Katherine and what *not* to say to her.

* * *

The next day, in the mid-afternoon, Maryanne goes to the offices, not knowing if Vera and the other woman will be there. But they are. The atmosphere is subdued, the talk quiet. She approaches Vera, who, she's glad to note, shows no sign of bruising or injury.

'How are you?' she asks, trying not to think of the spittle on the young woman's face and the sudden look of horror in her eyes.

'Nothing broken.' And then she adds, 'Body or spirit.'

'They were awful.'

'The police or the people?' Vera asks, her eyes hard. 'We shouldn't be surprised. We unnerve them.' She looks out over the room and begins speaking, to no one in particular. *'Das Leben gehört den Lebenden an* … Life belongs to the living, and those who live must be prepared for change.' She says this flatly, unemotionally, the poetry, this time, gone from the words. Vera is clearly in no mood for poetry. She sighs. 'We bring change. We unnerve them. They *think* they hate us. So they lash out.' She taps the table top with her fingers. 'Of course, we should have known.'

'It happened so quickly, they knew exactly …' Maryanne says, trailing off, looking at the women behind them, then shaking her head. 'How long did they keep you?'

'Not long. They told us we'd been warned. We had no right to hold the traffic up.' Here Vera emits a cynical laugh, which, coming from Vera, seems like blasphemy. 'The traffic? People are dying in the most horrible ways, blown into bloody bits and sinking into endless mud. The world is tearing itself to pieces, and all they're worried about is the traffic!'

They pause, Maryanne looking round the offices, noting once again the sombre atmosphere. The quiet talk. And it is only then she remembers Vera's hat. 'Oh,' she says, handing it over. 'You dropped this.'

'Ah.' Vera's eyes light up. 'I thought I'd lost it. I shall wear it on the next march.'

Maryanne nods grimly. 'You were calling something out to me. In the street.'

'Was I?'

'You don't remember?'

Vera pauses, collecting herself. 'It might just have been your name ...' And she shrugs her shoulders, as if to say, why not? It's as likely as anything else. Then she turns to look at the group of women behind her. 'They mean to scare us off. But they won't. They'll find out we're not so easily scared.'

And so it is a different image of Vera and the group of women that Maryanne takes home with her. It is still, when she thinks of Vera, a marvel that she can imagine things being different, and can imagine bringing about that change. But Maryanne also suspects that Vera and the other women have, quite possibly, all been reminded that change doesn't come easily. Never has. And sometimes it can get dangerous. You can be hurt. The trick, Maryanne imagines, is to use it. To use the hurt. And with that thought she leaves the building and merges with the footpath traffic. Down the street, past the site of yesterday's protest. There's no sign that it ever happened, but the echoes of the incident trail after her.

* * *

Ghouls. She can only think of them as ghouls. A smith with a black face watches her pass, hammer in one hand, wheel in the other, a furnace glowing behind him. Men and women from the boot factory, their faces tired, blank, sit on the footpath for their smoko. The coal merchant, arms and face black from coal dust, looks up for a moment while shovelling giant chunks of the stuff into hessian bags.

The sun is low in the sky, shadows are lengthening. Maryanne is almost home. She knows all these people, at least by sight. And they know her. Some days it's just the workers she sees, doing all the things that workers everywhere do. Nothing out of the ordinary. Other days, and it's not just the effect of witnessing yesterday's march, these moods come across her and it's all an underworld. And these aren't people, or workers doing all the things that workers do everywhere, but ghouls that stopped being people long ago. She knows them and they know her, and have watched her belly grow since she came back to her old neighbourhood. No doubt they've heard too that she's the Hun's whore and the brat inside her is a little Hun.

These streets are full of factories, warehouses and workshops, big and small. Workers' cottages are jammed in between: street after street, row upon row. Sometimes she and the workers greet each other; sometimes this mood comes over her, comes over everyone, this living deadness, and nobody's got the energy or the urge for hellos. And everything becomes a shadow world, everybody a ghost or silhouette. Maryanne too, just another shadow passing over the footpath. Just another ghoul. All of them underworld creatures in a waking dream as the afternoon sun sinks and shadows spread. Nothing quite real. But she can't take her eyes off them, all the same. It's not a nightmare. No, it's not frightening. It's almost marvellous. Almost wonderful. Like walking through a dark dream, the dream creatures looking up as you pass, the occasional eye asking: are you of the dream, one of us, or are you just passing through? We must stay here. But you, are you only passing through and can you really leave?

But they're not ghouls, they're people. And this is not an underworld, this is life. She stops in her tracks, the smell of the smoko trailing after her, the coal merchant's dust in the air, the clang-clang of the smith behind her. *Life!* The baby is still, and she can almost imagine it staring out from her belly, taking it all in, the world it will enter.

But where is *her* world? For this surely isn't it. Is it travelling towards her, or she travelling towards it? Over her shoulder, out of view, a silver jet prepares to land. A story begins, and Maryanne stands, stock still, a long shadow on a footpath of shadows, the story curled up in her belly, the egg that will give birth to it all.

10.

A letter is waiting for her on the kitchen table when she gets home. Katherine is out. She sits with the letter, puzzled. For the handwriting is Viktor's. She knows this from the notes they exchanged in the town during the brief time that was theirs. It is spiky, controlled writing. And the moment she looks at it she can imagine him compiling the accounts for the shop in this very hand. But the writing also brings with it an unexpected rush of emotion. Feelings she's almost forgotten clamour to the surface. *The father?* Of course there is a father, Vera: a father who once, in a dangerous, unguarded moment, told her she was beautiful – the only time in all her life anybody has ever said that to her, for she comes from a family that never wasted its breath on words like that. Yet the same Viktor stood in front of her in the gardens that overlooked the town, his fierce eyes as good as telling her that she was a crafty bitch for going and getting herself pregnant, who pronounced everything a mess and strode off, leaving her alone in the gardens, because they couldn't possibly be seen together.

Now, he is writing to her, and why is that? But even more puzzling is the return address: the military camp not far from the foundling home. Such a wonderful name it has: Broadmeadows. Once again, she imagines swaying fields of wheat and haystacks, but can only remember seeing from the train window Scotch thistle and scrub. Broadmeadows camp. What on earth is Viktor doing there? Has he gone and done it? Done something silly? Joined this mad march to death?

She tears the letter open and sure enough he has. *Idiot!* Her fist thumps the table. Did he forget he is about to have a child? Yes, Vera, there *is* a father. And she knows that in thinking all of this, that in registering that jumble of emotions that the letter has set off, she is allowing herself to indulge in the possibility that once the child is born, instincts as old as the stars will take over, and the child might see its father from time to time, and might even come to know him. Now this. *Idiot!*

He writes that the town now nods its approval in the streets, and that certain people have begun to speak to him again who haven't spoken to him for years. The feathers have stopped coming. Trade is booming. Even his mother lets slip occasional murmurings of pride. He writes that he doesn't expect her to feel or think any such things, and he's right. But she can also see it, that awful town. All feathers and spite. Its mineral waters bloodied, its gardens dark as death. Everybody staring at him in the street, in shops, at church. Ghouls. No wonder he broke under the weight of it all. How could he not? And it's only as she finishes re-reading the short letter, for his head, he says, is asleep even as he writes and he only has so many words in him, that she notices he has changed the spelling of his name. He is now Victor.

She could weep. Not for Victor. But for something that she can't even name at the moment, and is suddenly too tired to even bother trying to. Viktor is now Victor. The beast has won. Perhaps someone really did threaten to report him. Have him rounded up, like all those rounded-up neighbours all over the city who went from being neighbours one day to Huns the next. The beast roared, and Viktor bowed to Victor.

But she can now write to him, at least. He's even asked her to. Asked her how she is. And she *will* write. When the time comes.

The front door opens, and Maryanne stuffs the letter back into its envelope and slips it into her dress pocket as Katherine appears. The sisters stare at each other; Katherine doesn't need to ask who the letter is from and Maryanne doesn't need to tell her.

Besides, she doesn't have the energy. A long day makes itself felt. She barely has the strength to rise, but she does, and makes her way to the front room and the armchair that has become hers, the sound of children fighting in the street faintly audible as she closes her eyes. When she wakes, Katherine will have everything ready. A meal will appear. A pot will be brewing. All will be well. Here, at least. She drifts into sleep, to the comforting clatter of cutlery and plates, and her sister humming some distantly familiar hymn from their youth.

* * *

In the morning the sun is bright. She is rested, she is strong. She pours tea. The newspaper is on the table.

The Milhaus case still captivates the city. His trial goes on. The city rushes to the papers for the latest, gasping and hissing like children at a show, the caped villain of Milhaus pausing to laugh or sneer before going about his nasty business. A handwriting expert, Maryanne reads, has given testimony. The letter retrieved from the basket and the letters of Milhaus, he says, are in the same writing. Written by the same man. And still Milhaus proclaims that he was not even in the city on the day the letter was written and delivered, the date clearly inscribed at the top of the page. But there are no witnesses, and who will believe the word of a fallen god?

And so the evidence of the handwriting expert prevails. Milhaus is guilty before the judge even speaks. Condemned by the beast, the papers, the experts. All agree. And when Maryanne puts the paper down on the table, it's the memory of Milhaus's foot, frantically tapping, as if tapping out some secret message in code, that comes back to her.

What was he holding back? For she is sure he was hiding something, sure there is another story that isn't being told. *Innocent.* She hears that laugh again. Nervous. Unsure. Cuffed hands folded. An attitude of prayer. Foot tapping. Almost as though he were guilty of something. Or felt he was. And had come to the conclusion that guilt for one thing is no different from guilt for another. It's all one.

She bites her toast, drinks tea and looks out the kitchen window onto the small yard. The case is already decided. Just as Milhaus said. They will take him to those gallows she saw the Sunday before: the rope, the lever, the trapdoor – waiting just for him. All there is to do now is await that something final that everybody craves.

And will they be satisfied then? Feel the slightest remorse? Do the hounds feel sympathy for the fox? She has always sided with the fox. Even knows what it is to be the fox. Or imagines she does. *Give that to your fancy man!* People! They ruin everything. She folds the newspaper. Enough for one day. And the image of a fox she saw once in a city park comes back to her: keeping low, up against a wall, somehow doomed. Well, the hunt is nearly up; the fox awaits sentence. The dogs are in full cry.

* * *

Later that morning, Katherine having given her a list of what they need, Maryanne is standing at the counter in the local grocer's. It is an old shop, and Maryanne has been coming here for much of her life. She knows the husband and wife who run the shop. They know her. Enough to pass small talk. With knowing eyes, they've watched her belly grow but haven't said anything. As though it doesn't exist. Or perhaps they think that if they act as if it doesn't, it won't.

There is a small queue behind her and the shopkeeper is humming to himself as he wraps onions in a sheet of newspaper. The people behind Maryanne are chatting quietly in a sort of background murmur that Maryanne finds restful. Then the shopkeeper pauses, looking down at the next sheet of newspaper on the counter. He laughs. There is a picture of Milhaus in the centre of the page, and he stares at it, then looks up.

'We don't need a court to tell us what we already know, do we?'

Maryanne is staring at the photograph, thinking it is not such a good likeness (that in *this* photograph he does appear shifty), and when she finally looks up she realises the question is addressed to her. And, what is more, the shopkeeper is waiting for her response. And when she turns around she sees that the queue is also waiting. And as the silence goes on, the shopkeeper and the other customers begin to view her with suspicion. Then distrust. It's not a difficult question. The answer should be easy. So what is she waiting for?

And it's then that she realises that the question has become a test. Of loyalty. Or something else; she's not sure. But a test, all the same. And it is in this moment that their faces all transform, become warped. Mouths twisted, eyes of animals, noses twitching. The way the beast eyes her in the streets and squares. Sniffing her out, recognising with unerring animal accuracy that she is not one of them. And the longer her silence lasts, the more their suspicions are confirmed. She has been tested and failed. But what for? Her loyalty? Her patriotism? Her sense of duty? So be it. Let them fail her. She's never, never once – she could tell them, would love to tell them – called herself a patriot and distrusts anybody who does. She'd rather believe in God than a country. Or a football team. She is silent. A silence, along with the look on her face, that rings with something between cheek and pride. All eyes are upon her and she knows she has been called upon to say something that shows she is one of them, after all, and has failed. But, of course, they know she's not one of them. They knew it all along. She's the Hun's whore. Still, they gave her a chance.

And it is while she is contemplating this that she suddenly finds herself saying: 'And just what *do* we know?'

The shopkeeper plonks the wrapped onions in front of her. 'I know a guilty face when I see one.' And he points at the photograph in the newspaper. 'Guilty as the devil, that one.'

With this, the queue behind her erupts into agreement. And it is while this is happening that Maryanne takes her onions and drops them into her shopping bag, casually saying when they all fall silent, 'Oh, I don't know; he didn't seem all that bad to me.'

There is a sudden intake of breath throughout the shop. A kind of disbelief. They can't have heard right. She said what? Maryanne folds up her shopping list, forgetting all about whatever else she was going to buy, and puts it in her pocket. And as she turns to leave, she adds, 'And not so tall. Little boy, really.'

She leaves the shop with the sound of muttering behind her, and although she can't hear precisely what they are muttering – to themselves, to the other customers, to the shopkeeper – she can well imagine. And suddenly muttering seems like a good word, just right, for they've all got that muttering look about them.

Outside, she looks up to the sky and bursts out laughing. Oh, what the hell. They hate me anyway. May as well give them something to really hate me for. And talk about. It was her chance to show them she was one of them, after all. And she's flung that chance back at them. And would again, without hesitation. So, she silently says as if addressing them all: if I don't love my country, what do I love? She smiles. Would you like to know? Would you *really*? She asks this, staring back at the grocer's shop, the owner and the customers eyeing her as if she were dangerous: a stray dog, unpredictable. To be avoided. Or rounded up. Her smile broadens as she stands there in the street, slowly rubbing her belly. What do I love? Let me count them. I love this child, more than my own life. And I love my sister. And small animals. I think that's it. Oh, and those moments when the clouds part and step aside, almost thoughtfully, and we see the endless blue behind them.

She might have said that, and it might have been fun to watch their faces. But all that matters at the moment is that for once, just once, she has silenced the beast. And has walked from the shop, the beast staring after her, its mouth agape and muttering. A small win, true. But a win. One she'll pay for, she tells herself as she turns for home with only a fraction of the shopping she promised Katherine she'd do. Of course, she'll have to explain to Katherine why that is. So be it. Leaving the beast behind her, she imagines a slight smile on the face of the child as together they walk home.

11.

GUILTY. The word covers almost half the front page of the morning paper. She's never seen such a thing before. Nobody has. Almost half a page for one word. Black letters, stark as a scaffold. GUILTY. And it makes no attempt to explain itself: who is guilty or guilty of what. It doesn't need to. Like the words YES and NO, GUILTY doesn't need to explain itself.

That light-heartedness she experienced outside the grocer's shop the day before deserts her. She is heavy again, weighed down by this world. She can hear the roar of the beast, smell its medieval stench, see its scales shining triumphantly in the sun, the swamp dripping from it as it bellows to the sky. There will be death. Death it craves, and death it shall have. And the broken body of Milhaus will be returned to earth. Just as one day the beast will be returned to the swamp from which it came.

The paper sickens her. Sudden waves of nausea pass through her. She could almost vomit. Fears she will. Body and mind no longer separate, but united in disgust. And Maryanne, faint, powerless to quell this rising disgust with it all. She can feel the frenzy of the mob coming off the paper: roars of satisfaction, cries of rage and jeering laughter. Like some dark festival. And once again she asks herself: if *this* is the world, where is hers? Where is the child's? Not this, please, not *this*.

The nausea passes. The disgust ebbs. The moment fades. She reads on, beyond that stark, single word. Milhaus, it seems, will be sentenced the next day. And at this point she puts the paper down on the table, folding it as if to silence the thing. Outside, children are being dragged to school, the clang-clang of the smith's hammer a distant ring. She pictures Milhaus standing in the dock, the court as full as a football ground on a Saturday afternoon. And Milhaus the lone figure on the playing field. The crowd straining forward to see, hushed and breathless, as if expecting one last miracle, one last leap that will leave them gasping in disbelief. One last reminder of the days when he was as good as a god, before he fell and became a dark angel with crushed wings, foot tapping on the courtroom floor. Impatient for the thing to be over, and, like the crowd, longing now for that something final.

And, once again, the image of Milhaus, suddenly alone in the playground and wondering where everybody has gone, comes back to her. And she decides there and then to go to the court the next day to watch it all. Put herself through it. Somehow. So that he can see her, know that she's there, and know that Milhaus the Hun, who lifted them all to the heavens with every leap he took, who left them breathless then betrayed them, is not alone: that there is someone out there, after all. She need just be there, nothing more.

And it is while she is vaguely listening to the sounds of the day's activities outside that Katherine steps into the kitchen, sleeves rolled up from wringing out the washing before hanging it on the clothesline. For there is a breeze, she tells Maryanne, and it is a good day for drying. She sits and pours the last of the tea. Her forearms are strong, a glimpse of the different kinds of work she's done on farms and in towns out there on the land that Maryanne has barely seen and has no great desire to. And she dwells on this for a moment: Katherine and Maryanne, both born in the city, the same neighbourhood, but now living in different worlds. And she wonders if, by some strange chance, she were to come across Katherine one morning or evening in the bush, sitting round a camp fire – alone or with others, casual workers like herself – she would recognise her. Would she pass by and not even know her sister? Would this other Katherine be unrecognisable? A different Katherine altogether. Which makes her wonder who this other Katherine is, and if she's ever really known her.

Maryanne doesn't say what's in the paper and Katherine doesn't read it. They say little. It is enough that she is there, that they are together. For she is sure that if Katherine were not here, she would not have the strength to take them all on. And so the talk, or the lack of it, doesn't matter. It's just *being* there that does.

All the same, she suddenly throws a question across the table, one that she has never asked her sister before, but one she has long contemplated and thought about asking.

'Have you ever thought about getting married?'

'Married?' Katherine says, startled by the question. But it is also a response that suggests: my sort, Maryanne, my sort doesn't get married.

'Well, not so much married as having someone around.'

'A man?'

'Well, yes. Haven't you ever wanted someone around? Being there, with you?'

Maryanne has no idea what sort of answer she expects. In a sense, after the surprise of Victor's letter, she is almost asking herself the question, and asking Katherine is a way of contemplating it. Seeing how it sounds spoken, as apart from thought. And so she watches, half contemplating what her own answer would be.

Katherine looks down at her cup, turning it round and round in front of her. When she finally looks up it is with a touch of mischief in her eyes, an expression that says: you *did* ask.

'There was a man, once.'

Maryanne snaps out of her own thoughts and eyes Katherine. What? She's happy to be surprised by people, especially when she thinks she has them nailed. But her sister?

'*Was?*'

'Yes.' And the mischief in Katherine's eyes has given way to a slight smile. 'Is it so preposterous?'

'No. Of course not. It's just that you've never ...'

'Let on.'

'No.'

They stare at each other, silent for the moment. Neither sure who should speak next. Finally Maryanne, who can't stand such silences and always breaks first, speaks.

'When?'

Katherine, recognising that there is a story to tell and that it may be a long conversation, seems to gather herself before beginning. 'A long time ago. I was still young.' There is a touch of wonder in her voice, as though remembering someone she once knew. 'He proposed. Quite formal. I thought about it then, I did.'

'And?' Maryanne waits, eyes wide, as if, indeed, speaking to a different Katherine altogether.

'I said no. Obviously.' She pauses, as if it *is* another Katherine speaking. Or, rather, one whom she keeps to herself and is only now giving voice to. 'I'd only just set out. On my travels. I was sure that life, the country, was full of adventures. And I wanted to live them. *All* of them.' Her face darkens. 'But I also knew that getting married would be the end of all that.' She sits back in her chair, eyes on the ceiling. 'Oh, I thought about it. Of course I did. I'm plain. I know that. A plain girl, a plain woman. I knew there wouldn't be too many proposals. That this might well be it.'

She stops, nodding to herself, in recognition – at least, to Maryanne, this is how it looks – that it was, indeed, *it*. 'Mind you,' she says, picking up her thoughts, 'he was a plain man himself. A small farmer I did some work for. Didn't speak much. Usually left the talking to me.' Here, she laughs. 'Thought I was fascinating. Told me he could've listened to me all night.' She looks directly at Maryanne. 'Nobody ever told me that before. Oh, yes. I thought about it.'

She folds her sleeves down, buttons them and pats them into place. 'It was the proposal of a lonely man. Someone who wanted a voice around. And I could see why. It was a lonely-looking farm. On the edge of a plain. Nothing to look at. Flat. I'd have gone mad there. Besides, I wasn't a lonely woman. For the first time in my life I felt free out there in the bush. No rules.' She stops short. 'Well, just a few basic ones. And everything new. And always, always moving on. Every day an adventure. I wasn't giving that up. I'd only just started out.'

Maryanne can't believe that Katherine has never shared this story before. And while she's dwelling on this, she's also telling herself to never, *never* assume she knows someone, really *knows* them.

'Do you regret it?'

'No.'

Her answer, Maryanne suspects, is too quick.

'*Never?*'

Katherine raises her eyebrows. 'I think about it from time to time. But not enough to call it regret.'

This is not just a different Katherine, but one whom Maryanne finds it almost impossible to imagine. However wrongly, she can picture Katherine out there in the bush living this life she does. But being young and getting proposals of marriage? This is not a Katherine she's ever contemplated.

'I never went back there. Never saw him again. I sometimes wonder if he made a go of it. I doubt it.'

'Why?'

'His farm just had that look about it. Like it wasn't going to live.' She pauses. 'It was the proposal of a lonely man, on a lonely farm. The sort of place you pass through. On your way to somewhere else.'

A good place to end. Katherine rises, takes the shopping bag and nods at Maryanne, as if to say, well, there you have it. And after Katherine has asked what she needs, Maryanne watches her go, not so much a different Katherine as a mystery. What else has she got up those carefully buttoned sleeves?

No, Katherine, she might have said, you're not the ordinary run, are you? Nor am I. We're not. But – and this is the effect of their conversation – who is?

12.

An ancient clerk of courts, grained and gnarled, seems to emerge from the wooden desk at which he sits, desk and man made of the same material. He not so much rises from his chair as comes alive, like some wooden toy that suddenly speaks. And from the moment he rises, the constant hum of talk, the shuffling of feet, the scraping of chairs are silenced, and the judge enters the courtroom and takes his place.

Two policemen leave the room and everybody, apart from the judge, turns their attention to the door through which they've left. Those on seats lean forward, straining for a clearer view; hands, here and there, rest on the shoulders of those in front to steady themselves. Either nobody notices a stranger's touch or nobody cares. They are all one at this moment: eyes, arms, trunks and legs, surrendering themselves to this thing they have become. And motionless, scarcely breathing.

Maryanne stares out across the courtroom from her seat as if looking at a painted scene. No, not so much a painting, she decides, as a vast room of sitters, posing for a photograph, waiting for the white flash that will release them. And she wonders just how long they can stay like this. She smells smoky breath and sweet perfume, mingling in the dusty air blown in on a spring wind; feels the heat coming off bodies, filling the room, almost drugging her. And dream-like, she takes it all in, the sight and the smell, the expectant calm, and part of her surrenders to it, like a child at a show, just one of the crowd, waiting for the villain to appear.

Then the door opens and the policemen return, the cuffed Milhaus between them. The effect is instantaneous. Everybody moves as one, leaning further forward, straining to see more clearly. Mesmerised by the very thing they loathe, in the sway of some power, some force they themselves have created and now have no control over. Whispers ripple through the crowd, low mutterings and indistinct words. And, all the time, their eyes are fixed on the cuffed figure of Milhaus.

And what is it they see? A fallen angel, the mask ripped from his face to reveal the traitor beneath, dark and sinister, made all the more sinister for having once been theirs. Is it like looking upon the devil himself? A devil called Jack Milhaus that they once cheered as one, who lifted them to the heavens, left them breathless with wonder, then betrayed them? Or, for a moment, do they simply register what is standing before them – a young man who woke one morning to find himself at the centre of some all-encompassing madness: at first imagining that a few simple words to the right people would straighten things out; then gradually coming to the realisation that his life was no longer in his own hands, that everything had spun out of control and events had taken on a momentum of their own; and there were no words, simple or otherwise, he could muster that a sympathetic ear might listen to; that words, as he once knew them and used them, didn't matter any more?

Or do they see the boy, lost and alone on a darkening green playing field, wondering where the players and the cheering crowd have gone? Night coming in and no home to go to.

The judge's gavel comes down. The whispers and mutterings stop and a new, expectant silence fills the room. More urgent. And it is during this silence that Milhaus lifts his face and scans the crowd. There is something calm in his manner, just as there would have been, Maryanne imagines, in those few seconds before the siren sounded to start a game. And it is then, as he takes in the spectacle, that he sees her. She knows he does. For his eyes linger upon her. He gives her the slightest of nods, his head leaning to one side, and his brow wrinkling in thought, as if to say, can I trust you?

What follows lasts only a matter of seconds. Possibly a minute. No more. But it is like being physically struck. A blow. One that leaves her dazed. And although it all lasts only a moment, the impact of the judge's words, delivered without emotion, slows everything down so that events do not unfold in the usual, everyday time. Seconds could be minutes, and minutes hours. She's not even sure she hears correctly. Nothing is quite real.

His crime, the judge tells an unblinking Milhaus, who doesn't even look at him but stares straight ahead to some open field beyond the walls of the court, is heinous. Treachery. A betrayal of his people, his country and the thousands who have died in battle for the likes of him. There can be no forgiveness. The prisoner will be taken to a place of execution and hanged until dead. May God have mercy on his soul.

The blow is struck, falling with the sudden crack of the judge's hammer. The silent courtroom erupts into bellowed exultation. The white flash they've waited upon all through the strained silence to release them has exploded like a bomb ticking down to its set time. Maryanne is rocked and dazed: the sweet perfume, the smoky breath, the glare of the room – all unreal. The world is a dream and she enters dream-time. Everything around her slows: the cries and shouts in the courtroom take place out there in everyday time, in seconds and minutes, but not for Maryanne.

She is the one still, silent figure in the room, the unmoved observer at the centre of a sudden storm. All around her, arms are waving in joy, faces beaming the way they did when the war began, fingers pointing at the silent figure of Milhaus, who stares straight ahead as if still upon some playing field beyond the walls of the court. Shouts, jeers and laughter all blend and become one swirling wind of sound, going round and round the room, now louder, now softer. *God be thanked Who has matched us* ... And through it all the judge's hammer comes down again and again, trying to quieten the crowd, but has no effect. It is hopeless. The crowd will not be quietened. Like a runaway class, lost in an ecstasy of revolt, it cannot be recalled.

And, more or less unnoticed by the crowd, Milhaus is led away, disappearing through the same door he came in by. Almost incidental now, she thinks. They have what they craved, this crowd. His job is done. Like, she imagines, the inspiration for a story that is forgotten when the story is written: no longer necessary when it takes on a life of its own. And it is as she sits there, Milhaus and the judge now gone, the police beginning the task of emptying the court, that the judge's words – all the more stark and dramatic for being flat and unemotional in their delivery, like a dry lecture on a dry subject – come back to her and she feels the blow again. Nausea and disgust rise up in her. For although she dreaded the sentence and had prepared herself for it, although she knew in her bones, like the crowd, that those words would be spoken, that they were the very words they'd all come for, although she knew all of that, she wasn't prepared for the physical blow of the words themselves: 'hanged', 'dead', 'soul'.

The life inside her wriggles and kicks, almost complaining about the noise, impatient to leave, and she calms its protest with soothing hands. Then, slowly coming out of the shock, returning to the world of everyday time and motion, she looks around the room, the crowd thinning, the exultant bellows dying down. Then erupting into life, and dying down again. The world like some dark dream become real, and she passing through it all, observing and observed. It is, she tells herself, like passing through the circles of hell.

And as the room thins and she starts to leave, she notices someone coming towards her. His wig still on, his eyes, like Maryanne's, dazed. Milhaus's lawyer: the one he doesn't trust. She watches his progress, his eyes blank as if he too has been sentenced to death. And when he reaches her he nods, as if to say good day, then hands her a folded piece of paper with, she notices, an envelope tucked inside it.

'From Mr Milhaus. For you.'

'For *me*?'

'Yes.'

'But ... what is it?'

'I don't know,' he says. 'I'm just the delivery boy.'

With that he turns and leaves her, and Maryanne stands there, watching him stride away, impatience in his every step, wanting only to be rid of the room and the case that has consumed him and the city far too long. When he is gone she looks down at her hand, contemplating the note or whatever it is, wishing it wasn't there. For she fears this thing and dreads opening it.

13.

When Maryanne returns home and opens the door, Katherine meets her in the hallway, telling her that Father Geoghan is waiting in the front room.

'Father Geoghan?'

'Yes.'

'For me?'

'Who else?'

Indeed, who else? For as much as she might have thought that everything was settled at their last meeting, it wasn't. These people never give up. They wear you down. That is how they work. Katherine retreats to the kitchen, almost apologetically, suggesting that this is between Maryanne and Father Geoghan. And as Maryanne enters the room and takes a seat, he nods. Again, as if welcoming her into his home.

'A windy day for visiting, isn't it?' he says.

'It is.'

'Disagreeable time of year. You've been out, then?'

'Yes.'

'Where?'

'Out,' Maryanne says, giving nothing away, as if to say, that's my business. And you're not in charge of me, as much as you might think you are. At the same time her fingers rub the note in her dress pocket, the contents of which she read on the tram, her mind more on what it asks of her than on Father Geoghan.

The priest waits for her to go on, then realises she's said all she intends to. Brushing her abruptness aside with a wave of the hand, he starts upon the matter he came for. The matter they both know he came for.

'You've had time to consider what we discussed when I was last here?'

Maryanne nods. 'I have.'

'And carefully, I hope.'

'Quite so.'

'Good. It's a serious matter.'

'I'm perfectly aware of that,' she says, in a manner that suggests, you don't have to tell me. But Father Geoghan either doesn't note this or chooses not to.

'You visited the home I spoke of.'

'I did.'

'The sisters are very good, are they not?'

She shrugs. 'They are.'

He notes the shrug. 'The Sisters of St Joseph are devoted.'

'I've no doubt they are.'

'The child will be well looked after. And cared for. The sisters love their work. They love their children. All of them.'

Not *their* children, Father Geoghan, she says to herself, eyeing the priest once again as a scientist might a sample of insect life under a microscope.

'Your child will want for nothing, I assure you,' he continues, as if the matter were concluded. 'And when it is strong enough, and grown enough, we know just the right home. A good religious home. A good religious family.'

'You've thought of everything, Father.'

'We have to. Trust me, we know about these things,' he says softly, again either missing or choosing to miss the irony in Maryanne's comment, his words and manner quiet and intented to comfort. The howling three-headed dog nowhere in sight. And, seemingly assured that the matter is settled, he leans back in his chair and becomes expansive. 'And if, in time, the child shows an aptitude, a … shall we say a leaning towards the religious life,' and here he smiles, as if to say, who knows, we may be blessed with just such a child, 'then we have special schools for the special children. God's chosen. A rare honour, but one that falls on some.'

Until this point, Maryanne's mind has been on two things: Father Geoghan and the note in her pocket, her comments to him almost off-hand. But the casual way he mentions this, as if it were routine, which it may well be for the likes of Father Geoghan, changes that instantly. Did she hear right? Yes, she did.

She is now utterly focused on the priest in front of her. And she is no longer observing him as she might a vaguely interesting specimen, but rather as she might look upon some nasty discovery, some malevolence that's only just revealed itself: the right home, a religious family, a child with an aptitude, a leaning towards the religious life and, in time, just the school for such special children. The shock of the words is made more dramatic by the casual way in which they are spoken. A child with an aptitude, a leaning … A little priest and nun factory; a calling. That's it, isn't it? Maryanne nods to herself as much as to the priest. It's breathtaking that he can sit there and say all this as if it were the most natural thing in the world. A nice little racket you've got there, Father Geoghan.

And suddenly, the mystery of Father Geoghan is solved. And all the thoughts she's entertained about him – that he must surely at some stage have been a child, must at some point have just been little Kevin playing with his toys, before he became Father Geoghan and acquired the disease of fatal purity – are clarified. There never was any little Kevin. Perhaps nothing remotely like a childhood. You were farmed out, weren't you, Father? That's why you've got no hesitation in farming out others. And you showed a special aptitude, didn't you, Father? You were one of God's chosen. You heard the calling. Isn't that so?

At the same time, she's remembering that moment when Father Geoghan did the unforgivable and lost control, that moment when the mask fell away and something happened. When he stared back at her with the eyes of a man who has said too much. And it's not just the look in his eyes she now remembers, but something else. The pain of remembrance that she didn't notice then, but does now. And she knows now, or is sure she does, that the way she thinks of Father Geoghan – the plausible, persuasive, devious manager of God's business – is only half the story. For somewhere in there, there *must* have been a little Kevin. Of course there was. A little Kev who played games with friends, imaginary and real. An inquisitive little boy, like all little boys. And girls. All of them, full of questions. And little Kevin, little Kev, just another inquisitive child asking all sorts of questions about God. Who is He? And what does He look like? And where is heaven and can we all go there one day? There'd been enough curiosity to arouse the interest of the good religious family he'd been given to, and for them to mention it to the priest. Enough curiosity to be called a special interest, not to mention a special talent for the religious life. Enough to say the lad had been called. Did they tell him that God had called, and that God calls few? And did they ask him if he'd like to live in one of the many rooms in God's house? Did little Kevin drop his playthings, his tin soldiers, storybooks and board games, and jump at the chance? Was that the last time he was ever just a little boy?

It is then, and she will never understand what came over her, that Maryanne leans forward and lightly rests her hand on the priest's knee, as, indeed, Father Geoghan had done to her: an impulse to comfort the comforter. For who will comfort the comforter if she doesn't?

The priest looks down at her hand as if trying to comprehend one of the great imponderables. Human touch has fallen upon him. And not just any touch, but a woman's. And he seems at once stunned into immobility by the sheer cheek of it, the effrontery of the woman, and relaxed by the understanding reassurance of the act; at once soothed by the mother he never knew, and slipping under the spell of a cunning witch. Wanting to give in, to trust her, Maryanne imagines, but resistant and wary. Poor man, poor man, you gained cathedrals of wisdom but lost the years of wonder. But it is only a momentary glimpse into the mystery, into the heart of Father Geoghan, before he gently lifts her hand from his knee and places it back on her lap. He stares at her, no loss of control this time, forgiving her as he might an impulsive child. May even have taken the act as a gesture of consent. As if Maryanne were saying, of course, Father, you are right.

'So, Maryanne,' he says, as though nothing has happened, and speaking her name as if welcoming her back into the congregation, 'you've decided then?'

'I have, Father.' Her tone is almost wistful, tossed between anger and newfound compassion.

'Good, my child. I'm pleased to hear it. It's for the best. For you, for the child, for everyone.'

But as he speaks, that glimpse into the heart of the priest fades, and she remembers she is facing the man who, with an absolutely clear conscience, would take her child from her. And with that realisation the steel re-enters her, and she could kick herself for giving in to such sentimental nonsense. 'Oh, it will be, Father.' And here a distinctly no-nonsense note comes into her speech. 'I'll have the child here. In this house. With my doctor and my sister. And I assure you, Father, I will bring this child up myself to be whatever he or she chooses to be. Not what somebody chooses for the child.'

Father Geoghan is astonished, outraged, silent for a moment, then glares at her as if betrayed. As if she has led him on to believe she had decided upon the right thing and all was concluded. That only the details remained.

'So you have *no* shame?'

'The only shame would be abandoning the child to the likes of you.' Maryanne pauses for breath. 'You come into my home as if it were your own, and casually announce that you propose to steal my child for the child's good, and expect me to agree as if the whole matter were beyond question. And then, then you have the nerve to talk of shame!'

'*You* are beyond prayers, child, but your baby is not!'

'I'm not your child, and the baby will be mine. And will grow to be whatever it wants to be, beyond your grasping reach.' She rises. 'It will go to any school it wants to go to: state or church. Go to church, or not. Believe in God, or not. The child will decide! And you …' here her anger is such that she can barely speak, 'you will never get your hands on my child. Never! Now get out of my house!'

At what point did her voice rise with such rage? Her last words ring about the room as the priest struggles from his chair.

'God will deal with you.'

Maryanne strides into the hallway and opens the front door for him. 'God won't have anything to do with it. Nor will you,' she adds, eyeballing the priest as he steps onto the footpath.

And as he departs into the windy, disagreeable time of year, he stares back at her as if, indeed, looking upon a witch and longing for the days, his stare says, when we drowned the likes of you.

Then he is gone and Katherine emerges from the kitchen where she has been waiting and stands by Maryanne's side, watching the disappearing figure of the priest.

'I don't think we'll be seeing Father Geoghan again,' she observes.

Maryanne catches the hint of approval in her sister's voice, for although she was not in the room, she clearly heard most of what was said. Or enough, at least. And Maryanne recalls just how important that hint of approval in her sister's voice has always been. It's still there, the thrill of having done well in Katherine's eyes. Katherine might be the believer, nodding with the priests on this or that point, humming hymns about the house, whispering her prayers like a child before bed, but Maryanne notes, with a swelling pride, that she's still there when it matters. All the same, she's not convinced they've seen the last of Father Geoghan.

'I wouldn't be too sure of that,' she says, warily eyeing the street, as if he might reappear.

'I would,' Katherine says, with a certainty that Maryanne would dearly love to accept as the last word on the matter.

They linger in the doorway, the wind tossing leaves left over from winter and discarded scraps of paper and pamphlets into the air, the Yes and No of the day, the giant headlines of the hour, GUILTY and MILHAUS and DEATH, carried away on invisible currents down the street and over the footpaths, fences and yards of the suburb and beyond.

Out beyond the rooftops, unobserved in a distant patch of dark sky, a silver jet hovers before landing in another time – inside, Michael pondering the Yes and the No of the day, the trial of a traitor in time of war, a single mother shielding her child with the tenacity of a tigress, in the way a storyteller looks back upon history: a mixture of what we know and what we can't know and so have to invent. The whole thing a mixture of what, if and why not. Figures that are recorded in documents and family photographs, and figures that never existed, like the priest currently disappearing into the night.

14.

Maryanne has arrived in a quiet, green, expensive suburb just outside the city. A lumbering bus departs, continuing on its way behind her. She didn't have to come. She could have torn the note up and nobody would have known. But now she's standing beside the road, staring at the wide, curved driveway of a mansion on a hill.

She's never been here before, for there are suburbs in this city that are as foreign as distant countries and which nobody goes to except the citizens of these foreign places. And she wouldn't be here now, would not have made the journey, if it weren't for the note, which she wished, from the start, had never been given to her. And it's not true to say that she could have torn it up and nobody would have known. *She* would have.

The house and its grounds occupy an entire section of land between two streets. A long red-brick wall runs the length of the frontage, and, she guesses, all around the block itself. It is almost impossible to see inside. The outside world is not meant to. Only a tower is visible above the hedge, a tower, she imagines, from a ghost story: the kind of tower from which the spirits of lost children might cry out to the living.

The best view of the house is from the locked front gate where she is now standing, looking up the driveway to the front door, where a large black car sits waiting. Just to her right she can see the edge of a lake. With ducks, and is that a swan? Yes, a black swan. And heaven knows what else. A diving board and boats, perhaps. Even a boatshed. A private lake, a private country. And as she stares at the estate, at this private duchy, she finds it difficult to comprehend that only one family lives here, for there is room on these grounds for a hundred houses. And that sensation that this may as well be a foreign country as a distant suburb grows on her. There may even be a train station in there; it wouldn't surprise her. And she wonders what language they speak here. For it would be a language dotted with foreign phrases the likes of 'Tell the maid to clean this', 'What's cook doing?' and 'Where's that gardener?' The sort of language nobody uses, unless they live in a place like this. What language do they speak, indeed; what customs do they observe, what games do they play, what god do they worship?

She stands outside the gate, feeling a little like Tess at the gate of the d'Urbervilles: a waif with a likely tale. Except it's not a likely tale she's come to tell. She brings something else, and she's not sure what it is. And a feeling that she'd really rather not be here comes over her. The note she never asked for has brought her here. She lets out a tired sigh as she glances down at it in her hand. In fact, she is holding two things: a hastily written note and a sealed letter with an address, the one to which she has come, neatly printed on the envelope.

She has read only the instruction: 'Please, deliver this by hand to the lady. J Milhaus.' That is all it says.

She has no knowledge of what is in the letter, which Milhaus clearly wrote before arriving at the court, possibly intending to give it to the lawyer he didn't trust, to deliver or post it. But perhaps the sight of her in the courtroom gave him other ideas. Whatever the case, she has ended up with it, and she didn't want it from the moment she got it. And all she knows of the letter is what is on the envelope: a woman's name. It is printed neatly. A married woman's name. And not a mere 'Mrs'. She is titled. She is a 'Lady'. Furthermore, Maryanne knows her. Knows the name. She is a society figure. Married to one of those businessmen who are always standing beside prime ministers and governors in newspapers and magazine photographs. One of those, she suspects, with all sorts of political connections; one of those who live in a world in which somebody or other always owes someone else something. A world in which favours are always being chalked up or called in. The long arms of the law, she muses, smiling to herself, are nothing compared to the long arms of the rich.

And his wife, the lady whose name is on the envelope, is one of those women who are always mentioned in society pages, and although Maryanne rarely reads these things, even she is familiar with the name. A lady, a wife, a mother of three. Their life a sort of fairytale for the city to look up to. And the city does. A fairytale lived out in a castle and a kingdom hidden behind walls from the street.

She hates standing around like some miserable little domestic on an errand. Some witless little go-between. She sees a distant, silent gardener and an inevitable wheelbarrow. The house almost glows in the sun. The edge of the lake sparkles. The swan is still, floating upon the water in black mystery. She doesn't want to, but she finds herself admiring the place. Against her will, for why should she admire it just because it's big and imposing and sits on the hill as if it was always there and will remain there, unchanged, forever. But she finds herself admiring it all the same. It's like gazing upon an etching of antiquity. Still and perfect in itself, something timeless that renders the outside world irrelevant. Except for the note in her hand: a message from the outside world for the still and timeless one behind those walls. An intrusion, bound to be. Why on earth has Milhaus asked her to do this? Why should the story lead here? And does she really want to be the one to hand the letter over and disrupt the perfect stillness? For, whatever it says, she is certain it will be a disruption. And unwanted.

And just how does she hand it over, anyway? This is not a common, everyday house. There is no door in reach to knock on. She cannot open the gate. She can barely see the front door, at the end of the wide, sweeping driveway. It's mid-morning, plenty of the day left. The car could sit at the front door for hours. She could be standing here all afternoon.

The gardener is cutting back the spring growth, the wheelbarrow quickly filling. The car, glinting in the sun, is as imposing as the house. She could call to the gardener and give him the letter. But would he hear her? And should he receive it, anyway? Her instructions are to deliver it by hand. To the lady in question. She is here because Milhaus decided to trust her. And how desperate is that? How mad must your world be to trust someone you don't even know? She tells herself she has no obligation. Nobody would know if she turned and walked away. She's got herself involved in something that she doesn't understand. But she can't walk away, not Maryanne. She invited Milhaus's trust, its burden of responsibility. She chose, after all, to enter his world, to let him know he was not alone, and he has responded by trusting her. And this letter, whatever it may say, is the measure of his trust. But, and she's asking herself this for the first time, does she trust him? For she's feeling used and Milhaus's world is starting to look like a murky one into which she's blundered. One of those worlds in which somebody always owes someone else something. Just rip the thing up and go, the solid sensible voice of Katherine tells her, while another tells her that she *owes* Milhaus this much. *She* approached him. He chose to trust her and that trust must be returned.

Damn the letter! It is while she is weighing this up that her head begins to swim, her legs go all wobbly. Her face is cold and she reaches out to the wall to steady herself. Head down, she waits, counting from ten to one and back again. And, slowly, it passes. Her legs come back, the chill leaves her face and neck. Her breathing steadies. She lets the wall go and stands free of it. The wobbles gone. A cold sweat on her face and neck.

And she is on the point of giving up for the day when she looks down the driveway and notices activity at the front of the house. The car doors are open. A chauffeur is standing by. Children are climbing in, and the lady herself is talking to the chauffeur. Possibly issuing instructions; it looks like that sort of conversation. The chauffeur is nodding. The lady looks imposing. At this moment, to Maryanne, as imposing as the shining black car and the mansion itself.

Soon the car is moving at a stately pace towards the front gate. Towards Maryanne. Like an event approaching her, some sudden turn in her life that could amount to anything. And although she is seized with an impulse to turn and leave, something keeps her there as the car slowly approaches, a silver figure becoming visible above the grille, glinting in the morning sun. The gardener materialises. The car stops in front of her at the gate, its engine thrumming. The gardener opens the gate, eyeing her.

As the car eases forward, Maryanne waves at the chauffeur, letter in hand. The car stops. The chauffeur winds his window down and asks what she wants. A letter, Maryanne says. A letter for the lady. And straightaway the back window winds down, and a kind face, the very type of face that the age calls beautiful, the face of an English rose, is gazing at her with a slight, practised smile. And it seems to Maryanne that there's something royal in that smile: that she is one of those who are used to smiling at strangers at public events. And this woman at her gate, the lady no doubt imagines, is holding a letter of admiration or gratitude for a contribution to some charity or other.

She reaches out for the letter Maryanne is holding, a graceful hand, beautifully formed like her face, eyes bright like the morning, and Maryanne passes it to her.

'A letter from Mr Milhaus.'

From the moment Maryanne says this the woman's face darkens; the light in her eyes shuts down. The air of kind consideration deserts her and she looks frightened, as if the letter she now holds signifies some dreaded event, a sentence that has been hanging over her, a verdict long feared. And she stares at Maryanne as if to say, who are you?

A child asks, 'What's that, Mummy?' The window is wound up, shutting out the world. Nothing further is said. The car moves on, out of the driveway and onto the road leading into the city. Maryanne watches it leave, lifting her hand as if to wave or somehow take back the thing she has just given. But she knows full well she was never *not* going to pass the note on. For she knows that if she were now watching the lady's car disappear with the note still in her hand, she would not forgive herself. In the end we can only ever do *one* thing, and as much as we might weigh up other possibilities, it always comes down to one thing. And we can only hope it's the right thing.

The car disappears. The estate is all but deserted, apart from the gardener in the grounds and Maryanne at the gate. Her job done, the go-between walks across the road to the bus stop, with no idea still of what the letter may contain, but with the deeply troubled feeling that she has set something in motion. The baby wriggles inside her, and she feels exhausted. Wrung out. The lumbering bus that brought her here approaches in the distance. It stops, she mounts the steps. Legs heavy. Barely enough energy to find a seat. The bus pulls away from the red-brick wall, the hedge, the tower suspended above it all, and as she looks back, the whole estate – the house, the lake, the gardens like the forest of a foreign country – takes on the appearance of a dark forbidding wood, as dark and shady as the world of Milhaus, the lord, the lady and the whole fairytale life they lead is now beginning to look.

15.

It all happened very quickly. One moment she was standing in the kitchen, tired from the journey, the next she was curled up on the floor. When the table tilted, or seemed to, and the floor rose to meet her, she reached out to steady herself by grasping the table, but her hands found only the tablecloth: the tea-pot, cups and a small vase of flowers clattering to the floor as she fell. She heard the thud more than felt it, heard the crack of the back of her head hitting the floor, as if it were somebody else's head. And it was only later, sitting up in bed, that she felt the pain.

She's not sure how long she lay there, but she was still on the floor when Katherine returned from shopping. She remembers the shopping bag falling to the floor, onions and apples spilling onto the bare boards, arranging themselves like a still life. Odd how the mind works at these times, for as Katherine smoothed her forehead and spoke gently to her, she was noting how pleasingly the onions and apples had arranged themselves. What a silly business, falling about like that, but no great matter.

Katherine continued to soothe her with gentle words. She'd had a fall. Ups-a-daisy. Come on, up you get. Let's get you to bed. Somehow she rose, legs all wobbly, and stepped over the tea-pot and cups and shopping. Her arm around Katherine's waist and Katherine's around hers, they made their way up the hallway to her bedroom.

That was two days ago. The doctor came, the doctor went. All is well. She's had a fall. Bit of a knock on the head. No damage. She's been doing too much. She must rest and sleep. And sleep she has, the time between falling and sitting up now in bed feeling like no time at all. The back of her head is sore, her hip is sore. When she moves, the pain in her hip rises. A dull thud in her head returns from time to time. She sits up, drained as if recovering from an illness, but also calm. Almost at peace, like those delicious childhood days off school when sick. All is well, she tells herself. She is lucky. The pain will go. The lingering sick feeling will go. But all the same, as she looks through the lace curtain of the window onto the dull sideway of the house, she's asking herself, again and again, just what did she think she was doing? Running errands for strangers. And at the same time, she's wondering if she went a little mad for a while. For the whole city is mad, and why shouldn't its madness rub off on her?

* * *

Katherine comes, Katherine goes, bringing trays of breakfast, lunch and dinner: toast, soups, biscuits and occasionally cake. And, all the time, the newspapers, with their stories of protests and brawls, of rallies and arrests. All out there, in the far-away world of the beast. Maryanne now removed from it all. And she begins to like it. Bed: reading, dozing, eating, sleeping. This being waited on.

She doesn't go to the world any more. No loss. It's not hers, anyway. Never really was. But word of it comes to her as regularly as breakfast, lunch and dinner and the daily newspapers. And so it goes, for a week. A week lived in a half-world of wakefulness and sleep: night-time succeeding afternoon; afternoon, night. One day after another, until the pain is gone and she is strong again. Strong enough for two people, as she must be. And she's beginning to feel like two people, and is certain that the baby, safe inside the universe of her belly, is watching everything, registering everything, like – and here she smiles to herself at the image – a faithful, anxious dog watching over its keeper. We're in this together, this baby seems to say, you and me; now don't you forget that. And one day, when I finally leave the liquid heavens of your belly, I will remind you of this. But for now just remember that we're in this together, so hold on to me tight. And don't do anything foolish again.

Wise, Maryanne tells herself, this baby is wise. And she can almost feel its eyes on her, its wisdom radiating out from her belly in soothing waves.

This is all the world she needs. Not the baying, bellowing thing out there. She's finished with that. And it is while she is lying in bed, watching the morning sun touch the top of the lace curtains, more content and calm and utterly self-contained than she has ever been, that Katherine brings her breakfast. And the morning newspaper. And as she opens it, as if gazing upon the news of some far-away country, she sees it: MILHAUS FREE.

It is printed in the same bold large letters that the word GUILTY was. Somebody, it seems, has come forward. A witness. And it is only as she looks more closely at the paper and the story that she takes in some of the words: 'scandal', 'society lady', 'secret affair'. And from the moment she reads this the whole world of Milhaus comes back to her: the jail, the gallows, the endlessly tapping foot, the nervous laughter at her mention of the word 'innocent', the courtroom, the note, the house and the tower like something from a ghost story. The child crying out, 'What's that, Mummy?'

The lady, it seems, has come forward. *She* was with Milhaus through the day and the night and the morning when he was supposed to have written the note, and passed on the information. They had gone, the newspaper tells Maryanne, dwelling on every detail as if it were some sort of crime report, to a holiday town in the country. Slipped away, where nobody, it seems, gave them a second look. They were just another couple on a holiday. No society clothes, no society airs. Ordinary, really. Quiet, happy in their own company, minding their own business. Just anybody. Miles away. This is what she has told the police. This is her testimony, and who would doubt the testimony of a lady? Even a fallen one. Milhaus is free.

And Maryanne, scarcely believing the news and on the point of bursting into joyous laughter, imagines him walking from the jail. Morning sun bright on the buildings, trees, lawns and on Milhaus himself. All brighter and warmer and greener for having just walked out of hell's dungeons. Your *life*! Perhaps her words really did matter that day she visited. And was this that enormous decision he'd seemed to be circling? Freedom? Life, but at such a cost. And in the end, his life depended on the letter he'd written being delivered by hand to the lady: the very note Maryanne had carried like some miserable little go-between. She was the lifeline.

Perhaps, at first, he'd thought to be noble. To protect the lady. Decided that he couldn't ask his one and only witness to ruin herself for him. The man who had made her an adulterer. But perhaps Maryanne's words had hit home, and something inside him said he wanted his life. That, yes, he wanted to live. Perhaps all he needed was someone from outside to remind him of that. And perhaps he decided that he and the lady – and Maryanne has just learned from the newspaper that her name is Constance – might have a life, somehow. That they might come through. And have a real life, as apart from propping up a fairytale.

Then again, perhaps it was a goodbye letter. A final communication. Delivered as discreetly as possible. One that moved the lady to act. Unasked, unbidden. For Maryanne could so easily imagine Milhaus telling her she must stay silent. Must not ruin her life. And must think of her children.

But maybe a simple goodbye note changed all that and caused her to break her silence.

Whatever the case, Milhaus is free. He has denied the beast its pleasure. Walked away. Maryanne imagines him blending into the crowds as he leaves the jail behind him, disappearing into streets, lanes and arcades, into the depths of the city. No one giving him a second glance. Just anybody. Not a fallen god, not the face of the devil, not the one whose leaps lifted everybody into the heavens for a moment, but who in the end seemed to betray them all – but just anybody. Left, for the first time in months, to himself. To live: just *live*. She could sing. And the beast, feeling too short-changed to even give him a second glance or thought, looks about elsewhere. And it's not hard to guess where.

* * *

Over the following weeks, the newspapers and magazines talk of the lady in the same way they once spoke of Milhaus. She was the fairytale everybody believed in, the princess they needed to lighten dark times, a touch of home-grown royalty that made the wrong side of the world right; now she has thrown it all away on a mad whim and betrayed them. And betrayed herself, the whole grubby affair beneath her. A footballer? Why not the chauffeur? Or the gardener? Worse, she has betrayed her family, her children. She is a heartless mother. Immoral. The dark angel behind the fairytale, unmasked.

Madame X, the papers call her, after a painting as scandalous and infamous as the lady herself now is. A cartoon copy of the painting is printed in one of the papers: Lady Constance in a black evening dress, anything but constant, a strap fallen from her shoulder. On the streets they call her a whore. The princess whore. Milhaus's whore. The Hun's whore.

Maryanne is staring at a newspaper one morning in the kitchen, the cartoon, the image of Madame X, a continuing accompaniment to the many stories the paper runs. No wonder her face fell the moment Maryanne handed her the note. For from that moment, Lady Constance Vine knew what she had to do. Knew she had no choice. All the same, Maryanne wonders, staring out through the kitchen window onto the sideway, what must it have taken to come forward, knowing her whole life would be destroyed the moment she did? Knowing that she would be ruined. Of course, nobody could live with a death on their conscience, knowing they could have saved someone. All the same, what it must have taken. And what sort of a world of favours, favours owed and called in, did she have to contend with? Her husband a man who dines with prime ministers and the wealthy and heaven knows who else.

Maryanne sighs deeply and puts the newspaper down on the table. Milhaus is saved. At a dreadful cost, but saved. He will live. They will come through, after all. She could cry with joy. Or is it relief? Someone, at least, has evaded the clutches of the beast.

While she is thinking this, she is also dwelling on the photographs in the newspaper. The lady and her husband in better times: at the front of that house, children at their feet. The fairytale everybody craved. A touch of royalty on the wrong side of the world. And at some point her eyes fix on the face of Lord Vine, the happy prince of the happy kingdom. But he doesn't look happy. He is not smiling. And his eyes, far from content, squint at the camera with impatience. No, more than that: it is the anger of someone putting up with something he knows is beneath him. With a touch of contempt. No happy prince. And at first she simply thinks he was having a grumpy morning. It's a grumpy photograph. But she's also asking herself, just how much did he know? What sort of information, in the world of favours and debts that he moves in, came back to him? And having been informed that all was not well in the fairytale kingdom, what favours were called in? Were Jack and Connie found out, as all adulterers are? And when Lord Vine discovered the affair, did the smiles stop altogether? What wheels were set in motion, all rolling inevitably towards the figure of Milhaus? Then again, perhaps it really was just a grumpy morning. And perhaps we can read too much into a look. It's just a look, after all.

* * *

One evening, when she is better and feels strong and able, still living inside the self-contained world of mother and child, impervious to the madness around her, she walks down to the Exhibition Building, its dome glowing like those domes in exotic foreign places to which she has never been and will never go – those foreign places, one of which Michael, the son of the son she carries, has just landed in – and sits on a bench by the lake.

The lake is a red, orange and yellow blaze of evening colour: smooth and glassy one minute, tossed and stormy the next. For some local boys are throwing stones into the water, bits of tree branch, anything they can lay their hands on – shattering its glassy calm. And every time a stone lands, the flames leap, and cheers go up into the evening air. Then the water settles, the flames fall, the surface closes over and calm prevails once more. Until the next stone, and the next, on and on, until they tire of the game, drop their stones, cease their cheers and prepare to move on. As one, like a herd of animals or a school of fish suddenly taking off. A gang, finding their fun where they will. Then moving on.

But before they do, one of the boys suddenly turns in her direction, and stares at her, a stick in his hand. And at this distance, it is difficult to gauge his look. But there is something nasty in the child, and she could swear for a moment that, as he looks down at the stick and back towards her, that he is contemplating throwing it at her. Does he know of her? Has he heard of the Hun's whore? Has everybody? Even the children? Did a parent, an uncle or an aunt point her out in the street one day and say: 'There goes the Hun's whore.' Perhaps. But he's no sooner turned and given her the eye than he hears another boy calling out to him, and he swings round, banging his stick into the grass, and rejoins the gang.

She's seen them before, this gang, and she watches them leave the gardens with a heavy sadness that she can't properly explain. Did he really mean to throw the stick? Or is she making something of nothing? Children, she knows, from half a lifetime of teaching them, are instinctive creatures, often doing things that even they can't explain. He could have turned towards her for any number of reasons. All the same, he had the look of a bully, and there was something nasty about the child.

And it is while she is watching them depart, leaving the shady arches of the giant Moreton Bay figs and the leaping flames on the lake behind them, that she becomes aware of a large black swan paddling towards her.

Thoughts of the boy fade, and she finds herself staring intently at the approaching swan. She knows it's silly to think that animals and birds are similar to people. They're not, of course. They are simply what they are. And they don't care what we think. They take us for what we are, as they would a tree or a rock or one of the garden's foxes that she occasionally sees slinking low in the shadows. Just something in the world. Gauging if it's a threat or not. So she knows it's silly, but she can't help thinking of this swan, drawing near, as a dignified woman of what people call a 'certain age'. Proud, but not arrogant. Contained, but not exactly aloof. For this swan has picked her out and is gliding through the water towards her. And quickly too. With such grace and power. And no sign of effort. Maryanne smiles. For she could swear the bird is about to greet her. And she is quite prepared to respond. To chat with this lady of a certain age, whose plumage shines in the late sun, and whose feathers fall across her well-lived body like a black silk evening dress over the bosom and hips of a lady on her way to a show.

But, of course, it's silly. For when the swan stops by the edge of the lake, no more than a few feet away, its eyes fix on her like no human eye. And Maryanne feels on the point of apologising. I do you a wrong, Madame Swan. You are no mere human. You do not bay for blood and death, wail and brawl in the streets while bowing before those who have conjured up the darkness in you, flinging yourself upon newspaper columns of lies and death and tragedy, and all the time craving that something final you so fear. No, Madame Swan, you are better than that. No sense of tragedy, no wallowing in self-pity, no tears for yourself in those eyes, in that direct stare. You are beyond all that. Above it. Single and pure. And yet we turn you into us. Let us call a halt to that right now. Instead, *I* shall be *you*.

The swan eyes her a moment longer, lowers its beak and nibbles at the water's edge, then looks up and, as majestically as it arrived, glides across the water to a further shore. And Maryanne can't help but think of it as a kind of visitation. But not from the soul of someone who's died, for the dead have no souls. And they do not come back to us as birds or trees or mysterious green-eyed black cats. No, if it's a visitation, it is from nature itself. Nature: people, birds and creatures, small and large, going about their business. Just like the swelling in her belly that will one day soon emerge from her. And as much as giving birth frightens her, she tells herself that it is simply nature doing what nature does: nothing to fear, for nature has prepared her well.

The swan glides further away, single and complete. Moss consumed, feet working under water, black feathers shining gold and vermilion in the last of the day's sun. And as it departs, other swans appear beside it, squawking and screeching and bullying – an uproar of complaint and outrage. But *her* swan ignores them. Head erect, she glides on through foreign waters. To a further shore. Without complaint or self-pity. Just nature doing what nature does.

And she draws strength from that, from that creature gliding across the water to a further shore. If all manner of living things can do this, then so can I. I shall be you, Maryanne smiles to herself as she rises from the bench, and go about my business without complaint or fanfare. So just get on with it, old girl. And with that thought the child kicks, a real footballer's kick, and she breaks into laughter as she rubs her belly. She *knows* this child. They as good as speak. I will soon be too big for my world, it says. I will soon be ready. And this is what the kick says: just get on with it, old girl.

As she walks back through the streets to her house where Katherine is waiting, as she walks back observing the stares of neighbours, she is a black swan of a certain age, everything around her – houses, horses and people – to be met with equal curiosity. And as much as she might occasionally greet someone, offer a good evening or a cheerio, as if she were one of them, people are not taken in. The beast never is. Unerringly, it sniffs out those that are not part of it. So the neighbours look her up and down and silently pronounce her snooty. And what's she got to be snooty about? She's got a belly swollen with some bastard brat, and yet she walks about like Lady Muck, handing out good evenings and cheerios.

But it doesn't touch her. Maryanne glides across the footpath, black plumage shining in the late sun, enters her house and shuts the world out. When she sits in the kitchen, she tells Katherine about the swan, how it picked her out, stared at her and stayed with her. And Katherine snorts.

'It just wanted to be fed.'

This is the worldly Katherine, the no-nonsense Katherine, who knows nature in all its extremes. She shakes her head at her younger sister: too much imagination, she says without need of speech, always too much.

But Maryanne just stares at her, saying nothing. And the look goes on and on until it unnerves Katherine.

'Well, what are you staring at?'

Maryanne grins. 'Nothing. I just want to be fed.'

Once again, Katherine slowly shakes her head, silently pronouncing her sister 'smart', while she ladles a thick soup into a bowl and passes it to Maryanne, who takes it with a thank you, a thank you that both of them know is for more than just the soup.

Later, in her room, sitting up in bed and reading, vaguely taking in the sounds of the street (children squawking, mothers calling, the occasional racket of revellers spilling out of the corner pub in drunken chorus), she feels at a comforting distance from it all, gliding on through the foreign waters of this place and time she has fallen into. Determined to be contained and single, unruffled and calm, one of those who are passing through, back up through the circles of this place to the light of a further world beyond, where the screeching and squawking will become a distant clamour.

Part Three

A Separate Peace

December 20th, 1917 – March, 1918

16.

Outside, the beast is quiet. It's been quiet all day: voting day. The day the Yes does battle with the No to see which shall be victorious. She can picture it, voting booths all over the city, the grim faces of Yes and No standing at the front of town halls and schools and churches: life contending with death. They have been voting all day. A warm day. A bright one, now mellowing and slipping into evening.

Maryanne has been lying on the bed all day, legs parted. For hours she has been heaving and pushing, struggling to bring the baby from its own private heaven into the world. But it won't come. She is exhausted, resting before trying again. This is when she looks to the window and notes the changing colour of the day, hears the faint sound of children on the loose, a world carrying on as if nothing were happening. While, inside, this endless business goes on and on, and she's convinced she'll never be able to do it. It's beyond her. Nature is *not* doing what nature does. The child will not come. It will defeat her, this thing. *I can't* ... Did she say it or think it? Neither Katherine nor the doctor looks up. If she did speak, it's clearly a matter of no importance to either of them. For nature *is* doing what nature does. And whether she thinks she can or she can't is neither here nor there to the doctor and Katherine. She has no choice.

The doctor places a mask over her face and she breathes the gas in. Katherine watches. Maryanne doesn't know how long he leaves the mask there; she's lost track of time. The room goes hazy. Katherine's voice, asking her how that feels, is distant, like someone calling to her from a dream.

There is nothing, she tells herself, that she won't do to bring this baby into the world. But it's stubborn. Refusing to give up its own private heaven, staving off the moment of being born. And who can blame it? Who would want to be born into this world? And in her drugged state, she's wondering if it really could work like that: the baby, its mind already at work, independent of them all, staving off the moment of being born, fearing birth in the same way that it will one day fear death. And for a moment the two seem inseparable to Maryanne: birth and death, death and birth. Yes and No, No and Yes.

The pain leaves her; she is almost light-hearted. Almost feels she could rise from the bed and stroll about, leaving the job of bringing the child into the world to this other Maryanne back on the bed. And then the doctor tells her to push. And so does Katherine. It is like being dragged back into battle. Together they are telling her to push and heave and get the thing out of her. And that's all she wants. But it's huge, it's massive. It resists. She pushes, and the pain comes straight back. There are groans and now screaming, at once distant like Katherine's voice and loud in her ears, exploding from her like cannon shots. She never knew she had such screams in her. But she has never felt anything like this. Ever. And all the while the world goes on just outside the window, as if nothing were happening. She stops, she weeps. Tears rolling down her cheeks. It's impossible. How does anybody do this? *I can't …* She is crying. *I can't, I …* And the pain, this pain like nothing she has ever felt, explodes inside her again. And with every push, for they're telling her to push and push again, she feels she could pass out altogether. But she pushes all the same, until a pain shoots through her entire body and she imagines for a moment that she's been struck by lightning. No, lightning can't be worse than this. Give me lightning, anything but this.

Maryanne looks at the rubber mask, then at the doctor. 'More!' she pleads. 'More!'

The doctor weighs the matter.

'Damn you! Damn, damn, *more …*'

Sighing, sweat dripping from his forehead, he reluctantly reaches for the mask and once again places it over her mouth. And once again the room goes hazy. Katherine's voice is distant, the pain retreats. The mask is taken from her face; she starts to push again. She pushes and heaves, gripping the bed sheets, tears pouring down her cheeks, screams, distant and near, filling the room. This time she can just bear the pain. And so she pushes and pushes again. And just when she tells herself, again, that there isn't anything she wouldn't do to get this child into the world, she feels sure there's nothing more she *can* do. They're stuck, and they'll stay this way. Stuck. Just when she's thinking all of this, she hears Katherine's voice. Calling to her, calling out that she can see the head. She can see it! The baby is coming. Push, push! Like you've never pushed before. Now. This is it! Push!

Katherine's voice, the doctor's, both combine, calling out to her, a chorus of crying and yelling. Katherine is telling her that the head is coming, the shoulders, the baby is coming. It's ready. Here it comes. Push, push. And suddenly, as if a giant boulder has just rolled from her, fallen from her, she feels the weight leave her, the burden pass from her, and feels someone's hands, the doctor's or Katherine's, she can't tell, pulling the child from her into life, and straightaway hears its birth cries, either in protest or relief. Joy or despair. Or all at once. And who could blame it?

She opens her eyes. And there it is. A miracle. Covered in blood, eyes blinded by the light, the child wails in Katherine's hands as she holds it up for Maryanne to see.

'A boy!' Katherine cries, joy splashed across her face as if she has just given birth herself. 'It's a little boy. A dark-haired, beautiful little boy!'

And right away Maryanne is crying again: from relief, exhaustion, joy, sadness, she just doesn't know. Just let the tears come, a wise voice inside her says. Don't ask why. And just as the pain was like nothing she has ever felt, these tears are like no tears she's ever shed. So, this is it. This is how we all come wailing into the world. This is nature: bloody and brutal and unbowed. Pushing on through the pain. On and on. Doing what it does. And as Maryanne sinks into the bed it is with more than relief; it is with an almost vacant feeling that her job is done. And nature, nature doesn't even turn to acknowledge her as it leaves the room. She has merely done what any animal does without thinking: pushed through the pain, then got on with things. The tears stream down her face and she doesn't bother to wipe them aside. You did it, old girl. You did it.

Katherine washes the baby, chanting and crooning as she does so. 'Beautiful little boy. Look at that hair! Beautiful, beautiful ... Now go to Mama, little boy. Go to your mama.'

When Maryanne takes the baby she knows the moment is real, but there is still a part of her drugged self that imagines it might yet be a dream. The weight she carried round all year, the swelling she took everywhere, the dome she led with when she walked the streets, now lies in her arms and she knows her job is not over; it is only just beginning. The child opens his eyes briefly, closes them, then falls into a deep sleep, exhausted by the sheer effort of getting himself born. She holds him a little longer – his nose, ears, fingers, all perfectly formed – gazing upon him in disbelief, the well of tears inside her drying up. And as much as she might tell herself that this is just nature getting on with things, she is also cradling something that is almost impossible to comprehend. Where *did* you come from, little one?

Her eyes droop. A wave of exhaustion sweeps through her. The doctor takes the baby from Maryanne and passes him to Katherine, who places him in a crib beside the bed. The baby is sleeping. The bed is drenched, the child's private, liquid heaven now a bloody mess all around her: soaked into the sheets, and dumped in a bucket. She's vaguely aware of Katherine changing the bed, moving her about, washing her, changing her, but it's all still drugged and distant as though she were watching everything, not experiencing it. The lamps are dim, the room hazy. She leans her head back on a fresh pillow, lies on clean, crisp sheets and feels herself enveloped in comfort. She could sleep for days. The baby is beside her, within arm's reach. Mother and child, all the world she needs.

She drifts in and out of sleep, her eyes closed. Screams and protests float in from the street, both distant and near. The beast has been quiet all day; now the beast is roused. For whatever reason, it is baying. The sound of fighting enters the quiet calm of the sleepy room. Of course, the pubs are closing. The beast is spilling onto the streets in drunken chorus. It craves something, and it doesn't know what but it craves it all the same. She is vaguely aware of the voices of Katherine and the doctor in the hall. She is alone with the child. The room shadowy, the corners dark. Mother and child float in some starless space, open to the world. The street sounds, near and far, gather. Somewhere there is the sound of breaking glass. The lamps are dim, the room dark. Dark and open to whatever is out there.

And suddenly she's convinced that something *is* out there. Lurking. Hiding in the darkness. Watching, waiting.

Something is lurking there in a dark corner of the room. The beast ... the beast is coming. Muffled talk from the hallway floats over her like talk in dreams. The baby sleeps beside her. The room floats in darkness. There in the room's dark corners, the beast is lurking. Crouched in darkness. Invisible. But there, she knows it is.

And then she sees it. Watches it step from the shadows. Slouching forward from the darkness towards her, scales glowing in the dim lamplight. Head raised. Eyes shining. Mesmerising. The beast itself. She watches, spellbound, as it rears and stands on two scaly, thick feet. It craves something ... but it knows not what. It moves towards her and the baby, silent, light on its feet, a towering thing that somehow fits into the room. And straightaway she knows that it's not her that it wants, but the child. And she tries to raise herself in the bed, to do battle with the thing like the heroes and heroines of old, but can't. She can't lift herself, she can't move. And as much as she wants to scream, no sound comes from her. It nears: a giant, a towering thing. Eyes red and shining and flashing. She can neither raise herself nor call out. She is stricken. And the beast is now beside her. No, no, no ... Mute cries fall silently in the room. No, you don't; I won't let you ...

The beast looks down at the sleeping child, less than an hour old, sleeping the deep sleep of the newly born. The beast beholds it, eyes shining, then stares directly at Maryanne. I have come, it says. You made me, you created me, you conjured me up from darkness, from the pages of your storybooks and histories and drawings. You called, and I have come. How could I not?

And with this, the beast leans over the crib and gently lifts the child and holds him in its scaly arms, looking down in wonder upon him. The child shines. He is calm, at peace. Serene. Sleeping the deep sleep of the newly born. The beast is gentle. Careful. It cradles the baby, the shining one, then looks at Maryanne. You made me. You called, you conjured me up, a beastly thing, and I have come. But see, do you see that there is yet some good in the beast? Some beauty buried deep inside, some goodness just waiting to be released. And you have called it forth. Do you see, it says, there is yet some good in your beast?

It places the child back in the crib, gazes upon him one last time, as if gazing upon the blessed, heavenly state denied all beasts: a heavenly state half-remembered, as though it too once knew such grace, then turns away and lumbers towards the dark corner of the room from which it emerged, where it dissolves into inky blackness. The baby sleeps. The room regains its quiet calm.

Maryanne's eyes open. She is aware of movement in the room. Katherine is beside her. She is checking the baby, making him secure. And as she does, Maryanne raises her head to watch her with the eyes of a sleepwalker. Back to sleep, Katherine says. Back to sleep. Maryanne lets her head fall back into the pillow: soft and crisp and clean. Her eyes close, sleep overwhelms her. Drugged, glorious sleep. She gives in. Sleep, Katherine is whispering, smoothing her brow. Sleep, sleep ...

The deepest, the heaviest sleep of her life, so heavy she feels the whole weight of her body sinking into the bed, is broken by an unfamiliar sound. Cutting and shrill. Her eyes open to darkness before her mind is properly awake. There is an animal in the room, its cry sharp and urgent.

It seems, at first, to come out of a darkness thousands of miles away. Distant and out of reach. Beyond her. And yet she must close that distance. It is a cry, distant and alone, that is also a call. Is there anything out there? She turns her bedside lamp up, and tiny fingers, tiny hands, rise from the cot beside her, testing the darkness, and straightaway Maryanne's hand reaches out, closing the distance, grasping those little fingers, and the baby's hand seizes hers with an iron grip. Such strength. Such will. You, the cry, the grip of the hand, says. *You!*

She lifts the baby from the cot and cradles him, releasing her breast as she does. And the baby seizes upon her breast with the same fierceness with which he seized her hand. He knows exactly what to do. His will to live won't be denied. Nature will do what nature does. The baby's lips fasten onto her nipple, his hands grasp the breast. Mine, he says. Mine, as he draws the milk from her. And in that instant the baby's lonely cries that called from thousands of miles away are silenced. And straightaway she knows that she can bear being alone. Not lonely, but alone. She is accustomed to it, even prefers it.

She can bear her own solitariness, but not her child's. Just as she can bear her own pain, but not her child's.

At first feverishly, then slowly and steadily, the baby draws the milk from her. She feels the life draining from her into the child. Gladly. And oh, the bliss of simply lying there in the semi-darkness of the room, silence outside, feeling the baby's lips fastened to her nipple, and the baby's hands clasping her breast in such a way that says: this is mine, not to be negotiated nor gainsaid. Mine. And she gives it gladly, all she has. All she can. Unstintingly. And in that moment all distance is vanquished. Mother and child are one. The lonely cry is silenced. And the child knows that there is something, someone, out there in the darkness after all, to seize upon and grasp and feed from, and knows that he is not alone.

Slowly, like a tender lover's, the child's lips fall from her nipple. His hands fall from her breast. Sated. At last. Once again ready for sleep. But before he does, his eyes open, seemingly staring at her, then looking around the dim room. Seeing what? Blurred shapes, half-light? Hints of things and objects he will one day put a name to: Mama, breast, lamp? Dark, light? Day, night? Who knows? Only the child, and the child will forget. Then his eyes close, satisfied, and he drifts off.

An exhausted, sweet calm sweeps over Maryanne. A calm, a blessedness, the likes of which she has never known. This world they have created is all the world she needs. And she feels a kind of beauty. Not in her face or her figure or the grace of her gestures. But simply in how she now *is*. And so too there is beauty around her: in the child, the rose beside her in a vase, the early-morning chorus of birds in the street. All transformed by a child's birth. And this calm, this world that is enough in itself, where mother and child are one, is a sudden outbreak of peace. And a separate one: in which the beast cradles the child, the streets are quiet, the ghouls are gone. All is changed. And she knows she will not give *this* world up, this world that they have created together, for anyone or anything.

And so she sits up in bed, the child cradled in her arms, deep in sleep, the honeyed glow of the lamp lighting the room, exhausted but at rest.

* * *

Victor is born. That is one way of putting it. Of imagining it. For who she was, this Maryanne, and what she thought and how the child (who will not stay Victor for long, for the schoolyard will call him Vic) appeared to her are the things that were never recorded. What she thought and felt in her heart can only be imagined.

And as Michael walks from the airport to the train that will take him into the city of Paris, he can't help but think that the whole of his father's life was already curled up inside the baby Vic, just waiting to unfurl with the years, for he knows those moody, brooding eyes (which he has inherited), just as his grandmother may well have read in them the kind of child she cradled: all there in the eyes of the one-day-old baby. Vic's life. All our lives. Tales already written.

And at the heart of Vic's tale is a young woman who has not yet been born or entered the story. But soon will. Complete, ready to step into the tale when her time comes, she waits in a dance-hall dress, all light and laughter. Her name is Rita. Michael's mother. Waiting to be met at the end of a troubled decade in a dance-hall dress. Vic and Rita, Rita and Vic. The egg is hatched. A story begins. And will all that follows that first meeting, in a noisy, crowded dance hall just a few miles from where Maryanne lies cradling the child, come to life as though already written? An unhappy marriage, an unhappy family? A moody son, with his father's moody eyes. Each of the players stepping into the roles that were just waiting to be stepped into, and rarely, if ever, stepping out of them. And if Michael's mother, waiting at the end of a line of calendared years, had known any of this, known what was in front of her (the miserable, drunken nights; a miserable, drunken Vic, forever the fatherless child, conceived in the back room of a country school house), would she have turned and walked straight out of the dance hall, the light and laughter still in her eyes? But still there for someone else, not Vic: another Rita, another story? Would she have turned her back on that age-old battle of light and darkness and walked out there and then? Or would she have been drawn to Vic's brooding darkness all the same, and he to the light? And would they later tell themselves that among the struggle and the hurt and the damage they did to each other (and which they couldn't help but pass on to their moody-eyed son) as they stood in the inevitable rubble of an unhappy marriage, would they tell themselves that there was an intensity, a pitch of joy there too that they would never have known otherwise? While, at the same time, asking themselves if that is really enough to be left with after all they'd gone through?

Michael, with thoughts of the grandmother he never really knew and of his day-old father and the image of his young mother weaving in and out of each other, suddenly remembers a line of poetry by one of the new poets, about how parents pass on their failings and miseries to their children, even though they don't intend to. But isn't it the case? For all the best intentions, isn't it just the case? Like all these thoughts it simply pops into his head, drops in like a surprise visitor at the front door. He stands, half smiling, half mulling over the lines, in front of the train-system map and keys in his destination. It is a small everyday magic show he has read about and that he has been looking forward to, for with his touch, every stop along the way to his destination lights up and glows, indicating the route his train will follow. The journey he is about to take, already charted. His suitcase is beside him as he waits on the platform: notes, drafts of this and that family tale, an old typewriter – the world of the dusty suburb on the very edge of the city that they all eventually landed in, travelling with him. He takes his finger off the trainline map, the spot worn with years of repeated pressing, and the lights charting his journey go off. No longer visible, but already charted. We'll see. He turns from the map and enters the crowd, seeking out his platform.

* * *

With the tenderness of the beast itself, Maryanne lowers the baby into the cot beside the bed. Tucks him in, secures him. And straightaway the child, sensing security all around, falls into the deep sleep of innocence. A whole life in front of him. And if she were to say anything to Michael, currently making his way through a crowded train station, she might well say no. There are no lives already charted with the symbolic neatness of a trainline directory. No fates to be met. Not really. That's too much like Hardy, like Tess. Too *final*. Too neat. No, no fates to be met, only made. And just the beautiful or the unbeautiful unknown stretching before the child, the adventure of life in front of him.

Maryanne resumes the place she has occupied these last few weeks, happily confined after all, sitting up in bed, writing paper and pen in hand and begins: *Dear Victor …*

It is a short letter. The baby is born, the baby is healthy, the baby sleeps. She'd like to write about gardens and birds and flight – and back rooms and brooding eyes. Light and darkness. Dark and lightness. But although these are the thoughts that preoccupy her, she realises that she really doesn't know Victor well enough to indulge such an impulse. And this is why such things are never recorded. For that kind of confession, she decides, you need to know the person you are writing to, and she concludes that she doesn't know Victor. Not that well. Their meetings were brief. And apart from the one occasion when Victor forgot himself and pronounced her beautiful, they spoke little of the things outside the room. Whenever she asked about his life, he went silent. These things, his silence said, we do not talk about.

She pauses. The fact is, she knows so little about him. The games he played as a child, and whom he played with; the family stories he heard; the village his parents came from; the house he grew up in; those remembered moments of broken sleep in the night when the child imagined something fearful out there in the big, frightening world; the books he read, if he read much at all; the God he prayed to, if he prayed at all. Just *who* is Victor? *Who* is one half of the child? And how will that half emerge?

But if Victor is a mystery to Maryanne, that mystery is a small one, she imagines, compared to the mystery that he will become to Vic. And small compared to all that flows from that mystery: the loss, the anger and the damage. For at some point when the baby is old enough, he will surely ask himself – prompted by something someone says in a school playground, some teasing question – *who* in fact his father is. And, indeed, where he is. And what does he do? But his father will remain a mystery. The kind of mystery that grows with the years until his father becomes little more than a story and a figure in a photograph: a soldier standing awkwardly in a studio setting. Not so much an absent father as a ghost.

So much to say, but, in the end, so little that is said. Maryanne begins writing again. A short letter. The facts: the baby is born, the baby is healthy. Why bother with all the rest? The pain that was like nothing she has ever known before; the liquid of the child's private heaven that soaked into the bed and stained the sheets. And the screams. The screams, yes. Father Geoghan would have liked them. We are all fallen, she can hear him saying, but *you*, fallen woman, daughter of Eve, are truly fallen and your screaming, your pain, is your penance.

So just as there is no point in talk of gardens, birds and flight, or of back rooms and brooding eyes, there is also no point in talking of pain, tears and satisfied priests. It is a short letter. The child is born and sleeping. Oh, and the child's name is Victor, which the schoolyard will shorten to Vic. She adds that when everybody is rested and able, she and young Victor will visit a photographer's studio and photographs will be taken. He can be there too, if he wishes. For the child. And, if he does so wish, they must arrange a day and time.

She decides there is nothing left to add. Eight lines that could have been eighty or eight hundred. She signs off with a simple 'Maryanne'. No 'love'. That would be false. So much to say, so little that is said and recorded in the end.

She places the letter in an envelope, seals it and calls for Katherine. The door opens slowly, the room an oasis of calm and quiet, and Katherine steps softly across the floor. When

Maryanne hands the letter to her and Katherine sees the name and address on it, she raises her eyebrows slightly. A look that says: why? Maryanne looks back at her, unblinking. A look that says: for the child. It is a silent communication, one that is possible because, Maryanne notes, they *know* each other: she knows the games they played, the stories they read and the God they prayed to in the days when Maryanne prayed. They know each other, in precisely the way that she doesn't know Victor.

But perhaps that's not true, she tells herself as Katherine leaves the room. She knows a lot about Victor, really. She knows the way he displays a cloth, at least to her, how he strokes the cloth, remarks upon its colour and texture, and can turn the exchange into a kind of courtship. She knows things that, quite probably, no one else knows: not his mother, nor the woman he is engaged to. She knows and remembers clearly that moment in the shop when all pretence was dropped, when they each took off their masks and stood facing each other, and the public manner gave way to a direct look that told her what he was really thinking beneath all the talk of cloth, colour and texture. A look that was a question. A question she answered with her eyes, a direct stare that said yes, and which eventually led to a back room behind a school house. She knows the smell of his skin, and the sounds he made in those times in the small bed in her room: the collapsed groan that told her he was finished. And she knows that as much as he might pronounce her beautiful, he can also *turn*, stamping his feet and wheeling away; she remembers that moment of hard anger when he stared at her in the gardens and silently pronounced her a crafty bitch. And she knows the coldness in his heart, for which she will never forgive him, that was there when he wheeled off and left her alone, birds taking flight from their branches as he stormed away. Yes, she nods, she knows quite a lot about Victor. Things that, quite probably, no one else knows. Yet not well enough for her to speak of all the things that might have been said but, in the end, weren't.

When she receives his reply early the next week, he names a day when he can get away. And she writes back – a second letter, she remarks to herself, in as many weeks; more contact than she made in all of the past year – naming the day and the hour at a photographer's studio in the city. And when they all gather that day, the three of them, it will be the first and last time that the three are together, and the first and last time that father and son ever meet. One will remember; the other will not. For the child, the stranger in uniform photographed that day will become a ghost from history: one that will haunt the child, the husband, the father, and the old man Vic will become. An old man who will die at around three o'clock in the morning in a simple one-bedroom flat in the sub-tropical northern town to which he will retreat in his final years when everybody has grown and gone their separate ways. Was he lonely then? Or just alone? Did nature, retreating to some distant place where it wouldn't bother anyone, simply do what nature does?

Maryanne leans her head against a pillow, staring out the window, oblivious of all this. At some point she looks at the child, telling herself, don't fret. The child will live, you will die. And she tries to conceive of the child, grown and in a world without her, even old, and she can't bear to.

There is no need to look ahead into the future, she tells herself; just live these days. These days of wonder. Let that be enough. For it is: this separate peace they have created, this oasis of calm and quiet. She strokes the baby's head, smoothing the ebony hair that is yet to turn wavy, and closes her eyes, sinking into the soothing quiet of the room, the silence broken only by a snort and a long sigh from the sleeping child.

17.

There are trees in the background, sun on the leaves, and low shrubbery, lush and green. She can almost hear birds hidden in the branches. But the trees, leaves and shrubbery are all painted on a large canvas backdrop. They do not sway in the breeze because there is none. And the only birdsong to be heard is the whistling of the photographer.

He is instructing Victor on how to stand: one foot slightly forward, the other back, toes pointing outwards. Head high, hat tilted, hands just so as they grip a baton. Statues stand like that, Maryanne notes, sitting in a studio chair beside the baby, observing the scene. Statues, not people. It is curious to be looking at Victor again, after everything. She has learned that his engagement is finally off and that he is, as the phrase goes, a free man. But, of course, he's not. He's *theirs*, in that silly uniform that looks a good size too large, and they'll send him wherever they want.

But here he is, all the same. Back in the picture. Assuming his place beside her as he did a few minutes before, the missing figure in a family portrait. But is he? Just who *is* Victor? Does he really complete the portrait? For as much as three is a good number, as much as people think of three as a good number, a balanced one (the baby in between, mother and father either side), there is also something disturbing in his sudden presence. He is here, as they arranged, but she is not sure she likes the arrangement. For he disturbs the perfect balance of mother and child. In the weeks since the birth, she and the baby have created their own small universe: two heavenly bodies, one circling the other, held together by an invisible force that was born the moment the child was. And so, as much as he is here, she is asking herself if she really wants him in the picture, after all. Does he complete it, or disrupt it?

He brings presents. Is considerate. Seems changed. But when she looks at those feet, carefully arranged by the photographer, she sees them wheeling off in anger once again, leaving her behind in the gardens, the gift of her miracle flung back in her face. He brings clothes for the child: mittens and knitted jackets and tiny socks for winter. And for her his finest cloths from the shop, for her to fashion as she will. His eyes were soft when he greeted her, no sign of the look that pronounced her a crafty bitch. Instead, she sees the same eyes that, in an unguarded moment, saw the beauty in her that no one else had. But, for all that, does he complete the picture or intrude upon it?

She has time to contemplate this because the photographer, an artistic type in coloured waistcoat and floral tie, is taking his picture. Victor looks puzzled and seems impatient with the photographer's instructions, but goes along with things.

Maryanne observes him, her mind ticking over. There he is, solid, standing like a statue, looking awkward in his oversize uniform. Suddenly back in her life when he's been out of it for most of the year. No hint of apology. No sign of regret. Just back again. And although he's said nothing that might suggest staying on – he could be shipped overseas any time anyway – would she want him around if he suggested as much? Asked her to wait, gave her a ring to make the wait official? Would she want it? There he is, like some lost lord coming home to claim what's his, or what he assumes or hopes is still his. Come back to his domain. But why, she asks herself, why should she bow to a lost lord just because he's returned? Because it now suits him? The conceit! No, she won't. They've got on perfectly well so far, the child and Maryanne. Without the lord, and will in the future. They have created this small universe, mother and child, and she's decided she likes it that way. She's already used to it that way. And what is more, she's decided she *can* do this thing. Why should he be thought of as completing the picture; the picture feels complete as it is. And why should she bow to the lord just because he's back?

Besides, he is part of a larger story now. Victor is not Victor the small-town draper any more, but somebody else. Somebody in a grand tale. One that is worthy of both mother and child. And yet here he is, like a wayward character who doesn't know his place, stepping out of his role. No, it won't do: Victor is not Victor any more, but someone else. The pattern is set. The story written. His presence now is a sort of inconvenience. No, she's looked ahead into the years to come, and he's not there.

Victor stands perfectly still. To attention, almost. A statue, indeed. There is a flash. A white light, and the moment is caught. Maryanne, in her best hat, starched white blouse and navy skirt, takes her place on a chair next to where Victor stood. The baby rests in a cot beside her. Victor watches. She is blinded by one flash after another. A series of photographs capturing a moment, a meeting of three people that will not happen again: photographs that will be passed down through the generations and finish up with Michael (currently speeding towards the city centre and following his progress on a map on the wall of his carriage). Ghostly figures from a ghostly past, stories within stories attached to them: imagined and real, and no way of telling one from the other. And Maryanne, the storyteller at the centre of it all, deciding what was, what wasn't and what ought to have been: the egg that gave birth to a whole mythology.

Afterwards, she pushes the pram along the footpath, Victor walking beside her. It is a late January afternoon. Hot and dusty. An annoying north wind blows across the city. Sad banners – a Yes here, a No there – flap, lift and fall in the wind. The battle cries of yesterday's battle. The No has prevailed over the Yes. The Wart has lost, the voice of Ireland has held sway. And for that she thanks him, this Mannix with the cold eyes of God himself, staring at her belly, judging both her and the child even as he saves all those sons who would have been dragged off into an army and sent thousands of miles away to die in the mud. Yes, for that she's thankful. At least something good has come of these days of the beast. But still, a crowd is a crowd, a mob a mob, and the cold eyes of a judging God are just as cold for all that.

She stares at Victor as they walk, aware that she too is staring with eyes that judge: that judge him and find him wanting. For nobody was ever going to be able to put Victor into a uniform if he didn't want it. And all of those soldiers from this land, on the other side of the world from the war, all of those soldiers lying dead or shivering in the mud, are there because they took themselves there. Or does anybody, Victor or anyone, just take themselves off to a war? Or does the hounding and the bullying of the schoolyard simply re-emerge on a grand scale? The Wart could call for volunteers all he liked, but if nobody turned up to the enlistment offices there would be no army to send. No, nobody was ever going to put Victor in a uniform. But he went ahead and did it all the same. Idiot!

'When do you leave?'

'I don't know.'

'Soon?'

'Probably. We've finished our training. We can't stay. Could be tomorrow, could be next week. They don't tell you these things.'

She shakes her head, a gesture of impatience: with the heat, with him. A couple is arguing on a nearby corner. They're hot.

Everybody is: these dusty January days, like stepping out into an oven, are enough to drive anyone mad. Over the littlest things. But her impatience with Victor is not over some little thing. There he is in uniform. A soldier. A soldier, for heaven's sake! Surrendering his independence, his will, to a faceless army that won't even tell him what it intends for him until the last minute. No, her impatience stems from disbelief. *Why, Victor? Why?* But the question is left hanging, blown away in the hot, dusty air.

They stop at a tea-house.

'Will this do?'

She nods. 'It's as good as anywhere. How long have you got?'

'Not long.'

'Then it will have to do.'

They find a table, they sit, the pram beside her – Maryanne, Victor, the child – taking in the clatter of cutlery, the buzz of talk, the gentle whirring of a fan in the corner of the room.

He looks at the baby, listless in the heat. He is awkward, fidgeting with his cap. 'Your forehead. Your cheeks. And jaw: especially the jaw.' He seems pleased with what he sees.

The gardens of the town rise up in front of her: Victor is wheeling away from her, storming off, the pronouncement of crafty bitch in his eyes.

'You don't think he's yours, do you?'

He turns to her, stunned. 'I didn't say that. Besides, I do. Just right now, though, it's you I see. Not me.'

'I can see you.'

'Where?'

'The eyes.'

'Really?' He is pleased.

'He's got the eyes of a little brooder. Are you a brooder, Victor?'

The pleased look fades with the question. 'Why do you ask?'

'Are you?'

'I can be.'

She nods. 'You see, we know so little of each other.'

'Not *so* little.'

'But not a lot. What have you ever really known of me?'

He doesn't get a chance to answer because a waitress appears, hot and flushed, pad and pencil in hand. When they have ordered their tea and cakes, they sit in silence. Like a bored married couple. And for a moment, Maryanne has an intimation of the life they might have had. Or is it just the day? Besides, it's not a bored silence. It's a silence that comes of having too much to say, having too little time and not knowing where to begin. But above all, a silence that comes of once having had so much to say, but missing the moment when such things might have been said, indeed needed to be said.

He plunges in. 'Was it hard?'

She sighs. *Now* he asks. Only now. 'Yes.' It is a snappy yes, and Maryanne is suddenly aware of the lurking anger in her. The anger that has been there all the time. Not just with Victor, but all of them: his family she has never met, Father Geoghan,

Mrs Collins, *Mrs Collins, who lost her drawers*, neighbours who fling feathers at you in the street and pronounce you a Hun's whore, the shops full of accusing eyes, the door, the front door of the house that she couldn't approach one morning. Was it *hard*?

'Did you have help?'

'My sister. She's a bit of a pioneer. She knows everything.'

'Good.'

'Yes, it *was* good. At least someone was there! I couldn't have done it without her.'

'I'm pleased to hear it.'

Still no hint of regret or apology. He shows no sign of picking up the pointed way she speaks of at least *someone* being there. And 'pleased', he says. Pleased. Why, Victor? You never showed the slightest sign of caring. Why should you be pleased now? It's just your guilt speaking, Victor, isn't it? And instead of silently asking all this, she distils it.

'*Why?*'

'Why what?'

'Why should you be pleased?'

He is taken aback. 'Well, because ...'

'... it makes you feel better?'

'No ... I mean, yes, but ...'

She doesn't bother waiting for a more considered response. 'I'm glad it happened the way it did. I never thought I'd get through it all. Not really. I seemed to be just dragging myself from one day to another. And some days never seemed to end.

And some mornings I barely had the strength to begin. I didn't think I could do it. But I did. I had it in me, after all. And I'm so glad I found that out. But was it hard? You bet it was.'

He looks down at the child, wriggling in the heat. 'You came through. You both have. You found the strength in yourself. I'm pleased for you. Yes, pleased.' He pauses, a slight frown. 'At some point during the year I became aware that I was thinking of you, and what you might be going through, more than I was thinking of Lizzie.'

Lizzie, he explains, is the woman to whom he was engaged. The responsibility that weighed upon him so heavily that day in the gardens, that caused him to wheel off and leave her weeping, a blubbering mess in a public garden, in public view. A Maryanne she will never be again. But she nods; it is the first time she has heard the woman's name. The first time, in fact, he has ever spoken of her directly.

'So it's not entirely fair to think, and I'm sure you do think this, that I never had the slightest care—'

'Victor,' she says, slowing him down, 'it's been a year. A long, hard year. There are things I can't even begin to tell you because I wouldn't know how or *where* to begin, and because, well … honestly Victor, it's just a bit too late for all this. Don't you think?' And she doesn't say this with anger or resentment or any great emotion at all. She says it with the calm deliberation of someone stating a fact.

He stares at her long and hard as if the possibility had never occurred to him. '*Is* it?'

'Yes.' And this time there is a touch of sadness in her voice. 'Besides …' she waves a dismissive arm through the air, '… you're going soon. Going to heaven knows where. And heaven knows what. What is the point?' She slumps back in her chair. 'How simply awful.'

'Why awful?'

'*Why?*' She looks at him, astonished. 'Aren't you afraid?'

She turns away, on the verge of sobbing, determined to stamp it out before it starts. But, at the same time, registering that she does care. Not enough to call it love or change her mind, but enough to tell her that something fine and good has survived the mess of the last year.

He looks about the room, quite possibly searching for the words to express thoughts he's held for some time, but not spoken until now. 'You … How *can* I say this? You … come to look forward to it. To *want* it.'

She swings back to him, half puzzled, half knowing what he means. Half praying for him, half bursting with anger at him again. Idiot! He can't mean that. 'To want what?'

'*It.*'

Tea, cakes, are almost dumped on the table.

'They train you, day in and day out, week in, week out, until you actually start getting good at it. And you can tell you're getting good. And that's when you start to look forward to it. To try it out.'

Her eyes widen as she listens, and then she snaps. 'Can you hear yourself?'

He leans back in his chair, staring at the baby and nodding. 'Yes. I don't say this proudly, but because it is the case.'

'They've trained you to kill. And now you're looking forward to going off and killing Germans. Germans who could be your family, or some sort of family friends. Or just ordinary, decent people who have no choice because some nasty old fool has ordered *them* to go off and kill or be killed. Just like nasty old fools the world over. Or they might kill you. Have you thought of *that*?'

'Yes.'

'I suppose you'd like to try *that* out too?'

'You get used to the thought.'

'Do you?' She almost rises from her chair. They both stare at the uneaten cakes. 'That's how they want you to think. It's death they want. They love it. They're sick. All of them. And not just your generals and majors and sergeants. It's everybody. We've all got the same sickness. Just look around you. All that grieving and wailing.' Her voice grows louder as she continues. 'Deep down they love it. It's death they want. They can't get enough of it. Can't you feel it? And all the tears and weeping—'

'Sssh!'

'No.'

'People can hear.'

'Let them!'

'Keep your voice down!'

'I will not! You're a fool, Victor. A perfect fool. Just the kind of fool they want. And you believe all the muck they print in the papers, do you? Honour and duty? There's no honour, Victor. It all ends in mud and death! They *love* it. Everybody!'

Victor turns away from the eyes of the tea-house and stares at the child in the pram, sleeping through it all. Maryanne's outrage runs its course. There is a silence. The tea-house customers return to their talk.

'My eyes, perhaps. Yes. My eyes.'

'Your eyes, yes. I just hope he doesn't have your wits.'

Victor's composure suddenly collapses. He snaps. 'Do you ever let up?' Heads turn again. They are a scene. He doesn't care. '*Do* you?'

She sinks back in her chair, staring out the window at the hot, scrappy afternoon.

Victor continues. 'You really are your own worst enemy, you know.'

She sighs and closes her eyes. As if to say, yes, you are right. That was unnecessary. More than that, cheap and untrue. Why do we say these things? She opens her eyes and nods at him, and there is tenderness there, caught up in all the anger; how could there not be?

He nods back, a small peace is declared. When he speaks his voice is soft, sincere. 'Did it never occur to you that I came with the offer of a chance? To help?'

'A chance?' She shakes her head. Her tone is mellow as a sudden ache, and a sweet one, rises up in her. 'Victor, Victor, we *never* had a chance. Oh,' she corrects herself, 'we *might* have. Once. At the very beginning. If we go back and work through it piece by piece, we might find a point at which we had a chance.'

And it is here that he looks away, squinting his eyes, caught perhaps by a sudden pang of feeling that he seems, with all his will, to be fighting back in case he makes a spectacle of himself. And Maryanne fully understanding the riot inside him that he is trying to quell, concedes that yes, this might have once worked. And there is a sadness in her she never realised was there: for him, for her, for the child, for that orphan moment that they let slip from them when this thing might have worked.

He recovers, she recovers.

'I suppose there must have been a time, a moment when we had a chance.'

He nods slowly, reluctantly. 'But not now?'

She sighs, shaking her head. 'We missed it. No. Not now. Just look at us. You're about to march off to God knows where and God knows what, and I've found I'm stronger than I thought or I knew. And I've got a whole other life. And you, you have …'

The waitress suddenly appears and they both look up at her. She stares down at their uneaten cakes and untouched tea as if, Maryanne imagines, it were some kind of insult. The cakes, the tea, the place – not good enough for them. It's what she's thinking, all right. But she says none of it. 'Finished, then?'

Victor and Maryanne look at each other and nod without looking at her: both contemplating the question in ways the waitress never intended or thought of. The waitress clears the table. They rise. The baby wakes, crying: hot and thirsty. He sucks on a small bottle, eyes open, eyes on the stranger in front of him.

On the city street they stare at each other, as if to say, well, this is it. And, of course, it is. Maryanne sighs, a slight shake of the head.

'Be careful, Victor,' she says, leaning forward and kissing his lips. 'Write and visit. You can always visit. We'll be here. And *do* be careful.' She adds this as if saying: They've got you in their grip now. They don't care about you. You're just another tin soldier. Look out. And again she notes that something good and fine has emerged from the mess. 'Oh, it's not just the eyes,' she adds, looking at the child in the pram, the hint of a tender smile on her lips, 'it's the widow's peak as well. Can't you see it?'

He scrutinises the baby's face, smiles and nods, then leans over the pram and kisses the baby's eyes and the peak of black hair on his forehead that they both agree are Victor's. Then they face each other. Yes, they nod, this is it. He returns Maryanne's kiss, then swings about, slowly, almost thoughtfully, and gives a slow wave to the two of them as he makes his way up the city lane, now shaded, the sun too low in the sky to touch them.

18.

A cool change, one of those sudden cool changes, blows over the city, breathing life into the parks and gardens. People have come out of their houses, floating along the footpaths and drinking in the cool air, like flowering deserts drinking rain. She walks the baby through the parks and streets. It is her favourite time of day. The sun is low, the sky a peach glow. An hour ago everything and everybody looked wretched and scorched. Ready to wilt. Or explode. Creatures wandering through the streets of some sand-blasted desert town. Now all is changed and she could be walking through a freshly painted scene, mellow and serene.

She has walked up the hill towards the parliament and is about to turn for home when she sees a poster stuck to a tree: 'NO MORE WARS'. She gazes at the poster with vague recognition, then realises that the meeting that Vera invited her to is being held today. In the gardens, not far away. She can see the crowd as she reaches the top of the tree-lined street. Maryanne smiles: for the change in the weather; the happy accident of stumbling upon the meeting; the child, cooled by the breeze and kicking in his pram; and those few affectionate parting words with Victor. After all, they could be their last words, and it's nice to know they were good words: that some fine fondness emerged from it all. *Let us sing in gladness ...*

She turns the pram, and as she nears the gardens, she hears an amplified voice. A speech. Somebody is talking through a megaphone. The meeting has already begun. People are lounging on the grass, in groups or alone. It looks more like a picnic than a political meeting. It is as though the cool change, with its sweet breath, blown by some kindly god, has banished the beast for a time. For this is just a gathering of people, not a mob. Neither snarls nor howls rising from it, no scales in the sun, no ancient monster stalking the grounds. Just people.

And it is while she is surveying the scene and succumbing to its calm that she looks to the stage, vaguely taking in the words of a young woman, noting the voice is familiar, then realising she knows her: Vera, face shining with that impossible youth of hers, blonde hair tied back, crisp white shirt and tie like a schoolgirl. Vera, the girl from the posh side of town, with whom Maryanne really ought not to have much in common. But if this wretched war has done anything good at all it has thrown people together from all parts of the city who might not normally cross paths, smashed a few things that needed smashing and paved the way for the likes of this young Vera. Currently on the stage. Addressing the crowd as if she has been doing this for years.

Maryanne steadies the pram, applies its brake, shakes the child's rattle for him, then settles on the grass. Until now she has simply been taking in the spectacle; hearing, but not really listening. Now, she is. And noting that, even through the megaphone, Vera has one of those public-speaking voices that you listen to without really trying. It is a combination of what she says and how she says it. She's unafraid. So confident. A born public speaker. She wants to change things, and she just might. Vera and her kind.

'Jack Milhaus,' Vera is saying, 'woke one morning to read a small article in the newspaper. Just a paragraph. Nothing much. An unlikely story about military secrets, and spying, under our noses.' Here she pauses, lowering the megaphone for a moment and looking round at the gathering. 'We all know the story. He thought nothing of it. Just one of those odd stories that come and go. But it didn't go. And one morning they came for him. He was told that *he* was the spy under everybody's noses. He could have laughed at the madness of it all, but nobody was laughing as they led him away. And life became a mad dream. But it wasn't. It was real. Suddenly, this was his life. This was *who* he was: Jack Milhaus, spy, betrayer of his country, Hun. And the story grew and grew. Until it took over his whole life. And ours!'

Here she pauses again, letting her words sink in, calculating what next to say, for, amazingly, she seems to have no written speech. And Maryanne is both listening closely, as is the whole assembly, and admiring Vera, who seems to grow somehow the more she speaks.

'Until the whole city was turned against just one man and nobody stopped to think why,' she goes on. 'We were all meant to hate him, because the more we hated him, the less we thought and the more we were *theirs*! The hate-makers. This is what war does: turns ordinary, decent people into monsters! Nothing good comes of it. The sickness is mass hysteria. The symptom is Jack Milhaus. Or was. We must resist the hate-makers, those who will divide us for their own gain, as we must resist war. Must never let the hate-makers drag us into it. Never again. Join us on the peace march. We don't have far to go. Just up the hill to parliament. We must resist, and if enough of us do – at home, at work, in the streets and the parks – then there can be no war. Let our boys put down their guns, and let them do the unthinkable: just turn and walk away. Let our boys, and *their* boys, do what all armies long to do: turn, walk away and come home.'

Here she drops the megaphone again, the applause and cheers loud throughout the park, unsettling the birds, Maryanne notes, which rise from their branches into the air, then descend again. And it is then that a change seems to come over Vera, for she looks around her, silently, a long, long silence, taking in the crowd, the police in the background, as if wondering how on earth to begin upon what she next wants to say, or even if she wants to say it. But she finally does. 'I lost my fiancé and my brother to this awful war. It has taken them. And it will not give them back. I will not forget them, the sweetest, sweetest boys who ever breathed. My two boys. Gone.'

Maryanne is suddenly frozen. Shocked, she steadies herself on the pram. And it is not simply the impact of Vera's words, but how wrongly she perceived her. Oh, how quickly we judge, and how wrongly. All that impossible innocence wasn't innocence at all. And she can see the fight, the resolve, that was always there behind the innocent milkmaid face: the fight she showed when they cuffed her and spat on her – *They'll find we're not so easily scared.* But, the thought suddenly occurs to Maryanne, if Vera is not innocent then who is there left in the world who is? And at the same time, she's realising that she *wanted* Vera to be innocent, and made her so. For reasons both worthy and not: to be reassured that there still was such a thing, but also to feel more worldly than her, even superior. Superior enough to judge her quickly, and wrongly. That and more, who knows? And it is while she is asking herself this that she turns her attention back to Vera. To all appearances the same Vera, but utterly changed.

'No,' Vera continues, '*I* will never forget them. But the world will. That's how it goes on, this carousel of war and war and more war: *because* we forget! But I will not. Not one sweet moment.' She gathers herself. 'This whole bloody war,' she says into the megaphone, her voice trembling and echoing round the hushed gardens, 'can only make sense if we say no more death. We have worshipped death for too long. Stayed too long at this carnival of death.' She pauses, 'No more *us* and *them*. Never again. But only if we build a new world from the ruins of this one. And imagine we *can*. And only if we never let the hate-makers into our hearts again. So that no one, and no war, will ever take our loved ones, our brothers, sisters and friends away again. Only then will it make sense. But we have to *make* it so.'

The silence of the large crowd, Maryanne concludes, is louder than any applause. She has struck home. She has them. 'And Jack Milhaus,' Vera says, resuming, 'wherever he may be now, may he find a separate peace. Heaven only knows, he's earned it. May we all find a separate peace. Heaven only knows, we've all earned it.' There is a warm burst of applause, and Maryanne wonders where all that applause was when it was needed. 'Now join us. Let's march up the hill to parliament and tell them what we think. Let them hear our voices, loud and clear: NO MORE WAR, NO MORE WAR, NO MORE ...'

The crowd rises to its feet, cheering. Vera smiles, as if soaking it up like the last of the afternoon sun, drawing strength from it. The Vera she knows, and the one she doesn't. And, once again, she's telling herself: how quickly we judge, how quickly and how wrongly.

It is over a month since Milhaus was set free. A month in which the newspapers forgot about him, moved on and focused their eyes on the lady who came forward to save him and in so doing became the new sacrifice for the beast; she who was branded Madame X, and the Hun's whore. The princess who betrayed them and has now disappeared from public life. And, rumour has it, who has been banished from her mansion, from her children, from the whole fairytale life she led, and sent somewhere far away – perhaps until public memory fades and she can return, perhaps not. And Milhaus? Milhaus, the god who fell, has disappeared from public view, as if he never existed. And the whole episode, what was the Milhaus case, has suddenly become yesterday's news.

Maryanne watches the crowd form a line: slowly, smiling and laughing, as though they are at a picnic and about to join in a three-legged race. The line forms, the banners are raised, and the procession to parliament begins. And this time, Maryanne observes, the police don't move. They stay in the background, some even smiling. They don't move: the crowd is too large, their numbers too few. And at the front of the line is Vera, wearing, Maryanne notes, the hat she retrieved from the street when Vera was spat upon and fell to the ground. She is surrounded by other women, some of whom Maryanne recognises from the offices. But Vera is at the centre. This, it is understood, is her idea. Her march. At first she smiles as she greets the women and men around her in the front lines, then she turns to look up the hill to the parliament, becoming serious, that steely resolve, the fight in her behind the posh face, apparent again as she raises the megaphone to her mouth and begins chanting, the crowd joining in: NO MORE WAR, NO MORE WAR, NO MORE ...

Maryanne stands as they approach, and as the front row passes her, Vera drops her megaphone, stops her chant and waves. She is in her element. And the more Maryanne observes her, as she waves back, the more she becomes convinced that this is not the last time Vera will lead a march: to parliament or wherever else her cause takes her. What it must be, Maryanne marvels, not only to want to change things, but to imagine you *can*.

She turns the pram, the child now tired, his rattle resting on his chest, and walks back through a summer evening more lit with hope than any of the recent summers or seasons past. The beast has prevailed, but maybe the beast's time is up. For the worst in us can only sustain itself for so long. And perhaps people know, somewhere inside where their better selves lie, that they have lingered too long at the festival of the beast.

* * *

When Maryanne enters the house she is still in a contented, almost dreamy state. But Katherine greets her and immediately annoys her as she has over the last few weeks. For a short while Maryanne was in a world of grand ideas and passion and hope. Then Katherine opened the door and her world seemed to shrink. And that hopeful, dream-like state evaporates. Katherine is shaking the baby's rattle and making the kinds of baby sounds that, Maryanne has noticed, grown-ups make around babies. She thinks of it as baby language, and Katherine is speaking in some ridiculous baby language right now. And getting on her nerves. Katherine picks the baby up from the pram, almost snatches him, and walks to the kitchen with him, coo-cooing all the way. And it's not just the way

Katherine snatches the baby from the pram and all the coo-cooing baby talk that annoys Maryanne. The baby was rested; now he's all stirred up.

It's something she's noticed lately. Katherine picking the baby up whenever she pleases. Treating him like he's, well … hers. It's becoming a habit. One that annoys her. And she's dwelling on this, even brooding on it, though part of her knows she is being unfair, when they sit down in the kitchen.

'Been to have your photograph taken,' Katherine coos to the child. She turns to Maryanne. 'How was it?'

Maryanne barely hears, for resentment is rising in her: her world, so wide a little while before, so full of hope and boundless possibility, has shrunken, and she is slow to respond.

'Did you hear?' Katherine is abrupt, the big sister speaking.

'It was awkward,' Maryanne finally says. She is suddenly in no mood to talk about parting kisses, and fine and good parting words.

'And did the beautiful little boy behave?'

'He was perfect.'

Katherine beams and rubs the child's belly. 'Of course he was. Where's the knife and fork?' she croons. 'Who's looking good enough to eat?'

Maryanne stares at her, as if willing her sister to just stop it. Why, *why* must she behave like this? So, so … so hopelessly what? And she ponders this for a moment, and realises that what she means is so hopelessly *ordinary.* Just like everybody else. No, let's be honest. So hopelessly *common*. Knife and fork, indeed! She's always hated the phrase and the way it comes with cooing women going gaga over babies. Her child is above all that. She knows it, she just has to look at him. Her child will be noble. Was never born for such baby talk. And for a moment (and it will not be the last time), part of her actually believes the tale of his birth: a noble family, oceans of vineyards and the giant family door slammed in her face. A tragic tale. No, her child will *not* have silly talk showered upon him, and will not be the ordinary run. The way Maryanne herself and Katherine have never felt part of the ordinary run. But *this* Katherine, cooing over the baby and talking nonsense about knives and forks, has somehow managed to slough off the other Katherine altogether: the Katherine who lives out there in the bush with her swag and rifle, the very Katherine whom newspapers will one day call a pioneer. Far from hopelessly ordinary.

Katherine bounces the child in her arms, babbling nonsense. 'I'm going to eat you all up,' she cries. 'Yes, yes, *all* up'. And suddenly there is one bounce too many, one coo too much.

Be it tiredness, Victor, the tea-house, the revolting, uneaten, rock-hard cakes, Maryanne's doesn't know. But her annoyance bursts from her like a cannon blast. '*Leave* him!'

Everything stops. All smiles dissolve. Katherine stares back, silent and crestfallen. The fun suddenly gone out of her. The glint in her eyes extinguished. The child too is gazing at

Maryanne, a frown on his face. Katherine, still holding the baby (the nearest thing to a child of her own she will ever have), slumps back in her chair. And straightaway Maryanne wishes she'd never spoken.

Why shouldn't Katherine have her fun? Heaven knows she's had so little of it: Katherine, grown too soon, and Maryanne always walking in her wake, protected from the world. Unaware of it, even. Why, *why* did she have to say that? Such a harmless bit of fun.

'No,' Maryanne says, trying to fix the broken moment, 'don't leave him. Don't, please …' But the fun has gone from Katherine and she hands the child to his mother. A gesture that says: it is true, I have acted out of turn. Of course, the child is not mine. I have behaved like a silly aunt, babbling silly aunt talk. It won't happen again.

And Maryanne takes the child, almost reluctantly now, while Katherine, not knowing what to do with her hands, folds them in front of her. 'You're right,' she says. 'He should rest.'

They are both silent, almost afraid to speak. For there is a line of separation between them now that wasn't there a moment before.

'You were away a while,' Katherine says, her tone sombre.

'We went to a tea-house.'

'Katherine nods, still dejected.

'It was crowded,' Maryanne adds, a way of explaining the time it took.

'Of course.'

'And it *was* awkward, if you must know.' And she immediately raises her eyebrows in self-reproach. If you must know, indeed, she silently tells herself. Who is so hopelessly common now?

'You don't *have* to tell me.'

'No, that's not what I meant … He, he talked about offering a chance. Or, something like that. It was noisy and hot.'

Katherine looks up. 'A chance? For what?'

'For us, I suppose,' Maryanne replies, catching the lost look in Katherine's eyes, and again wishing she'd never spoken.

'What did *you* say?' Katherine asks, but there's no great heart in the question.

'I'm not sure I said anything. It's too late, anyway.'

'I suppose it is.'

Maryanne sighs. 'Since when did he care?'

Katherine nods, her voice flat. 'All the same, I won't always be here.' The child suddenly grins at her and she returns the hint of a smile.

'No, you won't,' says Maryanne: a thoughtful, drawn-out no, one (and Katherine will have noted this) that does not carry with it the hint of any suggestion that she needn't go. That she might just stay.

'You won't feel alone?'

Maryanne is still thoughtful, pausing before speaking. 'There'll be times.'

Katherine nods. 'There will.'

'And you?'

Katherine smiles, and though sad, this time it is a real smile. 'There'll be times.'

'You'll miss everything.'

'I will,' Katherine says, 'but I'll be busy.'

'You're welcome any time.' A way of telling her: what I said, just now, I didn't mean it.

'I know.' Katherine nods, understanding exactly what Maryanne both says and doesn't say. 'I know that.'

Maryanne smiles back, the moment still broken, but mended a little, at least. Glued back together. Like one of those cracked vases that still function but which bear all the marks of having been broken and reassembled and are never what they were.

The room hums in thoughtful silence. Maryanne rises, taking the child with her, leaving her sister motionless in her chair, her eyes lowered once again.

In the bedroom she changes the child, then releases her breast, which the child grasps immediately. Mine, it says, hands around the breast, lips fastened to the nipple. Mine. And when he's finished she places him in the cot, smoothing his brow, the dark V of the widow's peak that is Victor's, as he falls asleep.

All around the house is silent and still, apart from the child's breathing and the rising and falling of his chest. Katherine, she imagines, is still fixed to her chair, her eyes lowered. Maryanne takes the child's hand and feels his grip, even in sleep. At the same time she registers that yes, there will be times. Just as there will be times for all of them, even the child who, at this moment, can't possibly conceive of being alone. But there will be times when loneliness will come to him, as it does to everyone. And she tightens her grip. Not yet, little one. Not yet.

19.

As Maryanne smooths the widow's peak, the brow of her sleeping child, both at rest in the separate peace they have negotiated with the world, Michael makes his way up the steps of the Métro and the city begins to appear. When he reaches the top, it is all laid out before him. A feast, a fantasy come to life. Just as he imagined. And more. He lowers his suitcase and pauses, taking in the spectacle. And tired as he is after a twenty-four-hour flight, it's as if his senses – sight, sound, smell – have rarely been so alert.

He can think of only a few previous occasions when the world took his breath away like this. Once when he was a boy, when propelling a red leather ball through the air at great speed, when the pursuit of the perfect delivery (the delivery that, in all its perfection, would stop the suburb), consumed his days. On one of those days he was walking through the dark, shady caverns of the Melbourne Cricket Ground, down the steps towards the oval for the first time, when he stepped into bright, blinding, late-morning summer light, and the dazzling, green-carpeted playing field was suddenly spread out before him: white figures on the field standing perfectly still, batsmen perfectly still, the only moving figure that of the fast bowler swooping down upon the pitch – *something* about to happen. Now the city opens out in front of him. This too is one of those moments, and he pauses, senses alert, taking it in as he had that distant playing field.

Montparnasse-Bienvenüe. Strange name for a train station. The wide boulevard in front of him is cluttered with cars, scooters and vans: red, green, yellow, blue – a moving canvas. It is a dull winter's day in December. December. The very word for Michael is synonymous with summer, school holidays and cricket. But even on this dull day in a different kind of December, the boulevard is bright with colour and movement. The pedestrian lights change and overcoated workers cross, for it is still early in the morning. And it is while he is watching them that Michael registers that these people are going to work. That it is just another day. Just another crossing. And it occurs to him that he may be the only one pausing to marvel at the spectacle.

And it is a spectacle that is as foreign to the world of his father and the grandmother he never really knew as the landscape of Mars. For Michael comes from the age of silver jets, winters in December and a world made smaller by speed. And Maryanne's world is as foreign to him as his would be to her. And although she may well have been one of those who were thrown into a world that was not theirs, one of those ahead of their times, *this* world her true one, he's wondering if she would have wanted it. Really wanted it, had her wish been granted.

As he picks up his suitcase and walks towards the nearest cafe for breakfast, it is the question of just *who* she was and what her world felt like that preoccupies him. That and the dazzling spectacle of colour and movement all around him.

But there is also that distinct sense of bringing family ghosts to the table he sits at, as though generations of living have gone into this journey and this simple act. That the act of sitting at a cafe table in a distant foreign city is a layered one, made possible by the dead and the living. Maryanne and his father are part of that layering, just as he himself will be one day for those who will come after him. The generations are always weaving in and out of each other, constantly refining themselves, so that when occasions such as this arise, *everybody* sits at the table. For history – of a country or a family – is never dead. And history is not just the deeds or misdeeds of the dead, nor is it stuck in the past; it is alive in us. They – our parents, their parents, and the public figures they brushed with – are alive in us, flowing through our veins and living on in our memory and our thoughts, both casual and deliberate. *There* in even the simplest of daily acts.

And even the waiter's *bonjour*, it strikes him, is just such an act as well. He smiles. His voice is bright. But all part of the job, like the pressed white shirt, the vest and napkin over his arm. It's a greeting, and business. And whether he's right or not, Michael can imagine generations of waiters going into that simple greeting: one that also, in its manner of delivery, leaves Michael in no doubt that the gentleman is in charge.

He may be serving, but he is not servile. You are at *his* table. *Bonjour.*

In poor schoolboy French, the effort of which, at least, is appreciated, Michael orders. And when his breakfast appears (bread, butter, jam, croissant and coffee), his senses, once more, are alert as they rarely are. The world is made new by the simplest things. Adventure tasted and smelled in the simplest things. And as he eats, staring at the moving canvas all around him, he is aware of sitting at a crowded table.

But if history, of family and country, lives on in us and crowds our tables, *who* were they and how does this happen? How is it that they seem to be *there*: not so much seen, as presence that is felt. It is, he decides, a kind of reincarnation. They live on in memory and are recreated at the same time. And what we end up with is both true and untrue. An educated guess, an intuition. A leap of faith. And she's there, in front of him or beside him, Maryanne, at odd and surprising times, with that gentle smile she gave to the camera, which lives on in the two or three surviving photographs of her. An elderly, grey-haired woman on the brink of an observation that tells you she's watching you and that there's more than meets the eye to this simple old lady. With her shrewd stare. Her sharp, intelligent eyes. But who was she back then, when her belly was swollen with Michael's illegitimate father? For it was then, when the world turned in on itself, and went to war with itself, that she made the biggest decision of her life.

The traffic on the boulevard suddenly intrudes on his thoughts as a police car, siren blaring, speeds by. Crowds press to pedestrian crossings, the cafe begins to fill. The moving canvas changes before his eyes. The world, here and now, imposes itself. Maryanne has disappeared from his table. They all have: the grandmother he never really knew, his father, his mother, the child he was, and the stick-house suburb on the fringes of the city that they all came to. All gone, and yet always there. His table no longer crowded. He is alone, for the moment. All of them ancient history, and yet alive. Immediate. The past, but never gone. For better or worse.

Michael calls for the bill, and when it comes he produces a colourful note from his wallet and pauses to admire it before leaving it on the tray. He rises from the table and joins that moving canvas, crossing the boulevard and entering the station the grand trainlines depart from. A journey in front of him. The whole travelling world of the past coming with him. The new and the old, the past and the present, travelling side by side.

20.

Katherine is slow to come to breakfast in the morning. Unusual. She is always the first at the table, even prides herself on it. The early bird who never sleeps in. As Maryanne sits there, feeding the child, she gradually becomes aware of the sound of drawers opening and closing. She quickly understands. Then Katherine emerges from her room, her swag under her arm, and puts it down in the hallway. She smiles at Maryanne and the child, then returns for her tent and rifle, placing them alongside her swag. All her worldly goods. And Maryanne wishes she had a camera, for this is the complete Katherine.

Then she moves back into the kitchen, and the moment containing the complete Katherine is gone. The process has taken one or two minutes, and in that time neither Katherine nor Maryanne has spoken.

'You don't need me now,' Katherine finally says, sitting down in front of her.

'Don't I?'

'You *know* you don't.' Katherine's voice is soft, soothing, reassuring. 'Trust me. I'll be in the way.'

'Never.'

Katherine smiles, as if to say, thanks for the thought, but we both know I'm right. 'One day I will be. Best to leave before then.'

Maryanne is silent, a silence that she knows and Katherine knows is as good as a yes.

Katherine nods. 'My job's done now.' And she looks at the child, who she as good as brought into the world, whose first cries she heard as she held him up for Maryanne to see (a moment she will carry throughout her life, like her swag and tent), changed and grown already.

And Maryanne sees the changes, just as Katherine does too. Just as she sees the years rushing towards her, the baby growing up, the image of what he may become standing in front of her, while she and Katherine hover about as the aged figures they will be when that time arrives. It is a thought too exquisitely sad to be held for long. For it will happen quickly, and these days, these days that got the job done, will too easily slip from them.

Katherine shifts her gaze back to Maryanne. 'But I'll be back.'

'Any time.'

'To see you and the boy...'

'Your room will be waiting.'

'... when you least expect it.'

Maryanne smiles. 'Of course. We'll be happily ambushed.'

It is done. They nod. Katherine rises. 'I'll have to book my ticket. I'll be gone a while.'

'Breakfast?'

'Later.'

And with that Katherine kisses Maryanne and the child, then sweeps up the hallway and out the front door into the glare of the day. When she shuts the door behind her the house is quiet and strangely still. And suddenly the sight of Katherine's swag, tent and rifle, all her worldly goods, stacked in the hallway, waiting for her departure, is too much, and eyes stinging, Maryanne turns from them in case they see.

Late in the afternoon, when Maryanne returns from her daily walk with the child and puts the pram in the hallway, noting that the rocking rhythms of the pram ride have put the child to sleep, she hears a sound, a glorious sound, coming from the kitchen. A man's voice, high and rich. An orchestra. A concert, coming to her in melodic waves up the hallway. 'Sumptuous' is the word that comes to mind. And drawn to the sound – understanding the power of the siren's call as she never has before – she drifts, spellbound, to the kitchen.

When she opens the door the sound lifts in volume, the voice soars, notes hover and slide effortlessly in and out of each other, and the most heavenly music, a private concert, is all around her. And Katherine looks up from the kitchen table, tears streaming down her face, and stares at Maryanne, too entranced to speak. She lets the music speak for her. Words, golden as the music, fill the air: *angels guard thee* ...

The song rises to its climax, words and music linger, then fade into silence, followed by a scratching sound that repeats and repeats until Katherine, wiping her eyes, leans forward and lifts the needle.

'I saw it in a shop window and couldn't resist it.'

Maryanne stares at the rich wooden box that houses the phonograph – a magic box, she can't help but think of it as such – and looks back at Katherine, her eyes, like her sister's, still in rapture. 'How much did it cost?'

'Don't ask,' says Katherine. And she stares at it in wonder: a marvel of civilisation that brings to them such wonderful sounds. 'It's worth every penny.'

Maryanne smiles. 'It'll be good company for you. Out there, I mean. You won't be so alone. Not with that. You're right, it's worth every penny.'

Katherine shakes her head, then announces: 'It's not for *me*.'

Maryanne is astonished. 'You can't mean that.'

'I certainly do.'

'But it must have cost a fortune.'

Katherine smiles. 'Not quite a fortune. But look what it does. Did you ever hear such things? A concert, at home? What's a fortune compared to that?' She wipes her eyes.

Maryanne sits, staring at the magic, mahogany box. The disc of the recording still, the needle poised. The rich crimson lining shimmering before her. She's never owned such luxury. She rises, goes around the table, hugs her sister, then resumes her place.

'It's for those days,' says Katherine, 'those nights, when that little child has exhausted you, and you need a little luxury. And, believe me, there'll be plenty of them.'

Maryanne nods, stroking the mahogany.

'Shall we hear it again?' Katherine asks, pleased with her farewell gift. And she grasps the handle at the side of the phonograph, winds it up, and gently places the needle on the recording.

When the song fades, Maryanne lifts the needle and moves it to its resting place. The child, woken from his slumbers, begins to cry and Katherine picks him up from the pram and brings him into the kitchen.

'Meal time,' she says, passing him to Maryanne. 'Then we'll have to go.'

When they're finished, Maryanne places the baby back in the pram and pushes it up the hallway to the front door. Katherine follows her, swag and tent across her back, rifle in hand. Just before she reaches the door she pauses, gazing back up the hallway to the kitchen, her small room beside it, and the best room in the house just to her left. So much living in such a small space; rooms that hum and echo with it all. At least, these are the thoughts Maryanne puts in her sister's head, and she may well be right. For when Katherine looks at her and the child, it is with an expression that says: Give me a moment … The rooms, the hallway, the house – all will remain, but they will be different rooms when I next return. Give me a moment …

When she is finished, her moment up, she nods and the three of them make their way to the tram stop near the gardens and the parliament, where the Wart sits deep into the night, conjuring darkness from light.

* * *

The engine hisses steam. White clouds rise from its wheels into the overarching roof of the station. Like an animal, a horse stamping its feet, steam hissing from its nostrils, it is impatient to go.

Maryanne has strolled up to the engine while Katherine finds her compartment. The baby is in her arms. The platform is busy, travellers and well-wishers mingling, heads poking from compartment windows, last waves fanning the air. But at the front of the train, where the engine steams and stamps, there is no one but Maryanne and the child.

She nods to the driver, his head poked out from the cabin, surveying the scene as if he has assembled it himself and is directing it all, then she looks down at the child, fully expecting him to be resting or sleeping, for the child is a good sleeper. But he's not. The baby's eyes are wide open, staring intently at this black steam-hissing animal in front of him. Alive. Almost nodding to the child; the child acknowledging it and almost nodding back. For the baby's look is direct and unblinking: he is enthralled, completely under its spell, not so much staring at the engine as communing with it. When the driver waves to the station master, the baby's eyes shift to the driver, as if he understands everything that is going on. And, noticing the mother and the wide, observing eyes of the child, the driver looks down at them, just below the cabin and laughs.

'I think he wants to drive this thing.'

Maryanne laughs too and the driver looks back down the platform. Master of the scene: the one to whom everybody, at one time or another, turns; the one who holds everybody's fate in his hands; who will take them out into the world beyond the city, through the night and into the morning. The child looks from his laughing mother and back to the engine, steam once more hissing from it. Alive, impatient to be gone.

It is then that Katherine suddenly appears beside them, waving the steam from her face. 'What are you doing up here?'

Maryanne turns to her, her sister's presence almost an interruption. 'Don't you think it's splendid?'

'It's filthy.'

'I think I could be an engine driver. In another life. It's so wonderfully solitary,' Maryanne says as they walk towards Katherine's compartment. 'Oh, you've got your fireman stoking the fire there, but you're the driver. In your own world. Out there under the stars. Steaming through the night. Free.' She nods to herself and smiles. 'Yes, that's why they do it. They're free. Themselves. No other people. No chatter. Imagine it, just the odd cow looking up. You leave the platform, the crowds, the whole city behind, and soon you're under the milky heavens, released from it all. Released from your everyday life. Just this fiery, blazing thing and you, steaming through the night, trailing white clouds. Oh yes, I could do that. In another life. Couldn't you?'

Katherine ignores the question with a slight shake of the head that says, too much imagination, then gazes on the child. 'Here, let me have him a last time.'

'For now.'

'For now,' she says, taking the child and cradling him. 'Now don't you forget your Aunt Katherine,' she hums to the baby, 'because your Aunt Katherine won't forget you. She'll be thinking of you. Every day. You and those big brown eyes.' She smooths the baby's thick black hair. 'And that widow's peak, that Mama says is just like your father's.' Here she stops and looks directly at Maryanne, as if to say, one day he *will* ask about his father.

The station master blows his warning whistle. But Katherine holds on to the child, as if still trying to comprehend the simple, astonishing fact that he has come into the world and will live on into another one that she, Katherine, will never know. But I'll be able to say I was there, the pride in her smile seems to say, that I was there when you came into the world. I heard your first cries, and I too nursed you through your first hours and days. I was there when it mattered. And I will return, when you are walking and growing into the world, for the world is big and you will need someone to hold your hand while you grow into it. Your hand will rest in mine. *Angels guard thee* ... Don't forget your Aunt Katherine. She won't forget you.

She hands the child back to Maryanne as they climb into the compartment, and checks the bits and pieces of her world she came with and which go with her: her tent, wrapped; her swag; and her overnight bag. And, of course, her Enfield. No wonder she didn't bother replying to Maryanne's talk about being an engine driver. Katherine knows and has known for years precisely that kind of release and freedom. A tent, a swag, the open country. Cities, towns, the beaten path: they were never Katherine's. We're not the usual run. Never have been. Maryanne shakes her head, as if admonishing herself for never having seen it properly before: Katherine is a remarkable creature. And for a moment, she wants her big sister back. Just for one more day. Let it be as it was, just for one more day. The two women hug, the child nestled between them, feeling their bodies against him.

Katherine steps back first. 'Well, you know what you're doing.'

Maryanne can only nod, stepping down from the carriage with the child as Katherine turns and lowers the window, waving the soot and steam away with her hand.

The train shudders into life. Great belches of soot and steam carry down the platform; the animal, its impatience at an end, heaves and puffs into motion; and everything is suddenly moving. Katherine is being taken from her; Katherine is going. Her head out the window, hand waving in a cloud of steam and soot, she fades from view like a ghost. In a minute or less the train is gone, yellow lights and white steam slipping into the late summer twilight. Maryanne waits, watching it go. The platform empties. Katherine was here; Katherine is gone. She and the child are alone. And, Maryanne suddenly realises, alone for the first time.

When she looks down she sees the child's eyes fixed on the last of the departing train. Outside the station, they take their tram up the hill to the parliament, where they will alight for the short walk home through the park. Home. And once more it sinks in that she and the child are, indeed, alone. And she hopes she knows what she's doing. The tram passes the Post Office, tired banners for Yes and No still hanging there, no one having bothered to cut them down.

Maryanne gets off at her stop and begins the familiar walk home. She is dwelling on the memory of Katherine's face fading into the twilight, when she spots a man sitting on a bench in the park, his back to her, eating something. And she realises it's Father Geoghan. She doesn't have to see his face. It's him. And for a moment, she's a little taken aback. Even put out, for she thinks of this as *her* park, and Father Geoghan's presence in it isn't right somehow. It's almost as though he's intruding.

She pauses, watching the priest, who has no idea he's being observed, and her resentment fades. For he is a solitary spectacle. A black figure on a green lawn, staring out over the park. And as Maryanne watches him, she concludes that he is not just a solitary figure, but a lonely one. Quite possibly a man whose loneliness runs so deep he doesn't even know it. She doesn't know why she thinks this, only that she is convinced of it. It is an instinct, and one she trusts.

And as he stares out over the park, she can't help but wonder what is passing through the unguarded mind of Father Geoghan. What memories. For she has decided that he is more than a lonely figure: he is a sad one. Every now and then his hand rises, almost mechanically, and he takes a bite from his sandwich. But he seems barely aware of his hand or the sandwich. A few pigeons wander near and he tosses bread onto the ground for them. But, again, he barely seems to notice, and Maryanne can't help but feel that somehow this world doesn't touch him, doesn't move him, that somewhere along the line he lost the knack and this is the source of his loneliness: an isolation, a loneliness so deep he's unaware of it. Something he has simply got used to, like a limp, and doesn't notice any more.

Once again, her impulse is to reach out to him, but that would be futile. He is, she is sure, beyond reach. And has been for years. His hand rises, he takes a bite from his sandwich once again, barely noticing the bite or the sandwich. He tosses bread to the ground, the pigeons gather, but he pays no attention. He remains unmoved. This world does not touch him. *Believe me, I know!* She shakes her head slowly as she gazes upon him. What have they done to you, Father Geoghan?

He rises, brushes the crumbs from his trousers, and leaves the birds to their feast. And as he walks away, his shadow trailing him back towards his church like an old dog, he seems to Maryanne to be the loneliest figure in the world. Only he can't see it.

He leaves the park, turns into a street, shaded and dark, and is gone. And as much as Maryanne tells herself that she could have said something, made a meaningless wave, a peace offering of sorts, she knows he is beyond reach. But she carries the image – a black figure on a green lawn, staring vacantly across the park, his arm mechanically rising and falling, the pigeons gathering – all the way home.

21.

The Angel of Death hovers over the page, a strange presence in the air. A dark, supernatural presence. It has been summoned up by the times, and is near.

Maryanne registers a shiver as she stares at the newspaper. There they are: Milhaus, Lady Vine. Two photographic portraits, side by side, in the middle of the page. And the more she stares at the photographs, the more she feels the presence of the Angel of Death. They have that haunted look, Milhaus and Lady Vine, as the dead always do in photographs. As though they've been marked out for their fate long before, and have unknowingly gone about their days with the sentence of death suspended above them. And it is only afterwards, when the sentence has been carried out, that the dark angel becomes evident in their haunted eyes: there all the time.

She slowly shakes her head from side to side. She has long since lost her fear of God, because there is no God. So why this feeling of some supernatural force hovering near? Does fear run so deep, and is the God of Fear never entirely banished? Always there in some form or other: some superstitious instinct that you can't rid yourself of, left over after faith? The dregs of belief, living on in the superstition of the atheist?

Whatever the reason, that dark angel is near and rises from the newspaper in the haunted eyes of Milhaus and Lady Vine. Marked for death before they knew it. The sentence suspended above them even in those hours when they stole away to country towns or wherever they went for their time together. Death was there, and death was waiting. Now it is satisfied.

Maryanne moans, rocking back and forth. They got him in the end, after all. And the joy of seeing him set free has come to this. A short-lived freedom, short-lived joy. They got him. Of course. Now he's gone. It's like losing her shadow.

Together, it seemed to her, she and Milhaus had endured and come through the days of the beast. Entwined fates. For she'd had the feeling that if she could see him come through, then so would she. If Milhaus was saved, the child would be safe. The mother and child. If one came through, they would all come through. And, for a time, they did. Together, they endured the gaze of the beast and deprived the mob of its satisfaction. But they got him. And to have come so far, only to fall now, is cruel. Like the fate of those soldiers who fall in the dying hours of a war.

So, Milhaus is dead. We make these half-gods, Maryanne tells herself, we lift them up into the heavens, and then we tear them down. And the Milhaus that comes back to her now is the Milhaus that has just landed with a thud, with that lost look in his eyes. The boy standing alone in an empty playground, wondering where everybody has gone and if they will ever come back. And, at the same time, she's asking herself what difference she may have made. Enough for him to know that he was not alone, after all? That there was somebody out there? For he was alone in a way that *nobody* ought to be alone.

The account of the deaths of Milhaus and Lady Vine is long, taking up the whole page, and in the kind of detail unusual for the newspaper: the kind of detail usually found in those magazines that devote themselves to grisly murders in dark lanes or barren, windswept fields. But they can't help themselves, and the newspaper, knowing that this is its last chance to feed off the story of Jack Milhaus and his Madame X, lingers on the details just like a grisly magazine. It's grubby. And Maryanne feels the grubbiness rub off on her, because she can't help herself and can't help but read on.

It happened the day before. The lady and Milhaus drowned together. In the lake of the estate. The late summer heat drove them to its cool waters. The husband and the children were away; Lady Constance Vine, having been banished from the fairytale kingdom and forbidden contact with her children, as if she might pass on her fallen state, her stain, to them, had stolen her way back into the estate, just to see the children again, only to find them gone. And once there, alone, a desperate shadow of herself, she somehow summoned Milhaus to her side. How, the newspapers don't know. The caretaker heard sobs and crying. The lady could not be consoled. Where, where are the children? Where, where are my beauties? The tears were endless. And, at some point, the tears and the heat drove them to the lake. The caretaker, from his quarters, heard splashing and cries. A man's voice, the lady's cries. The cries and the splashing continued, then everything went quiet. Silence fell across the grounds. And, at first, he thought nothing of it. Then, disturbed and drawn from his quarters by the silence, he went out into the grounds. The lights of the house were on, the front door wide open. He walked to the lake. The water was still. There was no breeze, no relief from the heat.

As he approached the lake, where canoes and a small boat were moored to a wooden landing, he stopped. For there, by the water's edge, strewn on the grass, dropped in haste, was the lady's clothing. And beside hers, the gentleman's. But there was no sign of them, no ripple on the waters. No splash, no sight nor sound.

He stood by the lake, troubled, the clothes of the lady and the gentleman at his feet. When Lord Vine returned with the children later in the night, the caretaker met the car at the front door and told him all he knew. The children were sent inside. Their nanny put them to bed, the children soothed by milk, biscuits and stories.

It was a long night. The lake was drained. Garden staff were called back from their Saturday nights off, and manned the pumps. By first light, the stink of the drained lake already heavy in the warm air, the two bathers were revealed near its centre, where the water was deepest. His lordship and the staff waded out into the drained pool in gumboots, and eventually stopped, staring down at the couple.

Their clothes were strewn where they'd left them. The bathers were naked. She had her arms around his neck, the paper has been reliably informed; he had his arms around hers. They had dragged each other down into the depths. The staff were told to tell no one. Whether by pact, impulse, desperation or accident, Milhaus and the lady had died together. And lay all night at the bottom of the lake, entwined in each other's grip, only to be revealed at first light like muddy statues.

The staff were sent back to their quarters; his lordship and the caretaker disentangled the couple. With some difficulty, for death had made their grip on each other strong. They were laid down, side by side, in the shade of a garden shed until the police arrived and spoke at length to his lordship and the caretaker.

Maryanne puts the newspaper down on the kitchen table. Just how the caretaker's story reached the paper is never said. But she can imagine the situation. Or thinks she can. A reporter on police rounds snoops about, hears this and that, and, through a long night, eventually puts the strands of a story together. Or makes it up. Who knows?

Images of the lake come back to her, seen from the high iron gate at the front of the estate. Did they enter the water from the lake's edge or leap off a landing and from there swim to the depths, never intending to come back, or did things take on a life of their own, the persuasive cold currents of the water taking hold? The newspaper article is all the more disturbing to Maryanne for having seen the place. For she was the go-between, was she not? And did she not bring this about, with the best of intentions? Did she not pass the note to the lady, see the lady's smile drop from her lips and hear the child ask: 'What's that, Mummy?' And did she not walk to the bus stop with heavy steps, vaguely aware that she had set something in motion?

And so the Angel of Death feels near, and, for a moment, she even wonders if the dark angel hovered over her then: Maryanne, the go-between who handed the note over that set the whole story in motion. Was she death's agent?

She knows that's not true. From the moment the lady came forward, something was going to happen, and whether she handed the note over or somebody else did, things were set to unravel. But the God of Fear and Guilt dies hard. These impulses, Maryanne sighs, linger on, and before we know it, we're consumed with guilt and imagining the breath of the dark angel upon us, when, all the time, it's *us*; we bring these things upon ourselves.

It is late morning. The baby cries and she rises from the table and walks to the bedroom. Did they, Milhaus and the lady, in the end, succumb to that something *final* that the times craved? That the whole city craved? Did they all linger at the festival of the beast too long?

Maryanne picks up the baby and carries him to the kitchen, watching his eager hands reach for her breast, and feels the bliss of his lips attaching themselves to her nipple. She could swear the child is grinning, saying: Mine! All mine! And the sadness of the news mingles with the joy of the baby's cry.

At the same time, while the child is feeding, and the milk passes from her to him, a ghostly chorus of 'What's that, Mummy?' comes back to her. And the tower of the house that she imagined to be the tower of a house from a ghost story now has three children standing in it, peering down onto the estate grounds, where the spirits of Milhaus and the lady haunt the lake.

22.

It is March. Mellow days. The baby is three months old, and lies on a mat on the kitchen floor. There is a rattle, a cloth doll and a bear beside him. Katherine has sent them, along with money and books.

Victor's presents, the cloth and the baby clothes, turned out to be parting gifts, prompted by a mixture of guilt and genuine care, Maryanne has concluded. For Victor has disappeared from her life. Not slowly, but quickly. All their communications since the session at the photographer's and the tea-house afterwards have been letters, the last of which she now holds in her hands. She and Victor and the baby will never be together again.

His first, censored, letter simply told her that they'd been posted 'somewhere' in the New South Wales countryside and had a vague reference to what he was doing. All very boring and routine; not much different from the shop. It was good, he added, to be all together that once, at least. And they will always have the photographs. Even if the shots of him aren't all that good, and don't really look like him. And he enclosed one of them taken in the city studio in the January heatwave. He hoped that the child will appreciate his mittens and jumpers, and that she would make something fine with the cloth. Guilt and care. There was that much.

In his second letter he told her that he had been shifted back to Victoria. An army base down by the coast. Not far. Same job. Again, not much different from the shop. He would see the war out there. At least he wouldn't be going off anywhere and killing or being killed, Maryanne thought. There was that to be thankful for. And he sent money. Not much, but enough – along with money from Katherine – to help make ends meet. And she told him in reply that he was free to visit, that the child was growing every day. But he never did.

And now, this third letter. She's just finished rereading it. He is married. To the woman in the mineral-water town he was engaged to all that time: the woman he was engaged to whenever they met through their brief period together. And once again, she sees Victor in the gardens above the town: the look in his eyes telling her she's a crafty bitch, telling her of his commitments and responsibilities, then wheeling away from her on the sandy path and disappearing into the trees and down the hill into town, where his commitments and responsibilities were waiting for him.

So, they are finally married. One of those marriages, she can't help but feel, that come after two people meet, are happy enough but crave something more, then separate, go looking for that something more, and, not finding it, eventually get back together because, well, there was nothing better on offer.

They probably deserve each other. And she can't help but think that it tells her all sorts of things about Victor. A certain lack of imagination, ordinariness, or is it just laziness? The action of someone who is frightened of ending up alone and who settles for the bird in the hand.

Is she being unfair? Probably, because what Maryanne doesn't admit to herself is that she is a bit put out by the news. It is one thing for her to pack him off, it was another for him to go off and get married. For some reason she hadn't thought of that. If she didn't want him, surely no one would. But someone did. Or, rather, someone has *settled* for him. So be it. And she can't help but feel that there'll be times over the coming years when he will find himself back in that room behind the school house, pulling up his braces, forgetting himself for a moment and pronouncing her beautiful. A dangerous thought for a man with commitments and responsibilities. An imaginative moment for a man with no great imagination, except for dressing shop windows. But, all the same, perhaps the only moment in his life when he will feel he was at the heart of something immense, a fleeting moment of grace that he will never experience again. A tantalising, recurring hint of another life. A memory he will never shrug off, nor, perhaps, ever want to.

And is she any different, she wonders. Will she too not hark back to the moment of that impulsive pronouncement. *Schöne Frau*. And will that be Victor's finest moment? When the imagination he never realised he had was set free and he saw things he'd never seen before? Will it not be *their* finest moment? One to be kept in mind, to balance the anger of the gardens when he flung her miracle back in her face.

It is odd to be thinking and feeling these things. And Maryanne is surprised at herself. But, she tells herself, she shouldn't be. For isn't this always the case when somebody we assume will be there in some form or another suddenly isn't? Isn't it always then that they look their best?

She folds the letter up and places it back in the envelope. The last of Victor, for she knows there will be no more letters.

What she doesn't know is that when the child is older, and she takes him into the city to view the marvellous display windows of the largest and most famous department store in the country, it will be Victor's display windows that she and the child will be entranced by. That his flair for display windows, which she first noticed in that spa-water town, will bring him to the city. The owner of the emporium will notice his windows on holiday one summer and entice him to the city with the offer of the largest windows, the grandest canvasses, in the country. And Victor will follow, with, by then, a family. And live in a sprawling house north of the river, not far from the famous football ground known to the locals as Windy Hill, where Jack Milhaus, the god who fell, soared across distant Saturday-afternoon skies. And while Maryanne will think of Milhaus and the days of the beast from time to time, and always with a pang in the heart, for there are few things sadder than a broken god, she will never know that the display windows she and the child will thrill to see are the work of the boy's father.

Her time with him was not long, but long enough to change everything. And all that would remain of Victor are a few letters and one photograph, stored inside an envelope in one of Maryanne's drawers: Victor, staff in hand, ridiculously formal in that oversize uniform.

And the child, currently shaking his rattle and staring back at her from the kitchen floor, will know only the photograph in her drawer. Not the father. And, one day, she will have to explain: what happened and how it happened. Once upon a time, in a country mansion far away where she worked, she met the young lord of the house, and the baby Vic grew out of their meeting. But they could not stay together because they came from different worlds and were thrown apart. He went back to his world, and she went back to hers. Once upon a time ...

Part Four

The Beast Withdraws

Melbourne, November 12th, 1918

23.

The same crowds that cheered for war, that sang and rejoiced, *God be thanked Who has matched us with His hour*; the same crowds that hung from windows and balconies, climbed lampposts and stood atop motor cars and carriages, waving flags, now cheer for peace.

The same crowds that called for the blood of Milhaus have forgotten all about him. He served his purpose and is no longer required. The same crowds that turned upon the lady – who stained and destroyed the fairytale they all looked up to – and bayed for justice, branding her Madame X, now think little of her, if at all.

The same crowds that summoned up the beast within, and surrendered to it, that submitted to the dark conjurers of hate and death, hearts bursting with inexplicable joy, *Let us sing in gladness*, and that all made up that frenzied festival of death and war, all craving that something *final*, the very worst of humanity on display, now cheer for peace. And the beast? The beast, its scales shining in the sun, turns for one last look upon the cheering crowds, before slouching off towards the swamp from which it came, where it will lie down and brood and wait for its time to rise again, in twenty years, in a hundred, a thousand, a million years, conjured up by the magicians of darkness.

It is a public holiday. Maryanne and the child move easily through the crowd, which parts for a lady with a pram. The Town Hall clock strikes the eleventh hour, a day after the armistice. The city heard the night before, and, no doubt, many of the revellers are still here from the previous evening. Somewhere they are singing the Marseillaise. The crowd erupts. Peace, glorious peace. *God be thanked* ... The great war for civilisation is concluded. The Town Hall clock rings out the hour. Hats are flung into the air, boaters hoisted and twirled on walking sticks, flags raised.

And those not waving flags or hats join hands and form circles, and, on no command in particular, begin dancing. One, two, three steps in, hands raised aloft in hooray, and one, two, three steps back. The simple three-step, quite possibly invented on the spot, is repeated, over and over again. Soon more circles are formed, and they each revolve as if moving round some invisible maypole. Circles within circles within circles; hats, flags and hoorays filling the air. A dummy of the Kaiser hanging from a tree, the beast's parting gift.

The dancing continues as Maryanne pushes her pram through the crowd, gradually leaving the intersection behind: the same intersection at which the beast once rejoiced and bellowed in ecstasy. And it is as she is leaving the scene, the child alert and transfixed by the spectacle, that she hears a voice calling through the crowd. And at first she is only conscious of a voice calling out something through the hoorays and war-time songs. Then, slowly, she realises it is her name being called. And with that, she turns.

Face shining, eyes alight, cheeks with the morning still on them, but night in her eyes if you look hard enough, Vera comes towards her.

'At last!' she cries, her voice a mixture of relief and joy. 'I never thought it would come. Never thought the war would ever end. Peace,' she sighs, 'isn't it the most wonderful word?'

'Yes,' Maryanne says, 'yes, it is.' And, of course, it *is*. Never mind the same crowds ... the moment is infectious.

'Peace!' Vera sighs again, her face in sunshine and shadow, eyes bright but distant, surveying the crowd, every one of them with a ghost at their side. Then she looks at Maryanne, with a resolute air that is way beyond her years. 'We must make sure no one ever forgets. We must never let them. So no one will ever want to go through this again.'

She turns, waving to a group of women Maryanne remembers from the offices she visited so often, a haven when one was needed.

'I must go,' Vera cries. 'Come and visit; we miss you.'

Then she is gone and Maryanne, like Vera, running from group to group, has the desire to share the smiles, tears and excitement of the moment. She thinks of Katherine, wonders where she is. Last word, and money – big sister always – was from a farm in New England. And she may still be there, raising a mug of strong tea to the news. And, in the absence of Katherine, Maryanne leans forward, looking down into the pram, smiles and produces a sweet biscuit.

'A biscuit for my little biscuit.'

And the child's eyes light up as he grasps the treat and begins sucking and chewing on it with his new teeth. And, together, they look about them, soaking up the scene. You won't remember this, my little one, Maryanne silently intones. You're too young. But one day Mama will remind you and tell you that you were here, and that we listened as the clock struck the hour of peace and everybody danced.

Walking up the hill to the parliament she is free of the crowds. The child finishes his biscuit in the pram. He is a good child, doesn't cry much and listens when she speaks. She has started work, not far from home. Cleaning nearby guesthouses and the large terraces that face the Exhibition Gardens, where the dome of the main building looks like something out of Florence. Large terraces, where once a gentleman and his family would have lived, but four or five people now do in separate apartments. The work is good enough; she doesn't mind it. She can take the child with her. He sits on the floor while she changes beds and dusts the furniture, playing with his toys or the large, jangling sets of keys she's entrusted with, or the books left lying around. Occasionally calling out Mama, and holding up one of his toys. And when he's tired, she pulls out a drawer from a chest of drawers and he sleeps there. No, she doesn't mind the work. It's pleasant enough, the days pass and the money comes in. And just as well, because Father Geoghan was as true as his word. For when she asked for work at her old school, the walls went up and nobody wanted to speak to her or know her.

She turns at the parliament and walks through the gardens beside the treasury, the same gardens where Vera, megaphone in hand, spoke in the days of the beast. And from which the march left. NO MORE WAR, NO MORE WAR, they chanted. Now, they have their wish. But these days will not go quietly. Or quickly. And even when they *feel* like history, removed and distant, they will not be gone. Not these days. For the effects of these days will go on and on, ever expanding, rippling through the years and lapping up against the lives of those who never knew them. A black wave, ever-expanding, like night rolling back the light of day or a drop of black ink on a sheet of white blotting paper.

She wheels the pram out of the gardens along a sandy path that runs beside the lake, the swans composed and calm on the still waters. And as she passes, she eyes them, wondering which one is *hers*. She can do this thing, she has done this thing. She will continue to do this thing. And out of these days, from the days of the beast, she has produced this child. With eyes that can smile and laugh, but which also bear the imprint of a back room behind a school where he was conceived. Eyes that bear the imprint of the times. And these days. How else can it be?

But, in their way, they have come through. And the routine of the predictable life she seemed destined to live is gone forever. Her life changed in such a way that it will never be the same again. And isn't that what she wanted all along? The egg is hatched. A story begins ...

Epilogue

Paris, December, 1977

The silver jet that carried Michael from one side of the world to the other landed a couple of hours earlier, and now, after his breakfast in a street cafe, he is entering the Gare Montparnasse. Platform One. Where the grand lines are. His train, which will take him to a small, windmill town in Brittany, is already there. A silver train, an arrow pointed at the future. And he will ride time's arrow into it, simultaneously taking the past with him. Maryanne is part of the travelling world he takes with him, always there: past, present and future riding together simultaneously in the air-conditioned comfort of a TGV.

Her belly was the egg, and when it hatched so too did a family story. Everything starts with her, and everything that flows from those days when they all lingered too long at the festival of the beast flows from her. But Michael doesn't *really* know who she was and never will. It was too long ago. And the more distant the time, the more distant the inhabitants of that time, and the more difficult they are to know. And Michael, after long and restless bouts of sleeping and waking on the plane, has come to the only conclusion he can: that he won't even try to answer the question of who she really was. In her innermost self.

However much the past may rise up before us, and however much its ghosts may sit at our tables, however much it may haunt us at varying times, however much it may be present, it is also the *past*. And the more distant, the more mysterious. A closed door of an old house that occasionally opens, revealing different things at different times to different visitors. A house long locked up that we occasionally enter, sniffing out its smells, finding in the long-abandoned furniture, photographs and newspapers hints of what might have happened there: of who may have breathed their first or their last there. Hints of who its occupants were, before they upped and left and walked into history. Into the recent past. Then the distant past. Ghosts that we try to give substance and weight to, but who, in their inner selves, elude us, and remain ghosts and shadows all the same.

The thing to do is to make her up, the egg from which everything came, just as she made herself up. Just as she gave herself a story between two dates, a story that life never gave her – but *could* have.

Lightheaded with tiredness, Michael floats along the crowded platform, noting his fellow travellers: among them a young woman, seated on a suitcase, immersed in the morning ritual of her breakfast of a croissant and coffee. In the rising noise of the station, amid the movement and the announcements, she is still. Oblivious of the world, immersed in hers.

He stops at the engine, the tip of the arrow, contemplating its tinted windows, noting how far removed this silver capsule is from the steam and diesel engines of his youth. But, at the same time, guessing that his father would have had little trouble communicating, through the language of engine driving, with the French driver concealed behind the tinted windows. And he would have been familiar, within a few minutes, with the workings of the engine. Some things don't change.

But some things must be discovered anew and so Michael has determined that when he eventually turns his full attention to Maryanne, he will not even try to present her as fact. For the core of her, the heart of her, he will never know. And he will not even pretend to enter her times. For the times are too distant. He must release her from history, release the times themselves from history, and discover her and them anew: the heart of her, the heart of them. He must look past the duplicity of photographs, the unreliability of family tales, and the shifting meanings of written records. To *his* Maryanne. To *his* 1917. It will require, he decides, taking in the hum of the busy station, a leap into what he *imagines* to be her world, into a Maryanne of sorts, who probably never existed but who just *might* have.

So, where will the leap land him? Where does he begin? With her bearing. The way she carries herself. Why not? A simple defining feature. A beginning. A place from which to leap again. *Tall, that's how she looks. But she's not. It's the bearing* …

And the times, the spectacle of the city that she gazes upon. A heaving crowd, many but one, rising and falling on the waves of history. A time of ghosts and monsters: of the beast of storybook, scales glinting in the sun and the moonlight, stepping out of a dark fairytale and into the streets and houses of the everyday, the very spirit of the times, craving that something *final* that death delivers. Like stepping back three hundred years. Or three thousand years. Or three hundred thousand. To a time when beasts and monsters stalked the earth: all-powerful one day; skulking back into the swamp of creation and destruction the next, into long-craved oblivion, returning to simple matter. The same swamp from which the beast will emerge once again at varying times in history, summoned up by the death wish of deadly times, conjured up by magicians of darkness.

That is the city she looks upon day after day. A Maryanne who stays removed and separate, who has an egg to nurture and a family history to give birth to, which will flow down through the years, shaping the lives of those she will never even meet.

It is a beginning. And the end? Maryanne died in that suburb, built on that flat, dry land of Scotch thistle and scrub she glimpsed from the train on the way back from the foundling home: a suburb of stick houses and dirt streets. She died there, in Michael's room. He slept on the back porch: an adventure, glimpsing the summer stars above him before drifting off, while she quietly died in his old room. A white-haired old lady; his father, Vic, sitting by her side night after night whenever he wasn't driving engines, occasionally calling her Mama, and gently mopping her forehead in the heat. Michael barely noticed. His days were spent hurling a red ball into his back fence; day after day, eventually shattering the fence. Speed, he was chasing speed, while she embraced slowness: drifting in and out of consciousness, occasionally snapped out of her slumber by the crack of the ball on the fence. Then she was gone, the room was disinfected and became his again. Maryanne died in that suburb, in that room, and was buried in a pauper's grave on a hill. An anonymous mound.

The crack of the ball, the pursuit of speed, went on. He barely noticed the last of Maryanne. Time speeds on, bends, collapses into slowness, then moves again, taking us with it. We all end up there, in a future cluttered with the past, drifting in and out of consciousness, half-lucid, half-gaga, drifting into that something final, once so remote, but suddenly imminent.

Michael looks back along the platform. The young woman has finished her breakfast and sits, still holding her cardboard cup, staring at the scene, the milling crowd around her, as if only just noticing it. The young woman, like Maryanne, one of those who have the gift of passing through their times and their worlds without appearing to be touched by them. Separate from the heaving beast, but, all the same, rising and falling on the waves of history. Waves that have continued beyond those distant days of the beast. Waves that are still felt clear into Michael's times of silver jets and air-conditioned trains that speed into the countryside as if speeding into the future. And even though the children of that future will look back on the days of the beast, the days of the First World War, the great war for civilisation, in the same way that people at that very time would have looked back on the Battle of Waterloo (too distant to matter), the reverberations of those times will pass through them, and they too will rise and fall on the waves of distant history.

The platform is moving. People are pouring into the train. Michael joins them. The girl with the croissant and coffee cup has disappeared. Gone to wherever she will. He takes his seat. Slowly, almost surreptitiously, the train begins to move, quickly building to its maximum speed. Soon Michael is looking through his window onto the deep green fields of the French countryside, while bringing with him a picture of *his* Maryanne, looking directly back at him through the ages, resolute and independent, defying him to read her expression.

Notes for a Novel

This essay was written two years before *The Year of the Beast* was published, and appeared in *Meanjin*, vol. 76, issue 4, 2017

In the late 1990s I had a vivid dream about my old street in Glenroy where I grew up. In the dream my father (who is now dead), my mother and I were standing on the street, pausing in front of a vacant paddock and staring at the swaying grass. I knew, the way we know things in dreams, that it was summer. That it was a Saturday night in 1957 and from the colour of the sky that it was early evening. We all had our best clothes on: my father in a starched, white shirt, my mother in her best summer dress, and me in a striped shirt with a button-down collar that I'd forgotten all about until the dream retrieved it.

The dream was what we would now call virtual in its reality, the three of us a kind of *tableau vivant* that I felt I could walk around as I would a sculpture. The vividness and the urgency of the dream prompted a novel that, over three drafts, eventually became *The Art of the Engine Driver*.

I was convinced it would be a one-off book and would finally get this Glenroy thing off my chest: that my old street and my old patch of Glenroy, a rectangle of land about a mile long and a half mile wide, could yield only one book.

Almost twenty years and five Glenroy novels later I am half-way through the sixth and final novel in the sequence. When finished the six novels will span sixty tumultuous years of Australian history, from 1917 to 1977. EM Forster talks of different types of time in his classic *Aspects of the Novel*. There is basically everyday time that watches and clocks measure, and something that he calls time measured by value: by which he means those intense experiences that blur our sense of passing time and defy the clocks. Those sixty years that the novels cover – World War One, the Great Depression, World War Two, the tumult of the post-war diaspora, the Cold War, the Menzies ascendency and the rise and fall of Whitlam – is time measured by value.

They were written in no particular order, and, I think, can be read in any order. I started in the middle, went forward for the next two, doubled back to 1946 for another, then jumped forward to 1977. The novel I'm writing now, although the last of the six, chronologically speaking is the first in the sequence.

It is set in Melbourne in the last months of 1917, during the second conscription referendum. We call them referendums, but, in fact, they were plebiscites. The central character is a woman called Maryanne. She is forty, single and seven months pregnant. The child she is carrying is Vic, the engine driver, and pivotal character, in the whole sequence.

It is, like much of the series, drawn from family history. Or, more accurately, family mythology. My grandmother was Maryanne Carroll. She brought up my father, her only child, by herself. My father never knew his father. The family name, Carroll, comes down through the matriarchal line. Strictly speaking, our name should have been, and the spellings are various, Deuschke: my father's father, as best we understand, being German, from a small town in Prussia.

He was an absent father, a common phenomenon at the time. He was for many years an absence in the family history, and, to a large extent, still is. Although modern ways of tracing family history are continually shedding new light on things.

The task of fiction, however, is not to replicate the past but to reinvent it. One's loyalty is always with the novel itself, and the hope that what you create, although diverging from history, will contain a truth of its own. The constant challenge throughout all of the Glenroy novels has been to recreate the past and to find a style that does not simply repeat social realism, the style so often associated with working class, suburban tales.

This novel, however, like *Spirit of Progress*, is set before the suburb was born. So it not so much taps into the history of the suburb, as its pre-history. The events I describe in this novel take place in a Melbourne that existed exactly one hundred years ago. In *The Art of the Engine Driver* I knew the place and time intimately because I lived through it. The place and the time were at my fingertips. Not so Melbourne, 1917. That place and time are as foreign to me as revolutionary Paris or Dickens' London. And I made the decision right from the start that I would not even pretend to enter Melbourne in 1917: not to even pretend that I was leading the reader into anything resembling a faithful creation of that place and time. It would not only be false, it would be boring. Let the reader know right from the outset that this is an *imagined* Melbourne and an imagined 1917, and hope that it all rings true as fiction – not as social history. The novel is, above all, a work of the imagination. Martin Cruz Smith had never been to Moscow when he wrote *Gorky Park*. Borges never went to London; the London he writes about is drawn from Dickens. Novelists need to trust their imaginations and take those flights of fancy that are intrinsic to creating what you hope is a resonant imagined world that may as well be what it pretends to depict, and hopefully contains a kind of truth all its own.

For this reason, and because this is the way I work, I have chosen to do virtually *no* research while writing the first draft. I have done some, but very little. Research at this stage can be confining and deadening. The mind and imagination need to free, not weighed down by facts – most of which will prove to be irrelevant or unimportant in the end anyway. It is far more important at this stage to get the story rolling and the characters taking shape. Story, character and one informing, over-arching idea will hopefully give me the first draft. After that, I can go back and mine the history books, letters and newspapers of the age: when the story feels like it has taken on a life, and the characters are standing.

I am currently – late June – thirty-four and half thousand words into what I suspect is about a seventy thousand word novel. I have blocked out, on paper, the key chapters and scenes in the second half of the book. I like to work like this, there is no substitute for knowing where the story is heading and why. This doesn't mean that the story *will* go in the direction I have mapped out or that the characters will behave themselves and do what I think they'll do. It's good to have narrative foundations, but they must be accommodating. Must be flexible enough to incorporate all the changes that happen along the way because fiction, especially fiction works of novel length, are organic: the conscious and the unconscious, the planned and the un-planned, are constantly interacting. Things go to plan, then all of a sudden, things change.

For example, last week I started writing a section I had been looking forward to writing and building the story up to for some time. But the moment I started writing it everything changed. Maryanne, the central character, was meant to confront the towering figure of archbishop Daniel Mannix at the front gate of his house, Raheen, in Kew. I even drove out there and studied the place in preparation. But nothing of the sort takes place. The moment I started writing the scene the next morning it swerved off in a totally unexpected direction, and it is not Mannix who steps outside that gate on his daily walk from Kew to Saint Patrick's, but another character altogether. A character that had not even appeared in the book until that moment. But when I looked back I could see that her appearance had been written into the story. I'd plotted it without realising it. The unconscious had been one step ahead of me the whole time.

It's not entirely true to say that I've done no research so far. To an extent, it depends what we call research. The times were tumultuous indeed, the city in the grip of a kind of madness. When Bob Santamaria complained to Mannix one day during the Labor Party split of the mid 1950s, saying that he couldn't take the constant pressure of the moment any more, Mannix apparently scoffed, saying something like: 'This is *nothing* compared to 1917'. The whole country was divided down the middle on conscription. It's not unreasonable to suggest that this is the closest the nation has ever come to simply falling apart or falling into a kind of civil war within a war. Fights raged on the streets, rallies for 'YES' and 'NO' faced off against each other on opposing corners. It was an upheaval. So, how to depict this madness? Where to go to find the images I needed? Not history, I decided. I went to fiction. My preparatory reading was Dickens's *A Tale of Two Cities*, Balzac's tales set during the revolution, Milan Kundera's Prague both in 1948 and during the Soviet invasion, as well as Friedrich Reck's *Diary of a Man in Despair* about the mayhem and misery of the rise of Nazism in 1930s Germany. They gave me swaying crowds, massed madness, mob movement, and individual lives swamped by the waves of history in progress.

But, more than these books, there were two other key works that gave me entrée into *my* Melbourne, 1917: Sigmund Freud's brilliant essay *Civilisation and its Discontents* and Dante's *Inferno*. Freud's book was written in 1929. He makes no mention of the First World War and the death-wish madness it unleashed all over Europe, and the events of the 1930s in post-Weimar Germany are yet to happen. But I think it's reasonable to suggest that the essay is imbued with the experience of World War One, and pre-figures the outbreak of Nazism. Freud argues, compellingly, that although we may pride ourselves on being civilised and celebrate Progress – civilisation and Progress come at a price. We must supress the pleasure seeking, anarchic, primal part of ourselves or no cooperative social enterprise can be successful. Society would be dead in the swamp. For most of the time though, with the Ego and Super Ego in charge, society holds together, and History and Progress stumble and lurch, more or less, forward. But every now and then there is a mass outbreak of the primal and the Id erupts into pleasure seeking, death desiring life. For death, to the Id – the return of all life to indifferent primal matter – is the Id's ultimate pleasure: that something *final* that it craves. So Freud gave me my thematic framework and this is crucial, for we not only need to know *what* is happening when we are writing a novel, but *why*. Action, driven by idea, is the best, the most satisfying form of action. And so the crowds, the violent massed meetings across the city, day in day out, are depicted as just such an eruption. A beast, a leviathan made up of the very worst of humanity: a rampant Id. Freud also gave me my [original] title: *Festival of the Id* [later changed to *The Year of the Beast*].

But just as I needed an informing idea, I also needed an informing image, one that would hold true throughout the novel. Dante gave me this. Maryanne is seven months pregnant when the novel opens. The city around her, every day, is convulsed in an ecstasy of madness. And it is, to her, like being mad: like descending, every day, into Hell. Every circle of Hell she descends into is a variation on the one before and an intimation of the one to follow. I decided from the start to write the novel from two points of view: Maryanne's, and hovering above that, the omniscient authorial. The god-like perspective. She thinks of herself as descending into the circles of Hell, and over time I came to see her as a kind of Dante, seven months pregnant, making the perilous journey through the Hell of her city without a Virgil to guide her.

I'm halfway through, I think I know what will follow, and I even think I know how it will all end. Of course, things will change: characters will transform in unexpected ways, say the most unexpected things or *not* say certain things; the story will take the directions I've mapped out, and suddenly swerve off into unexpected directions. To borrow from Stoppard, I feel like a hiker. I know where I'm going, I have my compass and my general points of reference, but what happens along the way is another thing altogether.

Acknowledgments

Many thanks to the following.

Publisher Catherine Milne and Belinda Yuille at HarperCollins, my editor Amanda O'Connell, Jo Butler for proofreading, and my agent Sonia Land and all the gang at Sheil Land.

Dr Kelly Gardiner, novelist and Lecturer in Creative and Professional Writing at the Department of Creative Arts and English at La Trobe University, for helping me with information on the Women's Peace Army and the Women's Political Association; Toni Glasson for family history research; and Paul Lyons for casting a cold eye over certain sections of the book and finding a name for Father Geoghan.

Finally, special thanks to my partner Fiona Capp, for her constant support, suggestions and advice, not just in the writing of this novel but all of them; in this case, especially, for thinking up the title. And to Leo – the lion-hearted boy.